Sign up for our newsletter to hear
about new and upcoming releases.

www.ylva-publishing.com

BOOKS IN THE SERIES
THE LAW GAME

THE LAW GAME

ARCHER SECURITIES

by Jove Belle

DAUGHTER OF BAAL

by Gill McKnight

EVOLUTION OF AN ART THIEF

by Jessie Chandler

TABLE OF CONTENTS

Other Books from Ylva Publishing

Coming from Ylva Publishing

ARCHER SECURITIES

by Jove Belle

CHAPTER 1

The clinking of a fork against a wine glass sounded from the back deck. Laila stared at the kid, Logan, refusing to look away just because her uncle Samar had decided to make a speech. They'd been at it for almost three minutes, and the kid was going to crack any second. A small trickle of sweat worked its way down the side of his face.

"Thank you all so much for joining us today. We have happy news to share with you all, our friends and family." Samar's voice swam in the back of Laila's mind.

She already knew about her cousin Sia's engagement. That was the whole reason they'd gathered here today. She didn't need to forfeit her contest with Logan in order to watch Uncle Samar. And, since Logan was the thirteen-year-old son of the groom, he already knew and didn't really care either.

"Laila, what are you doing?" Christine stepped into Laila's peripheral view and tugged on her arm. She huffed out a sigh. "Come on."

"Can't." Laila refused to be the first to blink. She'd told the kid she could go five minutes, and while she was many things, a liar wasn't one of them. Christine yanking on her arm was annoying, but not enough to break her concentration.

"Are you seriously having a staring contest with a twelve-year-old?"

"No. He's thirteen." She was staring to prove a point. Not because of a contest. "And it sounds silly when you say it like that."

"That's because it is silly, no matter how I say it. He's a kid."

"So?" Laila still hadn't blinked, but it was getting harder not to look at Christine.

"As you know, my daughter has been dating Desmond for over a year now," Samar continued his speech.

When Christine darted a hand out and cuffed Logan on the back of the head, he yelped and flinched. Laila won their not-a-staring contest by default.

"Beat it," Christine said.

With his hand clapped over the spot where Christine had smacked him, Logan said, "This doesn't count. You didn't win."

Christine sighed, and Laila held the kid's gaze. She still hadn't blinked.

"I said get outta here."

Logan sulked but finally turned away. "Fine. You suck."

"Why did you do that?" Laila loved to win, but hated to win unfairly. When she beat someone, she wanted that person to know she was better.

"Because you're ignoring me, and I'm sick of it."

Laila looked at her date, finally letting herself blink. Her eyes itched. "What do you mean?"

"I mean, you brought me to your family barbecue, and so far, you gave someone a black eye, slammed a ball into that lady's nose, and now you're having a staring contest with a kid."

"Rafael asked for a sparring match, Maurine was blocking the net, and it wasn't a contest." Laila ticked off the points. Her cousin Rafael studied Jui Jitsu and had asked about Krav Maga, which Laila practiced. Of course they'd compared styles. If he were better, she'd have the black eye and he'd have bragging rights instead of the other way around. And their family volleyball games were never friendly. Everyone played aggressively, including Maurine—a distant cousin Laila didn't really know—whose nose got slammed. Maurine had paused long enough to check that her nose wasn't bleeding, and then she'd slapped Laila's outstretched hand to let her know all was good. The game had resumed.

"The point is, you've been ignoring me." Christine was beautiful, with long blond hair that she wore swept up in casual ponytail today. There was an ethereal quality to her beauty, and when she was pissed—arms crossed over her chest, body tensed and ready to spring, and glaring resentfully at Laila—she looked like some sort of goddess raining fire on a poor village that made the mistake of worshiping her on the wrong day. Divas usually weren't Laila's thing, but Christine was good in bed and willing to participate in some pretty kinky scenarios. The orgasms generally made putting up with Christine's weird social demands worth it.

Laila waited, unsure how to respond. She shouldn't have brought Christine here.

"Desmond is on track to become partner at his law firm in the next few years, and his son, Logan…" Samar droned on in the background, talking about Sia's bright future with Desmond and his son.

Christine looked at her, clearly waiting for something. Somehow, Laila went from having a staring contest with

Logan to having one with Christine. Except, she was pretty sure there was no way to win this one. Christine had a bad habit of using sex as a weapon, and based on the exasperated expression on Christine's face, Laila was dangerously close to the relationship equivalent of being put in timeout.

"That's it. I'm leaving." Christine stomped away, her heels sinking into the grass as she crossed the yard and made her way through the gate that separated the front from the back. Laila tried to decide what a normal person with normal emotions would do in this situation. Follow and apologize? Let Christine cool off on her own?

Sia slipped up beside her. "Think she'll come back?" she asked mildly as she sipped her beer.

Not sure what else to do with her hands, Laila scratched the back of her head. "I don't know." She shrugged. "Should I go after her?"

"You should." Sia nodded thoughtfully. "But I'd rather you didn't. She hit my future step-son and acted like a pouty brat in the middle of my engagement party."

Logan, Sia's future step-son, as she put it, went out of his way to aggravate people. But, he was one of the only people at this party Laila actually liked. "Sorry about that."

Sia shrugged. "It's okay. Besides, I've never really liked her."

"Really?"

"Nope. She's not right for you."

Sia had acted friendly toward Christine, but never particularly welcoming. Finally, at the Memorial Day picnic, she'd asked if Christine was really good in the sack or something. Laila confirmed that she was, and Sia had nodded the same way she was now, as if a piece of the puzzle had fallen into place.

Laila frowned. How upset was Christine? She wasn't sure, but it was possible that they'd just broke up. "She has a key to my place."

"So? You don't keep anything there that's worth stealing." Sia put her arm around her and drew her from the shade of a mature cottonwood tree toward the deck.

"What about my TV?"

"You don't watch it anyway."

"That's true, but what about sex?"

"You can still have sex."

"But not with her." That thought almost made Laila chase after Christine. She was really good at sex.

"No. You'll have to find someone new for that."

"I guess I could do that."

"To Sia and Desmond." Samar raised his beer in a toast, and Laila realized she didn't have a drink of her own.

Sia neatly pulled a bottle of water from an ice chest as they passed, twisted the top off, and handed it to Laila. She urged Laila up the stairs to stand with the group gathered there and spun her around to face the family and friends on the lawn. Laila, self-conscious about being dragged into the focal group, took a long drink of water just as Sia bent down and whispered to her, "Now, my maid of honor, drink to my wedding."

"What?" Laila sputtered. The drink she'd just swallowed was halfway down her throat, and Laila sprayed the people gathered to listen. Between the water and her confusion over Sia calling her the maid of honor, it took Laila a few moments to realize that she needed to apologize. People didn't like to be spit on. "Sorry, everybody." She smiled uncertainly at her aunt and two cousins as they wiped their faces with paper napkins.

Sia threw her a small glare as she hugged her dad. "Thanks, Daddy." She raised her bottle in a small toast. "And thank you all for coming. Desmond and I are so glad you could be here to share in our happiness. Now, everyone eat up. And have fun."

Desmond dropped his arm around Sia's shoulders as she spoke, a wide, proud grin on his face.

As soon as people stopped focusing on Sia, Laila grabbed her by the wrist and dragged her back down the steps toward the lake. Sia veered toward the boathouse, as was their ingrained habit. Once they were inside, Laila took a deep breath to calm herself before she said, "What the hell, Sia? Maid of honor?"

Laila didn't even believe in the whole idea of marriage. She thought long-term monogamy was unnatural, and Sia knew it, so why would she expect Laila to participate in the ceremony? This had to be some sort of sappy, sentimental request, and Laila sucked at both sappy and sentimental.

"Yes, maid of honor." Sia crossed her arms over her chest. "I'm getting married, Lai. Did you really think I'd ask someone else?"

Laila paused. She hadn't thought about it at all.

Sia sighed. "It has to be you. You're my best friend."

"Sia, I hate this stuff." Her understanding of emotions was mostly academic. Not that she didn't feel things. She did. But where most people's emotions were like a TV with the volume turned up, hers were muted and fuzzy in the background. They never came into focus long enough for her to really grasp them. "The maid of honor does a lot of important stuff, like giving a speech, planning stuff, and... and..." Laila's shoulders slumped. She couldn't even talk about it properly. How the hell was she supposed to *do* it?

"I know." Sia nudged her with her shoulder. "But you're still my best friend. This is what friends do, Lai."

Laila thought about that for a few moments. Sia was the only member of her family who made any sense to Laila. Her first clear memory was of Sia, her face scrunched up, red with anger, mouth open with the biggest screech that Laila had ever heard. She had been tiny and so loud. But when Laila had brushed the back of her hand over Sia's face—her skin had been the softest thing ever—Sia had stopped crying and looked at her with a broad, curious smile. Her mom had told her it was just gas, that Sia was too young for it to be a real smile. Laila knew, though, that her mom had been wrong. She and Sia just went together. Cousins. Partners in crime. Best friends. And now, apparently, her role in Sia's life had expanded to include maid of honor.

She dropped onto the wooden bench that skirted the inside front wall of the boathouse, and her shoulders slumped. "Are you sure?" Laila would do it. If it was important to Sia, she had no other choice. But Sia really deserved someone who would be better at it. "I won't be good at it."

Sia sat next to her. "Are you kidding me? Name one thing you're not good at."

There were lots of things Laila wasn't good at. Understanding people was pretty high on the list. Normally, she didn't care, but this was different. "You'll have to give me a checklist. Or maybe I'll buy a book." If she had a guide, she would be okay. "Do they have books about how to properly bridesmaid?"

Sia squeezed her in a sideways hug. "You bet. There are entire websites devoted to this kind of thing."

Of course! She could learn everything she needed to know on the Internet. "Yeah. I'm going to kick maid of honoring's ass."

"Yeah," Sia agreed, "you are."

"You really never liked Christine?" Laila didn't particularly like her either, but she always assumed her lack of attachment had to do with her own inability to relate. She'd never considered that Christine might actually be unlikeable.

"No. She messed with your head too much."

"She did?"

"She did. No matter what, she tried to make you think everything you did was wrong," Sia said.

"Huh." Sure, Christine bitched about everything from the toast being too toasty to the line at the movies being too long. Laila had just tuned her out and rolled with it. Most of the time, she was running through her list of objectives for the next day, or visualizing a new self-defense move she'd just learned. "I guess so. I didn't really notice."

"I know. Because you're too accepting. But it irks me when people take advantage of you."

"Why didn't you say anything?" Laila always told Sia what she thought of her boyfriends. Maybe this was one of those social rule things that she constantly screwed up. Maybe she wasn't supposed to tell Sia if she liked her dates or not. Not that it mattered now that she was marrying Desmond. Laila loved him. He was great at brainteasers and just laughed and tried harder any time Laila beat him.

"You weren't really into her. I knew it wouldn't last, so I didn't see the point in ruining your fun."

"Yeah, she was fun."

"No, she wasn't."

Laila laughed. "Maybe not with you. But I had a *lot* of fun with her."

Sia sighed. "We need to discuss this habit you have of mistaking great sex for a great relationship. It takes more than a regular dose of orgasms to lead to happily ever after."

Laila tried to picture another way to be happy for the rest of her life but came up blank. "I'm pretty sure you're wrong about that. Orgasms are awesome."

"They are. But they won't take care of you when you're sick, hold your hand when you're sad, or stick around long enough to grow old with you."

Laila wrinkled her nose. "That's what I have you for."

"True that, cousin. Now come on. My dad was telling me about a problem at work. He thinks someone might be stealing, and I know how much you love a good mystery." Sia stood and pulled Laila to her feet. Sia's dad, Uncle Samar, was the president of US operations for a multinational conglomerate called Archer Securities.

"He's right. A company that size, someone is definitely stealing. Several someones, actually."

"True. But this is more than missing pens from the supply closet."

As they made their way out of the boathouse, a couple of kids Laila vaguely recognized as cousins tried to make their way in. She caught one by the collar and spun him around. Sia pointed toward the house.

"Not today, boys. The boathouse is off limits during the party. If you want to take the bowrider out, ask Uncle Samar."

The boys ran off ahead of them, and Sia said, "I don't even know those kids. I swear, my dad invited everyone he could think of, from family to the guy who loads his groceries at Whole Foods."

"I'm pretty sure we're related to them." Laila locked the door, just in case. They normally left it open, but clearly that wasn't the best idea today.

"So, what are you going to do about Christine?" Sia asked. She stared straight ahead, and Laila appreciated that. She always did better with emotional stuff when people didn't look at her.

"I don't know. What do you think?" She scratched the back of her head and glanced at Sia out of the corner of her eye.

Sia shrugged. "You don't love her, do you?"

"No, of course not." Laila shook her head. She might love having sex with Christine, but that probably wasn't the same thing.

"Then you let her go," Sia said it in the same easy way that she ordered coffee in the morning.

"That's what you'd do?" Laila nibbled on the edge of her thumb, the skin right next to her nail.

Sia finally looked at her, one eyebrow raised. "I have no idea."

That was fair. Sia fell in love too easily. If she were like Sia, Laila would have married Christine months ago, and they'd be making lesbian babies together by now.

"I'll change my locks when I get home."

"Good idea."

On their way past the pool, they were both hit by a stray splash of water. One of the guys, a friend of Desmond, stood just a little straighter and smiled dashingly. Water dripped down his torso, and his hair fell in dark, wet curls over his forehead. Laila returned his smile.

"He's single, you know." Sia nudged her in the side.

"Yeah?" Laila turned her head and held his gaze a fraction longer. "What's his story?"

"Just ended a three-year relationship. His girlfriend complained he wasn't available enough and said she felt emotionally disconnected from him. He's an architect. Started his own firm last year and has pulled some major contracts since then."

"Workaholic. One who obviously puts in the time at the gym." So far, he sounded perfect. Someone who was that busy wouldn't make demands that Laila had no interest in fulfilling. "What's his name?"

"Gabe. He and Desmond went to school together. Want his number?" Sia paused at the base of the stairs.

"No thanks. I'll get it from him later."

"Christine who?" Sia shoved her arm lightly.

"Uncle Samar," she took the stairs two at a time, "your daughter tells me that you have a thief at Archer."

Samar raised his eyebrow and looked pointedly from Laila to Sia, who was a few steps behind her. With a shake of his head, he looked at the group of people he'd been chatting with. "Excuse me, folks. I need to have a conversation with my girls. Laila's got a quirky sense of humor, doesn't she?"

He turned and went into the house. Laila and Sia followed him through the kitchen and down the hall to his office. Once there, he poured himself a Scotch neat and stared at Laila as he sipped his drink.

It took her a moment to realize that this was his way of signaling she'd done something wrong. He was good like that, patient about her lack of savvy, and probably wasn't really upset. Just as Sia did, her uncle Samar took the time to explain when she broke social rules or misread emotional cues, and it really helped her to navigate future situations better. She thought back. She'd interrupted his conversation. That was rude.

"I interrupted. I'm sorry." Or, rather, she was pretty sure she would be if sorry was in her emotional arsenal.

"I appreciate that. Do you know what else you did?"

She shook her head.

"I work for a securities company, Laila. Every person I was talking to is an investor in Archer. Telling them we have a thief is bad for our public image."

"Oh." This was one of those subtlety things that Laila would probably never understand, where the truth wasn't always better. "I'm sorry about that, too."

Uncle Samar nodded toward the decanter. "Pour yourself a drink."

Sia beat her to it and poured one for herself and another for Laila. They settled on the black leather couch opposite Samar. His office was old-school classy, with a dark mahogany desk, floor to ceiling bookshelves to match, and a leaded crystal service for his liquor. When she was little, Laila would sneak into this room, curl up on the couch, and recite all the words that went with the office. Sumptuous. Luxurious. Decadent. Fancy. Stylish. The list went on and on, and over time, those words became just as closely associated with Uncle Samar as they were with the office.

As an adult, she still loved this room, and anytime she was feeling especially disconnected from herself, she would recite the list, very quietly under her breath, because people looked at her funny when she talked to herself out loud. Some day, she would have an office like this. Maybe not exactly—she wasn't crazy about the dark wood—but one that felt like this one. Laila sipped her Scotch. It was smooth in a fiery-apocalypse-in-her-mouth kind of way.

Laila waited politely for Uncle Samar. She hated the inaction, but he liked to ease into a conversation. Sia put her hand on Laila's knee and pushed down to stop her jiggling it up and down, something Laila wasn't aware she was doing.

"Dad?" Sia prompted her dad.

"Right. Archer. I haven't been able to pinpoint it exactly, but our figures are just...off. We expect a certain amount of loss, as you know, but the shrink in certain areas is well over the allowed amount."

Calling Archer a securities company, as Uncle Samar had, was an extreme understatement. Yes, they did some work in finance, including divisions in banking and commodities trading. But that was a drop in a very large, diversified global bucket. Archer Securities was an international conglomerate with interest in everything imaginable, from the US commodities market to overseas production of silks. Laila grew up listening to stories of Archer and still couldn't nail down what they did in precise terms.

Laila leaned in. This was something she could understand. "Which areas?"

"Home goods, food products, and electronics."

"Home goods and food? That's weird." Electronics was an area that invited sticky fingers, so that didn't surprise her. "Are they real losses, as in actual inventory disappearing? Or is it all on paper?"

"Neither. So far, everything I've looked at balances. The margins are just off."

"Can I look at it?" Laila tried to sound cool, but it didn't work. Stuff like this, solving a puzzle, buzzed through her like a live current. Always had. Sia called it excitement. Laila called it nirvana. Regardless, she was able to see patterns that other people missed, and it gave her a charge like no other.

Uncle Samar raised his eyebrows. "Do you have time?"

Laila owned and operated Hollister Investigations, a small private investigations service that had been funded almost entirely by Uncle Samar's capital investment. Without him, she would still have been able to start the business, but the outlook would have been much different. For instance, she would have been working out of her car rather than a small suite of offices downtown. And she would have worked alone rather than having two employees.

"Uncle Samar," she shook her head, "of course I have time for you." She'd paid back his startup loan within a year of opening the doors, but she certainly hadn't forgotten his generosity.

"All right. Come by Archer tomorrow. You'll have to work on site." With that, Samar finished his Scotch and set the tumbler on the low coffee table between them. "Now, come on. We have a party to get back to."

As they walked out of the office, Sia nudged Laila with her shoulder and said, "Never fear, Laila Hollister is on the case."

It was an old joke, left over from a childhood spent chasing down clues in the neighborhood as if she were a real life *Encyclopedia Brown*. Laila laughed. There was a lightness in her chest that she rarely experienced. It came from being able to do what she loved and help her family at the same time.

"That thief won't know what hit him."

CHAPTER 2

The shipping manifest showed twenty cargo containers arriving via barge from The People's Republic of China. Trinity tapped her pen against her teeth. Twenty containers full of soft goods—mostly pillows and those plush blankets that were really comforting when it was cold out—destined for a local chain store.

How many could she divert without being obvious? Typically, she worked with smaller quantities. A pallet here or there. When a company such as Archer was moving ten thousand pallets, the loss of one or two was written off. It took more resources to search for it than the value of the product.

But an entire shipping container, which was what she was contemplating at the moment, would throw up some red flags. There would be an investigation. No, it was better to siphon off a smaller amount than to go for the big haul only to have in-house security track it down and reclaim it.

That decided it.

She made a mental note of the delivery schedule. The entire container would arrive at the distribution center tomorrow, be inventoried, and then be routed to the retailer. Except for two pallets, one of pillows and one of blankets, which she earmarked for Open Doors, a local homeless shelter where she routinely volunteered. They would be delivered by the end of the week via a local transport company, along with an invoice for zero dollars.

After entering the information needed to generate a second manifest and execute the order, her work extension rang. She toggled her screen and tapped the button on her headset to answer the call.

"Computer services, this is Trinity. How can I help you?" Trinity kept her voice light, playful. People in the tech industry were notorious for being snarky and impatient. She was okay with snarky to a degree, but being impatient was simply rude. There was never a good excuse to be rude.

"You gotta help me. My boss needs this report for a meeting that starts in ten minutes. I've printed it at least twenty times, but it never comes out of the printer." The man, *George Harper* according to the readout that popped up on her computer screen, spoke with the unhinged desperation that colored the voices of most of her callers.

"Okay, George, I'm accessing your system now. Give me just a few moments." She typed in the commands that allowed her to control his computer remotely and then scrolled through his settings. "George, where is your desk located?"

"What do you mean?"

Like most of her callers, George worked locally, at the monolithic Archer Securities building that housed several divisions of the US operations. There were smaller regional offices throughout the country that stretched out from the main location like a spider web over the landscape. Archer's software, which sometimes moved with the speed of a hobbled elephant, provided Trinity with some basic information, such as which office a person was based out of, which department he worked in, and where his desk was located. It also indicated which printer his computer

was set to send material to. In George's case, his location
and the printer's didn't match up. Before she changed any
settings, however, she always verified the data in front of
her.

"Which floor are you on? Which side of the building?"
Trinity didn't understand why some people let themselves
get so frazzled before they called her. Sure, print the
document twice, just to be sure it wasn't working, but
twenty? Seriously?

"Oh, the fifth, next to the R&D lab," George said. His
description matched the information in the computer. She
changed the printer router to the correct location.

"Good. Could you try printing another one for me?"
Trinity waited, twirling her pen like a drumstick between
her fingers.

"Sure." George sounded skeptical. A printer whirred to
life in the background. "Holy shit! It worked! Thank you!"

Trinity laughed.

"Oh crap, I mean..." George stammered. "Sorry. You
didn't record this, did you? My boss would totally fire me
for swearing."

Of course she'd recorded it. That was part of the protocol
for working remotely. Any time her phone rang, the digital
recording activated automatically. George would have
known that if he'd paid attention to the recorded messaged
that played while he waited for her to answer. "Don't worry,
George. Your secret is safe with me."

"Great. You totally saved me."

"It's my pleasure. Is there anything else I can help you
with today?"

George paused. "Oh, I...I don't think so."

"Great. Take that report to your boss, and then you might want to head down to the second floor and check the printer in the southwest corner. I suspect you'll find a stack of reports just like the one in your hand. Take care, George."

Trinity signed off. When she started with Archer Securities in the IT department, she'd worked five days a week at the main site. Her desk sat in the middle of the bullpen, and she was surrounded by sweaty, competitive tech guys who acted as if they'd never seen a real live girl before, let alone talked to one. Now, almost nine years later, she was part of Archer's work-from-home program. It was perfect.

"Trinity?" Carol stepped into her office. "I'm going to take your mom to the park. It's a beautiful day, perfect for a picnic. Care to join us?"

At fifty, Carol was a robust woman with smooth, dark skin and a lyrical Jamaican accent. She grew up in Kingston with Trinity's mom, Ornella Washington. She'd moved to the US two years ago when Ornella's memory started to slide. Now, she worked full time as Ornella's primary caregiver.

"I wish, but I need to stay by the phone." Trinity could move about her house freely, but in order to venture outside her home, she needed to notify Archer. It was simpler to eat at home and remain available. "Do you need anything from me before you go?"

"Nope. Your mom is having a good day." Carol gave her a thumbs up. Ornella suffered from early onset Alzheimer's. A good day for her could mean she remembered who Trinity was or that she remembered to chew her food without reminders. Lately, her good days were becoming less and less frequent. Together, she and Carol had started the initial groundwork for moving Ornella into a dedicated care home, but Trinity wanted to hold off on that as long as possible.

Trinity slipped off her headset and stood. "Think she'll know who I am now?"

"It's possible." Carol squeezed Trinity's arm gently as she passed on her way to the living room.

Ornella sat by the window, her face turned up toward the sun, eyes closed, and a peaceful, easy smile just teasing the edges of her lips. In that moment, she looked like the mom of ten years ago, back when Trinity was still in high school and Ornella was still in charge of all her faculties.

"Hi, Mom." Trinity reached out and stopped just short of touching Ornella's shoulder. She waited, suspended mid-motion as she waited to see how Ornella reacted before she made physical contact.

Ornella inhaled deeply as she opened her eyes. She studied Trinity for a moment, a slight crease in the middle of her forehead, and then her clouded expression cleared. "Hi, baby. You look beautiful today."

Trinity let her hand drop onto Ornella's shoulder and exhaled. The moments between, when her mom had seen her but hadn't decided if she knew her or not, were the toughest for Trinity. She held her breath every time, as if waiting for permission to continue. Once, before they had really realized what was happening with Ornella, Trinity had touched her mom in a moment when she hadn't recognized Trinity. Her mom had cried out and jerked away. Now, Trinity knew to wait. Without the spark of recognition, touching her own mother was the same as touching a stranger without consent.

"No, I look like a computer geek. You, however, are very beautiful." She stroked Ornella's cheek with the back of her hand. She had the softest skin, two or three shades darker than Trinity's and free of makeup.

"Aren't you sweet."

Carol entered the room carrying a light jacket and a collapsible cooler. "Here we are, Ornella. Are you ready?"

"Oh, are we going somewhere?" Ornella slipped the jacket on and looked from Carol to Trinity and then back to Carol.

"Carol's taking you for a picnic lunch." Trinity tapped the cooler. "It's such a beautiful day. Doesn't that sound nice?"

"Oh, yes. I remember now."

Carol led Ornella to the door. "We shouldn't be more than an hour. I have my phone if you need anything before we get back."

Trinity waved as they left.

Early in her teens, Trinity had decided that she'd probably never have children of her own. She'd watched her own mom struggle as a single parent and didn't want to ever feel like she had to give up her own needs for someone else. Around the same time, she also tripped into her first relationship with another girl who made Trinity feel all sorts of things that her boyfriends never did. The realization that she was a lesbian simplified the decision to forgo having children. Yet, here she was, shaping her whole life to fit around the needs of another. What's more, she was happy for it, because a day taking care of Ornella was another day she got to spend with her rather than without.

Trinity's phone rang, and she jogged back to her office. This time, instead of work, it was a personal call via Skype.

She pushed the button to initiate the video, and Yvonne, her sometimes friend, sometimes lover from high school, popped up on her screen.

"Hey, babe!" Yvonne wore a beat up army green jacket with the sleeves rolled up, and her hair stuck out at funny angles. It was a stark difference from the way she looked before she ran off to Costa Rica with her environmental activist boyfriend. She used to be all lipstick, perfect makeup, and runway outfits. A few months after she moved, she'd sheered off her signature long blond hair and had kept it that way ever since. Now, she was relaxed, a little undone, and even more beautiful than ever.

"Hi. What's up with you?" Sometimes, when Trinity let herself think about it, her body ached with the loss of her friend. But that wasn't often because, if nothing else, Trinity was aces at blocking out those kind of emotional twinges.

"Adam is away on a secret mission involving some rare sea algae and several yards of that chain they use for the anchor on ocean liners." She waved her hand dismissively. "And I'm stuck here, alone and bored. Wanna fool around?" Yvonne waggled her eyebrows. They'd done that a few times, hooked up via the magic of a kickass Internet connection and video calling, but Trinity was working, and Yvonne didn't really look like she was into it.

"Nah. I'm on the clock." Trinity settled into her seat and kicked one leg up on her desk. "How's Central America?"

"Really, really good. I'm almost done with my next novel. Oh, and Adam's cousin, like, fifty times removed, is staying with us for the summer. She's this cute thirteen-year-old with nerd glasses bigger than yours. Seriously, she taught herself how to code. You'd love her."

"Oh?" Trinity cherished being able to talk to Yvonne, no matter the topic. But the idea of a geeky young teen who loved computers as much as Trinity hit a special place in her heart. The world of programming needed more female energy. "What's she working on? Any idea?"

Yvonne laughed. "I knew you'd be into hearing about her. You're so predictable in your dedication to all things geeky."

"Does that mean you don't know the answer?"

"She tried to explain it. Something super smart for some summer school project. I don't know. I mentioned you, and she got even more excited than you just did. She asked if she could email you."

While they were talking, Trinity pulled her lunch from the mini-fridge in her office and spread it out on her desk. Earlier, while on her morning run, she'd stopped at the co-op down the street and picked up a Greek yogurt, two of those delicious little oranges, and a chef salad made with organic veggies. She hated the yogurt, but her body liked her to eat it, so she did. As a special treat because she'd spent an extra fifteen minutes on yoga that morning, she'd also picked up a gourmet cupcake from the bakery.

"Sure, did you give her my email address?"

"Not yet. I wanted to check with you. What are you eating?" Yvonne leaned in toward her computer screen, bringing her face close, as if that would help her to better see Trinity's food.

"Go ahead and give it to her." As she spoke, Trinity held up her oranges and yogurt. "Plus salad and dessert."

"What kind of salad?"

"Chef, from the co-op."

"God, I miss that place. Remind me again why I moved here." Why, indeed. The cottage Yvonne shared with Adam was situated on a pristine beach, and Trinity had an excellent view of the surf in the screen behind Yvonne.

"Sex," Trinity deadpanned. Prior to moving to Costa Rica, Yvonne had shared Trinity's bed more often than not. Then she'd met Adam, fallen hard and fast, and three weeks later she followed him to Central America. She'd been there for two years and was still just as crazy about him as she'd been when she moved. Love sometimes worked like that.

"Oh yeah. That." Yvonne got this far away, blissed out expression on her face.

Trinity made a gagging noise, but she was smiling on the inside. "Stop it. I don't want to throw up on my lunch."

Yvonne laughed. "Sorry." Her expression sobered. "How's your mom?"

"She recognized me earlier. Carol took her to the park for lunch."

"Have you figured out what you're going to do?"

"Nope. Trying not to think about it."

"You have to eventually."

Trinity took a bite of her salad and crunched as loud as she could on the crisp lettuce.

"Stop it. You know I'm right. I wish I could help."

"You're right. Of course. But right now, in this moment, everything is fine, and that's enough."

Yvonne sighed, and Trinity's work line rang again.

"I have to go, Vonnie. Work." Trinity loved her job, but the timing sucked this time. "Love you. Miss you."

"Come visit."

Trinity sighed. "You know I can't. And I really do have to go."

"I miss you." Yvonne made a kissy face and then disconnected the call.

She always made the same plea for Trinity to visit, and Trinity always made the same excuse. With things as they were with Ornella, Trinity was grounded indefinitely.

The day passed in more or less the same manner as always. She answered calls, helped people, and left them with a smile in their voice instead of a frown. Between calls, she logged into an encrypted message board to see if her friends had posted anything new. There were two new threads.

The first read: *Housewarming 1208 S Hampton Ave Shreveport 7.22 BYOB*

Several people had responded, and she added her RSVP to the rest. *I'm in for a fifth of Vodka. The good stuff.*

The second message was similar, except this time it was an invitation for a baby shower. She agreed to supply an economy-sized package of diapers.

Then she set about researching who she'd just agreed to help. Obviously, she wasn't going to an event in Louisiana. A housewarming was code for a family on the verge of losing their home, and the bottle of vodka was her pledge of nine grand to the cause. But before she could fulfill her promise, she had to determine exactly who lived at 1208 S Hampton Avenue in Shreveport and, just as importantly, figure out which bank held their mortgage.

She'd stumbled across this group years ago when, arrogant and careless, she'd encroached on an Anonymous project. Rather than shutting her down, they'd put her through the paces and then turned her onto this collective of hacktivists who were dedicated to righting the balance of wealth in the US. This way, working together to save people from financial ruin, they were able to keep their banking transactions below the ten grand mark that automatically triggered an IRS notification. Collectively, they paid off some significant debts.

"Oh, hello there." Trinity's mom stood in the open doorway to her office. "I didn't realize I had company. How nice. Can I get you something to drink?"

"That would be nice. How about a nice glass of lemonade?"

"That sounds lovely. I'll be right back. My name is Ornella, by the way."

"I'm Trinity."

"Trinity? I always thought I'd name my daughter that, if I ever have one. It's nice to meet you." Ornella smiled in that soft, puzzled way that said she knew something was off but she couldn't quite put her finger on it. She tapped the door frame and then walked away, toward the kitchen. With any luck, she'd be back in a few with a couple of tall glasses of lemonade with chunks of ice.

Trinity turned back to her computer and was able to transfer the money from an off-shore account to the family in Louisiana before Ornella returned, this time with Carol. Trinity would finish with the baby shower later.

"Looks like I have two visitors today. How fortunate am I?" Ornella set a tray on the small coffee table and took a seat on the sofa that sat along the same wall as Trinity's desk. Carol sat in the armchair opposite. "I also found a lovely key lime pie in the refrigerator. I thought we might enjoy a piece with our drinks."

Trinity smiled, took the drink Ornella offered her, and spent the rest of the afternoon letting her mom get to know her all over again.

CHAPTER 3

The office provided to Laila at Archer was actually a hastily converted, but richly appointed, conference room adjacent to Uncle Samar's office. The space was typically used for meetings with his department heads and could only be accessed via a door to the side of his desk.

It was a small room but, like everything about her uncle, opulent. A dark mahogany table served as her desk, and, rather than the industrial carpet that would withstand nuclear holocaust found in the public areas of Archer, the floor was covered with a sumptuous wool carpet that felt remarkably like walking on air. Or small furry animals.

It wasn't enough to make up for the lack of exterior windows. Still, if she ignored the size—and the smell of recycled air—it was okay. Laila had definitely worked in worse, and this was a temporary arrangement, anyway.

She preferred her office downtown that looked as if it were pulled straight from the pages of a fifties-era crime novel. The door even had frosted glass with the business name etched in it: *Hollister Investigations*. The lettering had been an expensive indulgence, but it added the perfect touch. On the day it was installed, she'd posed next to it while Sia snapped picture after picture.

"Do you need anything else, Laila?" Uncle Samar asked. He stood beside her, just inside the open door, watching as IT Dude set up. Despite being a busy executive at Archer, he didn't make her feel rushed. Yet another reason to love him.

Her phone signaled that she had a new message, and she glanced at it. "Sia." She showed her uncle.

Scheduling appointment for dresses. Thursday at 6pm ok?

What a silly question. Why would Laila care when Sia went dress shopping?

Sure. Why wouldn't it be?

"Is everything okay?" Like a good father, Uncle Samar was always interested in the goings on with his daughter.

"She's talking about shopping." Laila shook her head. She and Uncle Samar shared a dislike for shopping and were collectively mystified by Sia's love of it. Laila's phone chirped. Sia again.

Your work schedule can be sketchy. Just making sure you're available.

Before she answered Sia, she turned back to her uncle. There was no reason to keep him waiting. "I think I'm good." She surveyed the table. The IT department had set her up with a sleek iMac, and she was excited to try it out. She'd been contemplating a switch to Mac for Hollister Investigations, and this would give her a good opportunity to see if it would be worth the investment. IT Dude was still there, checking her connection and setting up access per her uncle's instructions. He kept shooting her surreptitious glances as he worked. She smiled, and his cheeks flushed red.

There was a built-in, three-section whiteboard with storage space behind it. That was good. She'd use it to help visualize the processes here at Archer as she searched for the weak points. "Is it possible to get a printer installed in this room?" Some things were easier to compare when she had a physical copy in her hands.

"The printers are networked to the main printing queue. Everything comes out at the big laser printer in the middle of the floor." IT Dude picked that moment to overcome his shyness.

Her phone beeped with another message. She ignored it for the moment.

She directed her response to Uncle Samar. "It would be better, more discreet, if I could print in this room. I'd rather not give the rest of the floor access to every report I want to look at."

Uncle Samar nodded. "That can be arranged." He looked at IT Dude as he said it.

"Yes sir," IT Dude muttered, clearly not happy with the additional work order.

"Anything else?" Uncle Samar asked again.

She looked around. She had a landline, a small coffee station, and a remote that controlled something in the room that she had yet to identify. She'd figure that out later. "All I need now is a login and a brief tour to teach me how to navigate the system."

IT Dude groaned. Laila clamped down the urge to kick him. Her phone beeped. Again.

"You can call computer services and have someone walk you through it over the phone," Uncle Samar said. "The number is programmed into the phone. Before that, though, you should probably answer my daughter. She can be relentless." After giving her a brief smile, he left her alone to stare at IT Dude as he made hooking up a single-unit iMac look like much more trouble than one piece of hardware and two cables possibly could be.

She checked her phone. Three more messages from Sia.

Laila? Are you available?

Followed by: *Bitch, please! Don't ignore me.*

And finally: *Laila, this is part of being a maid of honor. Remember that? And how you're going to kick its ass? Man up!*

Realization of what Sia wanted from her finally kicked in. This wasn't normal dress shopping. She responded. *Tell me where.*

All the while, Laila watched IT Dude and waited. Her palms itched. It was always like this, the cagey, barely contained urge to dive in once a problem had been introduced. She'd waited all weekend—well, since the barbecue Saturday afternoon—to start her formal investigation into the discrepancies her uncle told her about, and the longer IT Dude prolonged his work, the worse the feeling got.

"I have to bring a printer from the IT department. On the other side of campus." IT Dude stared at her, his face blank.

"Okay." Laila swept the door open. She needed him out of the room sooner rather than later. Even without a printer, she could start poking around. "Get to it."

She returned his blank-faced stare. Friendly wasn't her strong point, and she was here to root out a problem, not make friends. IT Dude grumbled under his breath as he pushed his gray utility cart out of the room. A heavy, three-drawer toolbox sat on the bottom shelf, and one of the wheels spun wildly, making a squeaking noise reminiscent of Sunday mornings in a grocery store.

Laila released the door, and the hydraulic hinge at the top pulled it shut. She paced the distance from the door to the whiteboard and back again. She did her best work on her feet. First things first, she needed to check in with her office. She used her cell phone to call her assistant, Max, and as the phone rang, Laila made a mental checklist of items to review with her.

"Hollister Investigations. This is Max." Max was a skilled investigator and an excellent assistant. She was not, however, good at covering the phones. That's why Laila employed a receptionist.

"Where's Justin?" Laila didn't care where Justin, her receptionist, was so much as where he wasn't, which was at his desk answering the phones.

"I don't know. Something about a sick mom. Hospital. You know I suck at listening unless food is involved." Max sounded bored. Part of what made her so good at her job was her innate ability to convince others to underestimate her. Max was neither bored, nor a bad listener.

"Why didn't you let it go to voicemail?" That was, perhaps, not the best strategy in terms of responsive customer service, but it was better than turning Max loose on a potential new client.

"I knew it was you."

"No you didn't."

"Of course I did. You've been there long enough to get set up and now you want a report. You always check in about this time when you start a new on-site investigation."

"Huh." Laila thought she was less predictable, but when she mentally reviewed their last several cases, it had gone very much as Max described. "Still, you should let the service get it."

"Next time."

"Tell me what you have on Archer."

"I've already sent the full dossier to your email. The highlights include a banking division that's under investigation for illegal foreclosure practices, a private army based out of Sudan, and a dedicated kidnap and ransom budget with a top end of two million per incident." As Max gave the rundown, Laila's phone beeped with another message.

"Get me a list of any employees who have a mortgage through Archer." This wasn't a small ask, given the security protocols in place on most banking websites. She would request a similar list from her uncle and see how they compared.

"Working on it."

The FCC investigation into Archer's banking practices was interesting, but not alarming. The private army, however, that was…promising. Still, she was unlikely to find a link there. Conglomerated corporations such as Archer dipped into anything that turned a profit. A private army could be anything from contractors in the Middle East to an armed security company based in Hong Kong. Regardless, she would take a look at the details before she dismissed it.

"I want a full report on the security service." Private militia groups were generally funded under the budget umbrella of security.

"It's in your inbox." Max excelled at anticipating the needs of an investigation. She'd been scouted by several other larger investigation firms, as well as the security departments of a few corporations such as Archer. Each time, she chose to stay with Laila, earning her a sizable raise on her anniversary. Loyalty like hers was rare and deserved recognition.

"Tell me about the kidnap and ransom."

A K-and-R account was standard for a corporation the size of Archer. Most international conglomerates maintained a similar fund and also kept a professional crisis and hostage negotiator on retainer. In certain parts of the world, kidnapping an executive for the payoff ransom was a common entrepreneurial endeavor. One good ransom could often feed several families for a year or more.

"In the past twelve months, they refused to pay ransoms on six employees. One was released in the center of a town square in Bolivia, blindfolded and hogtied, 200 kilometers from the abduction site."

"And the other five."

"Also found in local town squares. Dead."

"Give me the workup on the families. Go back a minimum of five years for similar cases. Include information on the survivors as well." There was no earthly way she could review a detailed profile of all of Archer's employees. There were simply too many of them. They needed to narrow the field first. Five dead executives was as good a place to start as any.

"You got it, boss."

"What else do you have?"

"I've compiled data on all of the top executives. You'll find all but your uncle's in your email now."

Statistically, the higher an employee was on the organizational flowchart, the more likely he was to embezzle from the company. In order to be objective, she needed to see all of the information, including the file on her uncle Samar. Max knew that, so her withholding the file didn't bode well. "Why did you hold that back?"

Max paused, then said, "There's some...delicate information. I wasn't sure you'd want to see it." Max was as bad at tact as Laila.

Her phone beeped again. Laila needed to talk to Sia about this. The constant texting was distracting.

"Is it relevant to the case?"

"Mmm, hard to say."

That was enough for Laila. Unless her uncle was hiring twelve-year-old prostitutes or hosting illegal dog fights, she wasn't likely to care about his dirty laundry. Besides, he'd brought her in to investigate. Surely he'd anticipated that she'd need to look into him as well. "Send it."

"Okay," Max said, and the clicking of her fingers against her computer keyboard confirmed that she did it right then.

"Is that all?" Laila asked, and her phone beeped again.

"Almost. There's also a file on all the legal actions taken against Archer from the past five years, from several class actions all the way down to on-the-job-injury reports. Also, Archer has been targeted by several hacktivist groups. The data trail is sketchy, but there's enough to give you a general outline."

"Okay, good work. I'll be in touch." As awkward as the words felt in her mouth, Laila ended all of her calls with her employees with the words "good work." According to Sia, that showed that she cared, fostered goodwill, and bred loyalty. Max, who was too much like Laila, likely thought it was a giant wankfest, but Justin probably liked it.

Max, in her typical urbane fashion, disconnected without saying goodbye.

Before looking at the email files from Max, Laila checked her phone. Sia's text messages included the name and address of the dress shop, a link to a website for maids of honor, and a very succinct *You got this.*

Laila added the appointment to her online calendar, bookmarked the website, and responded with a smiley emoji. Sia said it was rude to not respond even if she had nothing to say. It wasn't fair to leave the other person hanging.

With that out of the way, Laila turned to her work. She spent the next several hours reviewing the information that Max sent. Until she got into Archer's systems, it was the only thing she could do. And, really, it was more about getting an overall picture of Archer as a whole entity. She'd always viewed the company through the rose-colored filter of Uncle Samar. The stories he'd shared made the company sound almost mythical in its perfection. She'd never find what she was looking for if he was her only source of information.

She started with the incidents that seemed to be the least likely source of the losses. Even though she didn't expect to find anything related to the kidnappings or the private army, it still helped with her overall understanding of the company. Without intending to, she saved the file on her uncle for last.

IT Dude returned with a printer just as she opened the file on the paramilitary employed by Archer in Sudan. She backed out of her work completely and stood far enough away to give him room to move, yet close enough to make sure he didn't mess about with her research. As he was leaving, a knock sounded from the door. Uncle Samar stepped in as IT Dude wrapped up his work.

"I'm headed out for a lunch meeting. Do you need anything before I go?"

"Yes, actually. I need the financial statements for those three departments. Home goods, food products, and electronics. An overview, plus detailed statements, going back at least five years."

When she finished speaking, Laila became acutely aware of IT Dude staring at her. It was different than the slobbering interest he'd shown her earlier. This time, he regarded her with open-mouthed astonishment. Uncle Samar, however, smiled at her with the same soft expression that he seemed to reserve for her and Sia alone.

"What?" She glanced back at IT Dude, who shook his head and looked away.

"Nothing." He pushed his cart out of the room, his gaze focused studiously at a point on the wall that Laila didn't find particularly interesting.

"What was that about?" Laila asked after IT Dude left.

Uncle Samar chuckled. "I imagine it has something to do with you tossing out orders to me. People here don't do that. They think I'm in charge."

"Oh. Right. Sorry."

"It's fine. Don't change a thing. Are you hungry? I'll have my assistant order a sandwich from the deli downstairs for you."

"Roast beef and a Cobb salad."

"Done." Uncle Samar backed out of the office, one hand on the doorknob. "I'll have her get those financial reports for you as well."

Rather than resuming her review of the files Max sent her, Laila called computer services for the tutorial on the workings of Archer's systems. Sure, her uncle would get her the reports she needed, but it would be much easier if she could access them on her own.

After twenty minutes on the phone with a pleasant man whose name Laila forgot as soon as he said it, she felt comfortable enough to work on her own. She thanked him for his time, disconnected the call, and returned her attention once again to her email. The only report left to review was the one labeled Samar Raje.

Before she could click on it, there was a soft knock at the door and a woman entered. She carried a stack of papers and a deli bag, both of which she set on the table next to Laila.

"Lunch. And work." She nudged the bag and the papers successively.

"Thanks. I didn't know I was hungry until Uncle Samar mentioned food."

"My pleasure. Let me know if you need anything else. I'm Ava, and you can find me just outside Mr. Raje's office."

Without a second thought, Laila tucked into her lunch. The file on her uncle could wait.

CHAPTER 4

The wind was cool against Trinity's overheated skin as she leaned against the railing that separated her from the Willamette river. With the water at her back and the greenbelt stretched out to her front and sides, she watched as children ran squealing through the grass. It was an early summer day that promised to be long and hot, but in that moment, halfway through her morning run, she was at peace.

To her left, a group of older people moved gracefully through their tai-chi routine, and she briefly considered joining them. Their peaceful, zen-filled presence was the perfect counterbalance to the light laughing from the children that she could just hear over the music in her headphones. This morning, she chose Bob Marley to ease into her day with the lyrical promise of "No Woman No Cry" in her ears. As delightful a distraction as tai-chi would be, her morning schedule limited the time she could spend on her run. Perhaps another time.

Arms stretched out along the banister, eyes partially closed, she luxuriated in the simple pleasure of the moment and tried not to think about the demands waiting for her at home. Between work and the ever-present worry about her mom, Trinity savored times like this. Having Carol there helped, but it didn't erase the fact that soon Trinity would have to make a more permanent decision about Ornella's care. Her health declined incrementally every day. Trinity wouldn't be able to pretend things were fine for much longer.

Right here, right now, the extra five minutes spent enjoying the light breeze off the water as it mingled with the scent of fresh bread from the bakery nearby wouldn't hurt.

It was perfection.

Of course, it couldn't last. With a heavy sigh, Trinity stepped away from the rail to resume her run. She only made it a few steps before a man, showing off for his friends as they tossed a football around, backed into her and almost knocked her to the ground. Trinity was able to catch herself, but he was not as lucky. He sprawled across the path at her feet. His friends stood a few yards away, laughing and calling out to him. With an easy grace, he rose to his feet, a charming, ready smile on his face. The football he'd risked injury—his own and Trinity's—to catch spiraled away in a lopsided, drunken crawl that spanned the length of the walkway only to peter out when it hit the grass.

"Hi." The man doubled his grin and ran his hands through his hair. It was short in the back, long on top, and the way it hung in his eyes was a little too much like a cultivated surfer look to be cool. "Sorry about that."

"No problem." Trinity didn't remove her earbuds, but she did offer him a friendly smile. Because she'd dallied too long enjoying the weather, she didn't have time for further delay. She bounced on the balls of her feet, a universal sign that she wanted to be on the move, not standing around. Still, there was no reason to be unpleasant, not with the voice of Bob in her head, encouraging her to embrace her fellow man.

The man brushed his hands over his chest as if knocking off dust after a hard day of work. He stuck out his hand. "I'm Dave."

This was where it always got tricky for Trinity. With his introduction, Dave had revealed his intention.

Rather than shake his hand, she held hers up. "I'm sweaty and need to finish my run." She went to side step around him.

Of course, he moved with her, stepping to the side to block her way. "Wait, what's your hurry? I thought we could get to know each other."

She stopped bouncing and planted her feet. With careful, controlled movements, she removed her earbuds, tucked them into the pocket with her mp3 player, and pushed her sunglasses up onto her head. Hands on her hips, she said, "Really?" She hated bullshit like this.

Dave's smile faltered. He tilted his head to one side and cast a fleeting glance toward his friends. "What do you mean?"

If she were at a bar, maybe she would understand his confusion. But here? On a jogging trail, covered in sweat? How could this guy possibly think she was interested?

"Dave, listen," she spoke in that sugary-sweet voice that she reserved for the especially stupid, "I'm sure you're a great guy—" she had an entire monologue ready about how she wasn't into him and that it clearly wasn't going to happen between them, with a bit about consent to tie it up nicely at the end, but he, of course, interrupted.

"Whoa there. Don't go saying anything crazy now." His smile morphed from frat boy to used car salesman—both tried too hard to be charming, but one was a bit shadier about getting what he wanted. He looked over his shoulder at his buddies as they howled with laughter. "Why don't you come hang with us for a while? Have some fun."

"Not going to happen." Trinity shook her head. So much for channeling the mellow of Marley. Men like this—privileged, entitled, white—made her crazy.

Dave shook his head. "Wow, look, you don't need to get wound up."

"You've got to be kidding me." Trinity wondered how wound up Dave would get if a man twice his size knocked him to the ground and prevented him from leaving, all in the name of misguided flirting. Until now, it had been such a lovely morning.

Dave faltered. Clearly he wasn't used to being shot down. He leaned in toward her and said, "I just... I thought we might talk. You know, exchange numbers?" His smile wavered. "You know?"

A couple of joggers stopped to watch the exchange, a man and a woman.

Trinity sighed. "Could you just step to the side? I'm officially late now."

She probably could have curtailed the whole encounter by telling him she was a lesbian, but why should she have to? "No" should have been enough. Not to mention, that approach could backfire. Some men considered it their obligation to "straighten out" lesbians.

"Dude," the male jogger stepped up, "let her leave."

Dave raised his hands up in front of him and said, "Whoa, everything is fine here. No need to get involved."

The man turned to Trinity. "Is that right? Is everything fine?"

Trinity walked around Dave, giving him a wide berth. "It is now. Thanks." She gave the couple her most grateful smile and took off without further comment.

The mellow high she'd felt a few moments earlier was officially busted to hell.

"I'm back." Trinity slipped off her running shoes and left them in the basket by the front door. Their house was old, built in the late 1800s, and had beautiful dark hardwood floors. When she was little, her mom had made Trinity take her shoes off because she'd track mud through the entire place without realizing it. Now, old enough to keep track of her own muddy feet, she still removed them every time she entered. It was a comfortable habit that reminded her of easier times. "Mom? Carol?"

"In here," Carol called from the kitchen.

Trinity headed toward the kitchen, the reusable shopping bag that contained her lunch swinging at her side. In the entrance to the kitchen, she stopped short. Her mom and Carol stood at the counter, lacing together the top crust of what looked to be a cherry pie. Trinity closed her eyes, took a deep breath, and then opened them again. "What's this?"

"Ornella wants to go to church this evening. She's baking a pie to take to the minister."

"Oh?"

For years, Trinity had accompanied her mom to church every Sunday morning and Wednesday evening. Recently, they were doing pretty good if Ornella realized where they were about twenty percent of the time. She hadn't requested that they attend service in too many months to count.

Tears swam at the back of Trinity's eyes, and she tried to regulate her breathing. Slow, easy breaths made it easier to keep things from spilling over. Church was something she'd thought was fully and completely past, yet here she was, watching her mom as she put the final touches on one of her signature pies. All so she could attend the evening service.

"Yes, baby. Don't look so surprised. We go every week on Wednesday. You know that." Her mom spoke with that same comforting sweetness that had carried Trinity through every hiccup and bump of her early teenage years.

Trinity's vision blurred even more. Then, completely without her permission, her tears spilled over. She crossed the kitchen, and Ornella engulfed her in a strong hug. For several moments, they stayed like this, with Trinity soaking up her mom. Then, after far too short a time, Ornella stiffened. The moment had passed, along with Ornella's awareness. Trinity pulled away, and her mom studied her with a guarded, cautious expression.

"Hello," Ornella said. "I don't think we've met. I'm Ornella."

Trinity gave her a wobbly smile and said, "It's nice to meet you." Then she turned to Carol and hefted her shopping bag. "I'll just put this in the fridge in my office. You two have fun."

Thirty seconds, give or take. That's how long she got with her mom before she turned back into a stranger. How much more would she have gotten if she hadn't taken an extended break during her run?

Trinity retreated to her office and dropped off her lunch, then ran upstairs for a quick shower. Nobody would know if she started work right after her jog, but she couldn't stand the feeling of sweat clinging to her. Besides, the few minutes with the hot water sluicing over her body gave her an opportunity to regroup. When she finished, she inspected herself in the mirror. The whites of her eyes were a crosshatch of red, contrasting starkly against her dark pupils and skin. A few drops of Visine helped. Her hair had grown out enough that she needed to get it straightened again. Or maybe she'd have it braided and weave in some deep burgundy highlights. Or maybe she'd cut it all off. That would certainly be easier. She sighed, something she seemed to do endlessly these days.

To work. That would help her to focus on something beyond her own state of affairs. She dressed and headed downstairs to her office. Her office line rang the moment she switched it on and didn't ease up until late that afternoon. During a lull, she logged onto her message board. Helping others, those who needed it even more than she and her mom did, made her feel better. Not quite right, but better.

It took a moment for her to put her security protocols in place and access the encrypted message board. There was only one new thread, this time about a birthday party for a single mom who lived in Las Cruces, New Mexico. So far, most people had responded with a bottle of wine or a six-pack of beer. One person had committed to a bottle of whiskey, Jack Daniel's.

Trinity opened a new tab in her browser in order to track down the woman. A birthday party was the pre-designated code for an individual in distress, generally financial, but not always. It took only a few minutes for Trinity to find her. She was newly single, left financially wrecked by the divorce. The ex-husband looked pretty nasty on paper. If the DEA was to be believed, he was fairly high up in one of the Mexican cartels. The woman had escaped to a shelter with her two children and was trying to put together enough money to relocate far, far away from him.

With the event authenticated, Trinity returned to the message board. *A pint of mezcal and a handful of limes. Anyone care to match?* The pint of mezcal was a straight forward message. A pint of anything equaled five thousand dollars. The fruit, on the other hand, was a lot more fun. Each lime—or any accessory, really—was a promise to do something intangible in terms of dollars, but that often turned out to be far more beneficial in the long run. She didn't often go this route. It involved paving new pathways, and that increased the odds that she might be caught. But after her morning encounter with Dave, she was happy to work out some of her male-focused frustration on this woman's ex-husband.

First, she did a search for property under his name throughout New Mexico and Arizona. In addition to the house he'd shared with his now ex-wife, there was another property farther north in Los Lunas, a suburb of Albuquerque. Nothing in Arizona. Very carefully, she dipped into the local utilities company for each property. She changed the account status for both from current to overdue, with balances in excess of ten thousand dollars each. He would receive one notice before the power was cut.

Because she liked symmetry, she posted a credit to the domestic violence shelter in the sum of the overdue amount for both of his properties. This, to her mind, was absolute poetry.

The trouble with cartel money was that cartel members rarely reported their earnings. He only had one vehicle registered in his name, so she put a clamp notice on that account. This meant that, at some point in the future, maybe today, maybe three years from now, whenever he was cited for a parking violation, the city would put a boot on his tire.

Her work extension rang, a call from another computer specialist. She didn't toggle over to her work screen, but kept chipping away at the ex-husband's online profile. Three limes—the power at his houses, the power at the shelter, and the wheel boot—weren't enough. She could do better.

"This is Trinity."

"Trin, hey! It's Becker. What's up?"

Becker had worked for Archer even longer than Trinity and was one of the people she called when she couldn't find an answer. He was generally upbeat and cheerful, was rarely stumped by her questions, and had a weird fascination with model airplanes—which he liked to talk about endlessly.

As Becker talked, Trinity revoked the ex-husband's license, created a new set of documents for the woman and her children, and arranged for them to be delivered to her via courier. She listened halfheartedly, catching snatches and inserting a well-placed noise of agreement as needed. Then he said something interesting, and all of her attention snapped to a clear, pointed focus on his words.

"...investigator. Apparently there have been losses."

"Wait. What? Backup. Losses where? And tell me about this investigator."

"Well, I haven't met her..."

"Oh." Trinity closed her eyes and practiced that conscious detachment that her yoga teacher preached. It did little to quell her desire to strangle Becker. It was just like him to bring something up that he knew little to nothing about and then leave her hanging with a bunch of questions and no answers.

"I talked to her, though. She called on her first day. I walked her through the basics of Archer's systems."

"How do you know she's an investigator?"

"She said she's here for a special project, and she's got access to *everything*. Plus, she requested financials from several departments, and she's got Samar Raje jumping through hoops. That man doesn't jump for anyone."

The threads Becker laid out could, in fact, mean the woman was an investigator. It could also mean that she was a ringer sent from Archer's office in Hong Kong, meant to take over Raje's position. The CEO, who was based there, liked to groom Archer's executives personally and then drop them into place when it was least expected. She hadn't heard any chatter about Raje being under scrutiny, but it was possible. Becker's conclusion about an investigator was a stretch, but worth checking out nonetheless.

"What's her name?"

"Laila Hollister. Oh, and she called Mr. Raje uncle."

Not a ringer then. She wrote the name on a piece of scrap paper. It wouldn't hurt to look into it.

"Listen, Becker, I need to get back to work. Chat later, yeah?"

"Sure, Trin. Bye." He always sounded a bit like a kicked puppy when she ended the call.

She went back to work on the birthday party. A woman in that situation likely had limited resources, so she generated a few giftcards to various clothing stores, grocery stores, and gas stations. After arranging delivery, she considered her work there done.

With an hour left of her work day, she had just enough time to verify her revenue streams were still flowing properly. Long ago, during her reckless early days of hacking, she'd run amok through several corporations, simply to prove she could bypass their safety protocols. Once she was in, she couldn't resist doing *something*. That's when she'd come up with an absolute genius bit of code she called "Housekeeping." It siphoned small amounts from every department each day. The amounts were small enough that no department head even noticed, but combined, the total dollar amount banked was staggering.

That's when she'd diversified and moved her funds to the Caymans. No matter what they showed on TV, those funds were untouchable by the US government.

Now, she was a little more discerning about how she applied her skills. She vetted the companies she targeted. They had to meet certain criteria, such as routinely engaging in unethical practices. Working for Archer, she'd stumbled across several practices that gave her pause, including such things as shifting labor forces to avoid paying benefits, falsely inflating expenses to minimize taxable income, and shifting hazardous waste to unregulated countries for disposal because it was cheaper to move than take care of it properly. With the money she gleaned, she was able to provide financial support for people who needed it.

CHAPTER 5

"This is how you spend your day off?" Sia nudged the stack of papers in front of Laila before flopping onto the couch next to her. "Come play with me. Desmond is off golfing with Daddy, and I'm bored."

Laila flipped to the next page of budget reports. Her search into the security fund had, as yet, proven fruitless. The answer had to be here. It had to be. "Busy." She grunted her response without looking up.

"Lai-la." Sia said her name as a prolonged sing-song that bordered on whining.

The numbers on the page swam in and out of focus, a sure sign she'd been staring at them for too long. She glanced at the clock. Three o'clock. "How'd you get in?"

"You gave me a key, remember?"

"Yes, of course, but it's for emergencies. Are you having an emergency?"

"Sorta. My fiancé blew me off for my father, and my favorite cousin ditched out on our regular Sunday morning brunch."

"Wait." Laila shook her head. "It's Sunday?" Surely she hadn't been working on this for that long.

"Oh, Laila, you didn't." Sia stood, took Laila by the hand, and tugged her upright. "This is an intervention. You need to put the work down."

Laila started to protest. So she'd lost track of a day. That wasn't so bad. She'd lost entire weeks before when trying to find the answer to a particularly delicious puzzle. While working her first official case as a PI, she'd lost almost ten pounds because she'd forgotten to eat until she'd wrapped up.

"No. Don't even try. You need a break, at least long enough to get some food in you." Sia sniffed. "And a shower and clean clothes. Damn, girl. How do you even stand yourself?"

Laila let herself be led to the bedroom. "Come on, Sia. I promised your dad I'd sort this out. The answer is right in front of me. I know it is."

Sia held up her hand. "Stop. First, you shower. Then we eat. We can talk over Thai." Sia left the room and closed the door behind her.

Since they were kids, Sia was first on the very short list of people who could penetrate the fog that surrounded Laila when she chased something down the rabbit hole. Probably because she never tried to change Laila, and she never really pushed to understand anything either. Too many times she'd heard "I just don't get you" from her parents before they died, from teachers, from almost-friends, from lovers. From everybody, really, except Sia. Her cousin never treated her as if she was a special project, something broken in need of repair. She simply was there. She called her on her crap and loved her no matter what. If Sia wanted her to shower and go to lunch, she could do that. Besides, Sia had promised to discuss it with her. That was always good. Her brain untangled things differently when she talked a puzzle through.

Laila rushed through a shower, skipped blow drying her hair, and crammed a hat on her head on the way out the door.

Sia insisted they walk to the Thai place that was about a half mile from Laila's apartment. About halfway there, after several attempts by Sia to start the conversation, Sia finally said, "Okay, fine. Go. But you're going to stay around long enough to talk to me about the wedding when you're done."

Laila paused mid step. Shit. She was being a bad friend again. "What's going on with the wedding?"

"Nothing... Everything... I don't know. Maybe nothing." Sia pushed a hand through her hair and, for once, looked ruffled instead of smooth and polished.

"Ummm..." Laila placed her hand on Sia's arm and signaled for her to stop. She pulled her into a hug. Just because Laila didn't understand the need for hugs, she definitely understood that Sia needed them. She held her, not too tight, but secure enough for Sia to know she was there. It was something she'd practiced, and she liked to think she'd gotten pretty good at it over the years. Sia snuffled into her shoulder and, after a few moments, pulled away.

"Thanks." Sia's eyes were rimmed with red. "I needed that."

"Okay, want to tell me what's going on?" Laila was pretty sure Sia wouldn't have brought it up otherwise, but she was bad at subtle communication. If something wasn't spelled out explicitly, she usually missed the message completely.

"Yeah. But let's order first." Sia started toward the restaurant again.

For the rest of their walk, Sia made light small talk. It was the kind of thing Laila sucked at, and as a general rule, she hated it. But this time she tried to participate. Clearly Sia needed something to fill the air between them.

They were seated with food in front of them before she tried again.

"So..."

"So...nothing really. Daddy just made a point that I hadn't thought about." Sia screwed her face up into an expression that landed somewhere between murderous and wanting to cry.

"What?" Laila was intrigued. Uncle Samar tended to make good points, regardless of whether the other person wanted to hear about it or not.

"Well, Desmond and I talked about a pre-nup, of course, but I simply refuse to sign one."

"Why?"

"Because, it's like we're admitting defeat before we even start. I hate that."

"I know. But it's the only thing that makes sense." Laila couldn't imagine just handing someone access to all of her financial security. Emotions were flawed, and people were fickle. Sia's inability to see that, frankly, surprised Laila.

"I just can't do it, Lai. I can't."

"Okay, so what did Uncle Samar say about it?"

"He thinks I'm being stubborn and foolish. I hate when he disapproves. You know how he gets. Sullen and brooding."

Laila hesitated to make the offer. Even though her uncle sometimes responded to Laila easier than Sia, it wasn't without cost. Uncle Samar didn't like the idea of them double teaming him, and it made him draw away for a time. And then there was the way Sia reacted when Laila was able to succeed where she'd failed. Overall, it made for some tense family gatherings. But, if it would help Sia, she had to do it. "I could talk to him."

Sia tilted her head and studied Laila, looking at her long and hard, with a contemplative expression on her face. "No. Not this time."

"Okay. What else can I do?" Laila would ask Max to look into Desmond, regardless of Sia's answer. Max was able to find dirt, no matter how well it was buried.

"Just listen when I need to vent?" Sia asked.

Laila nodded. "I can do that."

"Thanks," Sia said. "Now, tell me what's going on with your investigation."

Laila took a bite and chewed carefully. She needed the moment to mentally reset to the new topic. "Not much at all. Everything I've looked at looks fine."

"Tell me." Sia gestured with her fork for Laila to keep talking.

"I've looked at all the outlier information, like the international security budget and practices. There's some shitty things happening with that, but nothing that adds up to unexplained losses."

"What do you mean, shitty?" Sia adopted the look she got every time she didn't like what she was being told. Like Laila, she grew up with an almost fairytale view of Archer, only she clung to it a little tighter than Laila.

There wasn't an easy way to say that Archer refused to pay ransoms on several employees who ultimately were executed because of it. Still, she tried to soft sell it. "Just some issues with operations overseas that resulted in on-the-job injuries."

"Do I want to know the details?" Sia stopped fussing with her food and pinned Laila with a probing stare.

"No, Sia, you really don't." Laila wasn't capable of letting go of things easily, but Sia had always had that skill. If someone she trusted said she didn't want to know, she didn't push any further. She liked to remain borderline naïve about life. Whereas Laila, no matter how painful, ugly, and messy things got, well, she just kept picking at it like a scab. She refused to leave it until every last bit was uncovered.

Sia nodded slowly. "Okay. What else?"

"Then I looked at the employees who have loans through the banking division. There are a lot."

"Why look there? People get car loans and home mortgages all the time."

"Agreed, but money does strange things to people. For instance, what if somebody got really far behind in their mortgage and blamed Archer? Would that person then steal from the company?"

"I get it. What did you find?"

"Nothing. Or rather, nothing notable. The interest rates for employees are amazing. And the few examples where an employee got behind, the company restructured the loan without adding any additional fees. There's even a handful of cases where they forgave the loan."

Sia stopped mid bite. "Forgave the loan? What does that mean?"

"Maybe I'm calling it the wrong thing. But without digging too deep, it looks like the mortgages were paid from an account called 'Home Assistance.'"

"Did you ask Daddy about that?"

Laila shook her head as she shoved a forkful of noodles into her mouth. She'd been talking too much and her food was sitting there sadly neglected. "Why would I?"

"It's just that he's never mentioned anything like that. 'Home Assistance'? That's the kind of thing he would have told us about, isn't it?" Sia tilted her head to the side, almost as if it was a genuine question. She was right, of course; it was exactly the kind of promo-op story that Uncle Samar would have told them when they were kids. Anything that painted Archer as the hero was common dinner-table discussion.

"Yeah, okay, I'll ask him tomorrow." It wasn't really her uncle's department, but he should know enough to find the answers for her.

"What else have you looked at?"

"There's another account, 'Housekeeping.' Every department contributes, but there doesn't appear to be any balance to it. I just keep staring at those records. I know the answer is there. I just need to find it."

"You might be right. But don't do that thing where you get so tied up that you forget to look at everything else."

"When have I ever done that?"

For the remainder of lunch, Sia teased Laila about the many, many times when she'd latched onto an idea and refused to let go.

After, Sia dragged her across town to look at a venue for the reception. Sia drove, leaving Laila free to stare out the window and roll the facts about Archer through her mind. When they arrived, Sia slowed, but didn't park.

"There's no way we can have the reception here." Sia wrinkled her nose.

A block over, a line of people trailed down the sidewalk and around the corner. They had the ubiquitous uniformed appearance of the homeless—eyes downcast; clothing that hung from their frames, layered and dirty, making them look more like urban scarecrows than humans; bodies hunched over, sometimes shielding their mountain of personal effects piled high in an abused shopping cart. It was clear why Sia dismissed it out of hand, but it was also troublesome.

The line shuffled forward, and the first few people entered a building. The sign above the entryway read Open Doors. As people entered, others left, looking a little brighter for the briefest moment. Several clutched fluffy blankets to their chests, despite the heat of summer.

"We should help," Laila said.

"How?"

"I don't know." Laila never knew the answer to social problems such as homelessness. They were too abstract in nature. She wasn't able to simplify it into terms that allowed her to solve for the variable. It seemed that there was no magic integer to make it all better.

"Open Doors. Let's look them up later. We can send them a check." Sia stroked Laila's arm. Somehow, she always knew when Laila was in danger of being sucked down the rabbit hole.

"Good." Laila nodded. She liked this solution. "Now, how many other potential venues do you have lined up?"

It wasn't how she'd planned to spend the day. Then again, she hadn't even realized what day it was. She still hadn't looked at the websites Sia had sent her about being a maid of honor, but she was pretty sure spending an afternoon looking at reception halls was a good thing to do.

"Three more."

"Then we best get to it."

CHAPTER 6

"Hey bee-otch! Don't you ever leave that room?" Yvonne yelled her greeting, but Trinity still struggled to hear her over the loud calypso music blaring in the background. She held a glass filled with cloudy white liquid and topped with a stereotypical tiny umbrella. Her hair had been gelled and spiked and dyed bright pink at the tips. It was all very jarring.

"How many piña coladas have you had?" Trinity laughed because this version of Yvonne—the one who drank a little too much and rode life close to the edge—reminded her of the way they used to be, back in high school before things like money and bills and a mom with a slipping grasp of reality pushed the fun to the side.

"Umm..." Yvonne swung her arm out wide away from her body and stared at her glass, her brows drawn together. Liquid sloshed over the edge, and she snort laughed. Drunk Yvonne was considerably less ethereal than the sober version. Her expression brightened, and she proudly announced, "Five!"

"Vonnie, babe, I love you, but why are you drunk dialing me?" Not that she didn't appreciate the momentary distraction. She'd spent the morning running checks on all the code she had in place throughout Archer's systems. It was buried pretty deep, but a good coder—especially a hacker—would be able to find it. Since she'd confirmed that

Laila Hollister was in fact a private investigator brought in to research shortages at Archer, Trinity decided to take a minute to ensure it couldn't be traced back to her. It was tedious as hell to go through keystroke logs, but necessary under the circumstances. She was about two-thirds finished.

"I called you?" Yvonne asked, looking more at her drink than at Trinity. "Right! I called you. Adam's cousin is here, and she wants to talk to you." The grown up version of Yvonne rarely drank, smoked pot only on occasion, and did neither when she was responsible for a minor, making her announcement a bit perplexing.

"She's there?"

"Yeah!"

"And you're drunk?"

"Yeah!" Yvonne smiled stupidly and then frowned. "Oh, I see what you did there. Her mom is here, so I am not required to be a responsible adult. We're having a barbecue, and Adam's whole family is here, plus half the neighborhood too. Did you know that my neighbor three doors down is a bartender? She makes excellent drinks."

Trinity shook her head. "Nope. I had no idea."

"Anyway, do you have a minute to talk to Graciela?" Yvonne swiveled the laptop and Graciela's face swam through the picture. When the movement stopped, she was looking at the corner. She could just make out a Bob Marley print on one wall and a collage of black and white photos on the other. Before Trinity could comment, the screen swished the other direction and came to a stop on Graciela.

"Hi!" Graciela smiled and waved. "I hope you don't mind."

So far, Trinity had only communicated with Graciela via email. This was their first face-to-cyber-face meeting. Her enthusiasm charmed Trinity.

"No, of course not. Hi." Trinity smiled.

The noise of the party dimmed in the background. "I kicked Yvonne out and made her close the door. Those people are nuts," Graciela said affectionately. Clearly, she was fond of the others even if she would rather discuss nerdy stuff than party with her family.

"Good call. What's up?" Trinity glanced at her clock. It was after two; no wonder she was hungry. She grabbed her lunch and spread it out on the desk. She could eat and chat with Graciela at the same time.

"I just wanted to let you know that I tried that code sequence and it totally worked. I got an A on the project." Graciela wiggled in her seat with excitement.

Graciela had sent her a logarithmic equation she'd designed to catalogue her music collection. The assignment had been to create a program that allowed her to search and prioritize data across several categories. Not a particularly complicated project, but a good way to gauge the skills of the students who made it into the summer STEM program.

"Congratulations." Trinity smiled. "Well done."

"It's too bad you don't live here. Yvonne is awesome, but she doesn't get this stuff. Nobody does, really."

Trinity had felt the same way at Graciela's age. It had seemed as though no one understood who she was. It sucked. But then she'd found her people online, and that helped. She wasn't the only coder in the world who wanted to use what she knew to help others. The day she'd realized that had been...everything. Suddenly, she had a community. A place where she belonged.

Graciela was still a little too young for a full induction, and Trinity wouldn't share her not-so-legal tricks with someone she barely knew. But some day, maybe, if she continued to show interest in coding, Trinity could groom her. A protégé, perhaps. The idea of perpetuating a legacy appealed to her.

"I know, but believe this—it really does get better. I promise."

"Yeah, that's what everybody says." Graciela sighed.

The chatted for a while longer. Trinity told her about a few of the apps she'd launched the year before, including a keychain app that stored system passwords and required thumbprint identification to access. Graciela asked a few questions about the code, her eyes flashing with excitement and possibility. To encourage Graciela's development, Trinity challenged her to develop a similar program that could be used to store cheat codes and other data for video games. She promised to help her over any bumps that might crop up.

When the conversation naturally ended, Graciela said, "Okay, I'm going back to the party. Thanks again."

"You bet. Bye." Trinity waved, as did Graciela, then she disconnected the call.

Distraction over, Trinity returned to her project. She fell easily into the rhythm of reading line after line of base-level code. When she looked up next, it was two hours later and she was almost finished.

A crash of breaking glass, followed by Ornella yelling and Carol crying out in pain, came from the kitchen, just loud enough to be heard over the tribal music playing in Trinity's headset. She spun herself away from her desk, tore off her headphones, and sprinted toward the kitchen.

Carol leaned against one wall, clutching her left arm. Blood seeped around her fingers and ran in a steady stream down her arm. It dripped onto the ancient linoleum that Trinity refused to replace because her mom still recognized the kitchen as hers.

Trinity put one hand on Carol's shoulder. "Are you okay?"

Of course she wasn't okay. But it was the only thing Trinity could think to say in the moment.

Carol's pupils were blown wide, and her face was ashen, a layer of dry white over her normally deep, robust brown. She nodded toward the other side of the kitchen. "Help your mom."

"Who are you people? Why are you in my house?" Ornella screeched, her voice filled with the panicked edge of the truly terrified. In her hand, she clutched their longest, sharpest chef's knife. The blade, along with Ornella's hand, was splattered with blood. "Answer me."

Carol's cell phone sat on the island, next to a rolled out pie crust and the flour sifter. The glass pie pan, one of four that Ornella had used for as long as Trinity could remember, lay on the floor, broken into pieces. Trinity held her hands up in front of her and said, "I'm going to call for help." She motioned toward the phone. "Will you let me do that?"

Ornella's whole body shook, and her eyes were wild with fear. Her mom—her sweet, gentle, kind mom who baked pies and went to church and taught Sunday school—had attacked a woman who grew up in Jamaica with her.

"Who? Who are you going to call? You don't belong in my house." Ornella shrank back against the cabinets, but brandished the knife higher and waved it at Trinity. It was meant to be menacing, but all Trinity wanted was to cross the room and pull Ornella into a hug. Her heart broke to see her mom so confused, so desperately trying to make sense of the intruders in her kitchen.

"The police. Let me call the police. And an ambulance. Is that okay?" Trinity spoke softly, using the same soothing tone Ornella had used with her when she was a small child. As she did so, she reached again for the phone. This time Ornella allowed her to pick it up. She dialed 911 and set the device for speaker. That way, Ornella would be able to listen to the conversation as well.

"Nine-one-one, what's your emergency?"

"Hello, my name is Trinity Washington, and I need an ambulance to come to my home."

"The police," Ornella yelled. "You're supposed to be calling the police."

Adding someone with a gun to an already fraught situation was the last thing they needed. She glanced at her mom, who stared back, eyes wide with too many frantic emotions to identify. Trinity took a calming breath and then said, "Could you send the police as well?" She gave her address, never breaking eye contact with Ornella.

"Okay, Trinity, can you tell me the reason you're calling?"

Trinity paused for a moment. How could she describe the scene without setting her mom off? Worse, what if the police came in with a shoot-first-ask-questions-later attitude? If Ornella were a young black man, that would surely be the case. Those statistics spoke for themselves. But Ornella wasn't young or a man. Would black skin be enough justification for an adrenaline-filled cop?

She didn't have a choice. Carol needed help. And so did her mom. "My mother has Alzheimer's, and she cut her health care aid with a kitchen knife. She doesn't recognize either of us at the moment."

"I've dispatched emergency services, and they are on the way. Can you stay on the phone with me until they arrive?" The operator spoke with detached professionalism. It did very little to calm Trinity.

Trinity nodded slightly to Ornella, silently passing the question off to her. Ornella gave her a tight nod, and Trinity said, "I believe I can, yes."

"That's good. Can you tell me about the injury? The person is cut, you say? Can you tell how deep?"

She glanced at Carol. Blood still dripped from her arm, but not as rapidly.

"I don't know. She sliced her arm."

"Can you put pressure on the wound?"

Carol smiled weakly at her.

"She's holding it with her other hand."

"That's good," the dispatcher said, the faint sound of fingers tapping against a keyboard sounded in the background. "Is there anything nearby that you can use as a compress?"

"Yes." Trinity grabbed a dishtowel from the drawer and passed it to Carol. When she lifted her hand away from the wound, the flow of blood increased dramatically before she pressed the cloth to her arm.

The dispatcher continued to ask questions, and Trinity answered as best she could. Was there anyone else in the house? No. Was the front door unlocked? No. Was someone available to let the first responders in when they arrived? She wasn't sure.

After a point, it became clear that she was simply talking to keep Trinity calm and on the line with her. At no time did the veil of confusion lift from Ornella's eyes, nor did she interfere with the phone conversation or prevent Trinity from helping Carol.

"Okay, Trinity, the police are almost there. You should be able to hear their sirens."

Trinity focused. She forced herself to listen beyond the sound of blood rushing through her ears. There! Faint, and then growing louder, she heard the distinct wail of a police cruiser, followed by the squealing of brakes. The siren cut off abruptly, but another one sounded in the background, moving rapidly in her direction.

"Yes. They're here."

"Excellent. Can you let them in?"

"Yes." Trinity moved toward the door.

"No," Ornella said, her voice strained. "The other one." She pointed at Carol with the knife.

Trinity disconnected the call. In a fugue state, she watched with a sense of detached disbelief.

Carol held the door open wide. Two police officers stood on her front porch, their guns holstered. That was a good sign.

"You called nine-one-one, ma'am?" The first officer, a young black woman, asked.

Carol looked at Trinity, clearly expecting her to answer. Her whole body seemed to sag against the thin side of the door. Trinity stood in limbo at the edge of the kitchen, the no-man's land between the kitchen and the living room. She wanted to comfort Ornella and Carol but couldn't.

"Yes. My mom has Alzheimer's and forgot who we are." Trinity gestured toward Ornella who had backed herself even tighter into the corner of the cabinets. It made Trinity's heart hurt to watch her. "And she cut Carol with a kitchen knife." After saying it two times, she still couldn't quite believe the words as they left her mouth. "She needs an ambulance."

"She's still armed?" The female officer bypassed Carol, hand hovering over her holster, as if preparing to remove her service weapon from her holster. The other officer, an older white man, did likewise.

"No, no! It's not like that. She's scared. She's waiting for you to help her. Please, don't hurt her."

The officers entered the house as the ambulance pulled up. In moments, her house was full of emergency personnel. The officers, bless them, didn't shoot Ornella for being black and holding a knife. The paramedics quickly assessed Carol and guided her out of the house to the ambulance.

"Ma'am, I'm Officer MacDonnal. Are you able to answer some questions for me?" He spoke with a gentle, caring lilt to his voice.

Trinity nodded. She looked past him to the kitchen. His partner, the woman, had coaxed the knife away from Ornella and guided her to the table.

"My partner is speaking with your mom now, but I need to hear from you about what happened here today."

"I..." Trinity stopped and took a long, deep breath. "I was in my office, working, when I heard yelling. I came out and found my mom with the knife and Carol holding her arm, bleeding."

Officer MacDonnal nodded and made notes in a small Moleskin journal. "Any idea what set your mom off?"

"No. She's never done this before." If Trinity had heard about this after the fact without the benefit of seeing the wild, frightened look in Ornella's eyes, she never would have believed her mom capable of such an act of violence. Ornella loved beautiful things. She was gentle and encouraging. She had a lifetime's worth of practice at turning the other cheek. Nothing about this made any sense.

"You said she has Alzheimer's?"

"Yes. Early onset. But even when she forgets, she's still calm. She becomes overly polite. The way she was when I found her, paranoid and on edge, that's just not her. She's been upset before, when she forgets, but this..."

He scribbled down a bit more and then touched her hand briefly. "I'm sorry this has happened to your family."

"Thank you." Trinity fought against the torrent of emotion flooding her system. She needed to think about this like an equation, like a broken sequence of code that she could fix. But every time she considered it, the only obvious conclusion—a dedicated care facility—made her heart break just a bit more. The thought of Ornella in one of those places was unconscionable. What kind of daughter would she be if she did that?

"I need to talk to the other woman. What is her name?"

"Carol?"

"Right. You said she cares for your mom?"

"Yes. She moved here from Jamaica last year to help my mom. She's like family."

"As soon as the EMTs finish with her, I'll get her statement to determine if she wants to press charges."

"What?" That jerked Trinity out of her haze. "Press charges? Why would..."

"She was assaulted," he said mildly, his voice surprisingly free of judgment.

Trinity closed her eyes briefly as she nodded. "Of course."

"Assuming that she doesn't, do you have an alternate care plan for your mother?"

Trinity had done exhaustive research into the different facilities available locally, to the point that she knew the names of the directors and the fee schedules. She knew which places conducted routine outings, which places had gardens, and which places were only slightly better than the nightmarish state institutions that were dismantled as part of JFK's deinstitutionalization program. She knew which places had the most reported cases of abuse, which places had the lowest turnover of staff, and which places smelled of antiseptic and desperation.

She knew every conceivable detail *except* which place could be a believable substitute home for Ornella. The moment she'd dreaded and put off was finally here. She had to make a decision. There was no good solution, just varying degrees of Trinity as a bad daughter.

"I've looked into a few places."

"Have you checked availability? Started the paperwork?"

"Sort of."

"Here's the deal: in situations such as these, when there's a potentially violent situation, we have to remove the aggressor. In this case, that's your mom. I could call social services, or if you had arrangements in place, we could transport her to a facility."

Before she could catch herself, a small sob escaped Trinity. Then she took another deep breath to bring herself back under control. She nodded. "Can you give me a few minutes?"

She had a list, prioritized by a complicated set of factors, printed out and stuck to her bulletin board with a cheerful yellow pushpin.

"We can do that." Officer MacDonnal nodded and smiled sadly. He turned away and keyed the mic attached to his shoulder epaulette. In a hushed voice, he requested an additional ambulance.

Trinity glanced around her house. Her mom sat at the kitchen table, talking quietly with the female officer. She looked calmer but still not herself. Visible through the open front door, Carol sat on the inside ledge at the back of the ambulance. The EMT had dressed her wound and started an IV. Unlike Ornella, she looked a bit frantic and unsure of the situation. That was fair. It wasn't every day she got attacked with a kitchen knife.

Trinity made her way to her office, where she pulled down the list and dialed the top number. It was a smaller, private facility that specialized in creating a home-like atmosphere while still ensuring quality medical care. They catered to individual needs and provided creative outlets to match the patients' unique voices. For example, much of Ornella's identity was wrapped up in baking, and this was the only place that would allow her to continue doing that.

After a five minute phone call and a sizeable bank transfer, Ornella was officially a resident. Trinity had filled out the preliminary paperwork months ago, with the hope that she'd never have to actually use it. With the arrangements made, she went to her mom's room and attached ensuite and packed an overnight bag. She included Ornella's favorite flannel nightgown, along with some basic toiletries. Tomorrow, she'd take more, but this would get her through until morning.

When she returned to the living room, Officer MacDonnal was the only other person left in the house. Ornella and the female officer were outside on the front porch.

"Here you go." She gave him the address and contact information for the facility, along with the bag.

"Good. We're waiting for another bus to transport your mom."

"Bus?" Surely he wasn't relying on Tri-Met to carry Ornella across town.

"Ambulance, sorry."

"Oh." She still didn't understand. Why not simply drive her there in his car?

Before she could ask, he said, "The back of a police vehicle can be traumatizing, even for someone who is in full command of her faculties. The effects on someone in your mom's shape would be...not good."

"I see." She didn't. She didn't see at all, but that seemed irrelevant. A second ambulance pulled up to the curb.

After saying a few words of sympathetic encouragement, Officer MacDonnal left. Trinity shut the door behind him, closed her eyes, and listened to the silence filling her house.

For the first time since hearing the glass break, Trinity allowed herself a moment to break down. She slumped into the sofa, dropped her face into her hands, and tried to come to terms with everything that had happened in the past thirty minutes. Just like that, her life had changed irrevocably.

CHAPTER 7

The phone rang, and Laila grabbed it from the table before it could sound again. For some reason known only to him, Uncle Samar had checked in with her the last three times it rang. He had remarkably good hearing.

"Hollister," she answered with clipped professionalism without looking up from the report she was studying.

"When are you going to wrap this up? I miss you." Max lasted about three seconds before she laughed. It was a well-established fact that she preferred to hold court over the office without Laila there to spoil her fun. Justin, the receptionist, didn't share Max's opinion.

"I'd finish faster if I had the report I requested." She flipped to the next page of her printout. She'd spent the last two hours staring at shipping manifests from the local distribution center and was starting to go cross-eyed.

"The full workup is in your inbox," the sound of fingers on a keyboard came through the line, "now."

"Anything interesting?"

"No. Your future cousin-in-law is pretty boring on paper."

"Perfect." That was exactly the answer Laila wanted. Still, she'd take a look when—*if*—she finished with the reports currently on her desk. "Anything else?"

"I also sent you a supplementary dossier on your uncle."

Laila sighed. What else could Max possibly have dug up? "Do I even want to know?"

Max snorted. "As if *no* is ever an option to that question for you."

"Fair point."

"Do you want the highlights?"

"No. Thanks."

They stayed on the line for a while longer as Max briefed her on a couple of other open cases they were pursuing. They'd reached the point where Laila needed to seriously consider bringing on another investigator.

After they wrapped up their briefing, Max said, "Seriously. Finish at Archer already. Justin is too sensitive to be any fun."

"Working on it," Laila said. "Good job and stuff. Bye."

"Whatever." Max disconnected the call.

The report on Desmond was as boring as Max promised. Laila printed out a copy and added it to the growing pile of paperwork for her uncle. A few hours later, after even more manifests and bills of lading, plus a backache from hell, Laila was at an impasse.

She gathered her notes, along with a short stack of reports, and moved to the door separating her office from Uncle Samar's. With a polite knock, she opened the door and stepped through. Luckily, Uncle Samar was alone. He glanced up from his computer and smiled.

"Laila, what do you have for me?" He skipped the small talk, and Laila appreciated that. It was lost on her, anyway.

"Just a few questions." She pulled one of his guest chairs around to his side of the desk. It was heavy and left drag marks on the carpet. Uncle Samar watched her with a bemused smile on his face. She shrugged sheepishly and dropped into the chair next to him. "Can you tell me about 'Home Assistance'? How does that account work, exactly?"

She thumbed through the reports to find the correct page and then brought it to the top of the pile. In small print, highlighted in yellow and circled with red ink, about halfway down the page, she found the entry she was looking for. She tapped it with her index finger.

"Let me see that." Uncle Samar slipped on his reading glasses and held the report at arm's length. "Hmmm...that's interesting. I'm not familiar with this."

As president of US operations, it was Uncle Samar's job to be familiar with everything. His answer troubled her.

"How many times did you come across this?" He asked, wearing a tight frown as he studied the data.

"As you know, I went back five years. In that time, I only came across it a few times." Six, to be precise. She found the other entries in her stack of paperwork and showed them to her uncle. "You're sure this isn't an Archer program?"

He gave her a look, the one he reserved for the times when she said something he thought to be especially asinine. "Positive. This doesn't meet the criteria we have in place for charitable works."

"And it couldn't be anything else?"

"No. Without having a forensic accountant verify the origin of funds—a process I will initiate as soon as we're done here—I'm at a loss." His frown deepened.

"What about this: 'Housekeeping'?" She brought the next report to his attention. "There are hundreds of small transaction in every department that I checked. The funds are transferred into account labeled 'Housekeeping,' without any indication of why."

"And you're assuming it's not for housekeeping services?"

"I thought of that, but if that's the case, then what about this?" She pointed to a line item on the ledger labeled "janitorial and maintenance." "Each of these entries has a corresponding invoice, as it should, whereas the 'housekeeping' entries show the money leaving the department, but doesn't have any paperwork to balance the expenditure."

"Hmmm..." Uncle Samar took the report and set it with the other one. "You say this 'housekeeping' shows up across departments?"

Laila nodded. "The ones I checked, anyway."

"Laila, I don't need to tell you how serious this is. If at all possible, I'd like to dig deeper without involving our in-house accounting team. Do you understand?"

"Of course." She didn't blame him. She wouldn't want to face questions about it without having the answers either. "I have a guy..."

She half expected him to decline. Surely he had a forensic accountant available to him. Surprisingly, he considered her words for a moment and then said, "Contact him, would you?"

"Will do." She considered how to describe Ivar. He was unparalleled at what he did, but he was also unorthodox. His methods tended not to be a good match with a corporate office environment. "He prefers to work from his home office."

She left out the part where his home office was in his mom's basement and that he generally worked in his underwear. She'd learned that the hard way.

"He'll need electronic and physical copies of the accounts. He goes between paper and computer."

Uncle Samar's forehead creased. "That could be a problem. Information like that is restricted."

Laila nodded, thinking. "I understand, but really, Uncle Samar, you don't want this guy in your office. He can do what you need better and faster than anyone else, but he will disrupt everyone around him."

Not that he meant to be disruptive. Ivar genuinely didn't understand people. They confounded him, even more than they did Laila. They were simply too unpredictable. Ivar dealt in yes or no, true or false, black or white. He didn't do shades of anything, and he didn't do subtlety. If he had a thought or a question, he said it. Forget about social niceties.

Uncle Samar nodded decisively. "I'll prepare the files myself."

If he was willing to do that rather than delegating to his assistant, he was *very* serious that no one else learn about their removal from site. So how did he plan to get the documents past security?

"Do you bypass security on your way out?"

"No. They check my briefcase just like everyone else's."

"That's a problem."

"Not really. I'll ship it to my home address."

"Security doesn't check parcels?" That was a giant loophole in procedure.

"No. I'll address that tomorrow." Samar sent his admin an instant message, requesting she set up a meeting with the head of security for the next morning. "It looks like I have more issues than I realized."

Side by side, the discrepancies in the numbers over multiple accounts, the inconsistent shipping manifests—a point she had yet to raise with Uncle Samar—and the gap in security protocol, the problems looked larger than life. In reality, they were all so small individually that they only became apparent under extreme scrutiny. Still, he was right. He needed to address it.

She had three more talking points, and only one was good. She shuffled the pages and brought the relevant reports to the fore.

"Okay, what about this? See these shipping manifests? This is just a handful of the transactions. There are regular deliveries to various places around the country with a zero total due. None of them show up as an expense in a corresponding category."

"Let me see that." Again, he took the papers from her.

It had taken Laila a minute to see the pattern. On the surface, they were innocuous pieces of documentation. What made them stand out, or rather, what made their legitimate counterparts stand out, was the additional checks and balances. For instance, when the executive admins sponsored a girls' volleyball team by donating equipment, there was a shipping manifest, similar to the ones Uncle Samar was evaluating now, along with a ledger entry on the department expenses.

"It's almost always food items or household goods, such as blankets, clothing, and toiletries. Except these two," she pointed to the standout manifests, "for computers and tablets. The shipments go to a handful of charitable organizations, mostly homeless shelters, including one here in town called Open Doors."

"I'm familiar with that organization, but it's not on our list of approved charities."

"So, this probably isn't a legit donation?"

Uncle Samar studied the forms, shaking his head slowly. "It certainly looks legitimate, but none of these are approved transactions."

"How can you be sure?" Not that Laila doubted her uncle. Certainly, he should know about any large-scale donation program.

Uncle Samar removed his reading glasses and looked at her levelly. "Laila, I know I raised you girls on stories of the great things Archer does."

She nodded.

"And those stories were certainly true, but the acts weren't purely philanthropic. Yes, we sponsor many humanitarian efforts, but we do that with an expectation of a return on the investment. That means we publicize everything. If this were an approved Archer initiative," he raised the papers slightly and then set them down on the desk, "then there would be sound bites and articles and as much spin as we could milk from it."

That made perfect sense, but Laila was pretty sure she didn't like it. It felt contrary to what she'd believed her whole life. It wasn't that she was angry at being deceived; such an emotional reaction really wasn't in her wheelhouse. It was more a sense of disappointment, similar to how she'd feel if she suddenly realized that she'd been calling blue green. It was unsettling to be wrong with such a fundamental belief.

She didn't even try to explain all that to Uncle Samar. "I'll swing by Open Doors when we finish. See if I can learn anything."

"Good. What else do you have for me?"

Two more things. Neither particularly bad, but one certainly had greater potential to be explosive. She opted for the easiest subject first.

"Sia mentioned how concerned you are about her decision not to sign a pre-nup."

"Yes..." He gave her a dubious look.

"I'm with you on this one. Desmond seems like a great guy, but still." She handed him a manila envelope labeled "Bells." "At least I was until I saw this."

He quirked an eyebrow. "Bells?"

"You know, wedding bells? I didn't want to be obvious, just in case Sia happened to see it."

"Mmm." Uncle Samar flipped open the top and slipped the contents out.

"Sia doesn't know about this, but I asked Max to do a full workup on Desmond. There's information in this file that Desmond himself probably doesn't remember. The part I thought you might want to see is on page three."

She waited while her uncle flipped to the appropriate place.

"Do you see, down at the bottom there, his net worth? His family is loaded. He chooses to live on his salary rather than dipping into his trust. He's a self-starter."

"That does speak well of him, doesn't it?" Uncle Samar reviewed a bit more and then returned the report to the envelope. "Thank you for this."

Based on his expression, Laila couldn't tell if it helped him or not. She shrugged. "It wasn't just for you."

He nodded. "You have something else for me." He gestured toward her last file.

"Yes." Laila moved the chair back to its normal position and remained standing. She wanted to be able to see Uncle Samar properly for this part. More than that, she wanted him to be able to see her. "You know one of the first things I did when starting this investigation was request reports similar to that one," she pointed to "Bells," "on all of the senior officers, including you."

His facial features tightened, but he didn't respond.

"It would have been irresponsible not to." She paused a beat. "I just...I wasn't trying to find out. I want you to know that."

She set the last envelope on his desk.

He pinned it down with his fingertips. "Who else has seen this?"

"Nobody. Well, Max, because she compiled it. But I haven't shown anyone else."

He relaxed incrementally.

"I *won't* tell anyone."

"Thank you."

Laila scuffed her boot against the carpet. She didn't know what to say, but knew she needed to say something.

"You know Sia wouldn't care, right?"

"No, I don't suppose she would. But your aunt and I made the decision years ago to keep this private."

"She knew?"

"Of course."

"Wow." That...Laila hadn't expected that. Before her aunt died, they'd shared a traditional, conservative Indian marriage. Or so Laila thought. If she'd known about Samar's relationship with the man in the photos—or any man, really—then they weren't as conservative or as traditional as she'd thought. That her uncle had been closeted for so long, that he still believed he needed to remain that way, seemed like such a waste.

"If there's nothing else?" Her uncle's voice was brusque.

Laila shook her head, surprised. She'd never been dismissed in quite this manner before. "I'll let you know if I learn anything from Open Doors." And then she turned and left.

Chapter 8

The line for the evening meal stretched around the perimeter of the room and out the entrance. There always seemed to be more people than food, no matter how aggressive they were with their fundraising efforts.

"Hey, Trinity. Good to see you back." A woman with a wide smile and an even wider rucksack strapped to her back squeezed Trinity's hand.

The first time one of the clients at Open Doors touched her, it had freaked her out. Of course, she'd been twelve at the time and Ornella had dragged her there to get her off the computer and out into the world. Everything freaked her out back then. Everything but code and equations.

Today, though, it made her smile. She stepped around the table to pull the woman into a warm hug. "How are you, Jane? Staying warm and dry?"

Even though it was summertime, warm and dry was always a concern for someone living on the streets.

"Oh, you know how it is. I get by. How's your mom? We sure do miss her."

Trinity moved back to her spot in the distribution lineup and grabbed a carton of chocolate milk and another of juice. She held them up to let Jane choose as she answered. "She's good. I'll tell her you asked after her." Trinity used her practiced, emotionless tone. It would be far too easy to cry, and the people here had far bigger problems than hers.

They didn't need to see the privileged volunteer fall apart at the drinks station.

Jane took the chocolate milk and said, "You do that. She's a good woman."

Not for the first time, Trinity considered disclosing Ornella's true status. It wasn't something she spoke of casually, and certainly not with someone only tangentially involved her life. Besides, she still felt a little raw from moving her to a dedicated care facility. Despite reassurances from friends, family, and the professionals she'd consulted, Trinity felt like the worst daughter ever. She'd promised Ornella she'd care for her, and now she wasn't.

Trinity smiled and nodded and thanked her.

"You take care, hon." With that, Jane took her tray and moved to the dining area.

Trinity spent the next hour or so handing out beverages and purposefully not thinking about Ornella. When meal service ended, she gathered up the remaining cartons and carried them to the walk-in cooler in the main kitchen area. They didn't always have individual drinks. Sometimes it was milk by the gallons. Sometimes it was concentrated frozen juice that had to be mixed with water. Sometimes it was cases of sports drinks and sodas donated by the local distributor. She hated giving out the soda. It was nothing but corn sugar and death in a bottle. Nevertheless, it was always a big hit with the clients.

After cleaning up, Trinity made her way back to the dining room. She liked to spend a little time sitting with people as they ate. Sharing a meal with a person made him more human, and she liked the idea of breaking down the barriers between economic groups. That was something

Ornella had taught her. For her mom, it was a fundamental lesson, right up there with remembering to brush her teeth at bedtime.

As she made her way around the room, pausing to chat briefly with people as she went, she noticed a woman standing near the entrance. Her back was to Trinity, displaying long, silky black hair that was pulled up in a ponytail. It curled gently at the ends. Between the salon sleekness of her style and the designer labels on her clothes, she clearly wasn't looking for a free meal.

Then, as if bidden by Trinity's thoughts, the woman turned, her profile illuminated by the warm light coming in through the streaked glass of the street-side windows. She wore dark sunglasses that, if Trinity had to guess, cost more than the other people in the room spent on food in a year. Combined.

There was something familiar about her, but at this distance, Trinity couldn't say what. As she moved closer, the woman removed her sunglasses and turned to face Trinity.

Laila Hollister—the investigator hired by Archer who Trinity had researched earlier that week.

Smiling her best, Trinity crossed the distance between them, hand outstretched in greeting. "Hi, you look a little lost. Can I help?"

"Hello." Laila shook her hand and paused as though she'd forgotten what else she wanted to say. She stared at Trinity, her expression both dazed and intense at the same time. It was the same look some guys got right before they propositioned her. Open Doors was hardly the place for an illicit hookup, and Laila, hot as she was, needed to be on a do-not-touch list for Trinity.

"Are you interested in volunteering here?" Trinity prompted. That couldn't possibly be the reason. The coincidence was simply too improbable, and Trinity played the odds.

"What?" Laila continued to pump Trinity's hand up and down. "Volunteer... No!"

Trinity glanced down a their still joined hands.

"Oh, sorry." Laila gave her one more firm shake before she relinquished her hold on Trinity. She dipped her fingers into a pocket and pulled out a business card. "I'm Laila Hollister, and I have a few questions about some deliveries that were made to this location."

The headshot on her website didn't do Laila justice. In the photo, she looked almost ordinary. The woman before her was anything but. She had striking dark eyes and a penetrating stare. The intensity in Laila's face made Trinity want to play.

Trinity took the card without looking at it. "I'm Trinity. I don't know if I can be of help, but I'm happy to sit and chat with you for a few minutes. Can you tell me what this is about?"

As she guided Laila toward a semi-empty table near the back of the dining room, another volunteer drew her attention away for a moment. With a taut smile, the volunteer said, "I've got to run. My mom gets pissed if she has to watch my kids too long. Are you okay for me to go?"

Trinity vaguely remembered a story about court-ordered volunteer work, several small children, and an unsympathetic family. She returned the smile and said, "That's okay. I'm sure we'll be just fine."

The other volunteer slipped away as Trinity returned her attention to Laila. There were several open seats as the dinner crowd tended to rush through the meal and hustle to get an open bed for the night. Open Doors had a limited number of beds and didn't hold them. They were first come, first served, and the queue was a few blocks over at a different facility.

When they were comfortably seated, Trinity said, "So, what brings you to Open Doors? An investigation, you say?"

Laila scrunched up her face and cocked her head to the side, clearly puzzled. It was adorable, and Trinity wanted to giggle at the unfiltered honesty in Laila's expression.

She shook her head. "Right, right. I'm conducting an investigation for Archer Securities. Their records show several significant donations of goods to this organization."

"Oh really?" Trinity blinked innocently. "Well, that's certainly generous of them. Please thank them on my behalf." She smiled sweetly.

"What? No, you don't understand." Laila's tone was tinged with frustration. "They didn't donate them."

"Well, that doesn't make any sense. How did they get here if they weren't sent here?"

Laila made a slight growling noise under her breath, and Trinity internally squealed with delight. Laila was exactly the distraction she needed to take her mind off things with Ornella.

"That's my point. They shouldn't be here."

"I'm sure they're not here anymore. Most donations go out as soon as they come in." Trinity folded her hands on the table and gave Laila a satisfied nod.

"You are very frustrating." As soon as Laila finished speaking, a panicked look crossed her face. "I'm sorry. I'm not supposed to say things like that."

That was interesting. Who would encourage this delightfully refreshing person to do anything other than be herself? "Why not?"

"It's rude?" Laila paused. "Isn't it?"

"I suppose some might see it that way. I don't."

"Seriously?" From anyone else, Trinity would read that question as sarcasm, but the crack in Laila's voice and the confused tint in her eyes made Trinity pause.

Something shifted inside Trinity with that question. She was happy to toy with Laila over her investigation, but the distress in that single word took the fun out of teasing her otherwise.

Trinity nodded, for the moment dropping the plastic shine from her expression. "Very much so."

Laila almost smiled, one side of her mouth pulling up slightly. Trinity stared at her for a beat longer and then slipped back into the role of vapid tormentor. "So, why are you here looking for things that aren't supposed to be here when they aren't even here?" She was right. This was fun.

"Let me start over. You see, over the past few years, several pallets of goods have been shipped to this organization from Archer Securities. The items weren't donated by Archer, but they were shipped with a zero balance invoice nonetheless."

"Well, that's certainly a conundrum." Trinity couldn't help it. She was impressed that Laila Hollister, Investigator, had made it this far. She decided to up the ante. "Are you sure they weren't doing some routine *housekeeping*?"

She put just the slightest emphasis on the last word. To anyone not in the know, it would have been undetectable. Laila, however, was definitely aware of the significance. Her eyes opened wider for a fraction of a second.

"Trinity, was it? What did you say you do here?"

"Yes, Trinity. Trinity Washington." She pulled her own business card from her pocket. "And I'm doing it. Or rather, I'm done doing it."

Laila took the card. She glanced at it and back to Trinity. The moment of realization was so beautiful. It couldn't have been better if Trinity had scripted it. All it took was the slightest of seconds, and Laila did a double take. She looked at the card again, slightly slackjawed, then back to Trinity.

"Trinity Washington. IT Specialist. Archer Securities." Laila's voice was almost deadpan, but the light in her eyes betrayed the speed with which she was calculating the importance of this new information. "That's interesting."

"Isn't it?" Trinity nodded along, careful to keep her expression blank. "What are the odds that you, a contractor for Archer, and me, an employee of Archer, would meet here? A place where Archer has apparently *not* been donating goods. That's one for the record books."

"It really is." Laila gave her a predatory smile.

If Trinity hadn't spent time verifying that there was absolutely no way to trace her code at Archer back to her, the look on Laila's face would have been terrifying. As it was, Trinity had to remind herself to breathe properly and not look away.

Laila stared at her for several moments, clearly waiting to see what other information Trinity would volunteer. Trinity forced herself to meet Laila's calculating stare. With every second that passed, the light of understanding sparked a little brighter in Laila's eyes. Perhaps this wasn't as much fun as she originally thought.

Finally, Laila tapped Trinity's business card sharply against the table. The sound echoed around the room. "It was nice meeting you, Trinity. I'll let you get back to whatever it is that you do here."

They stood at the same time. Laila was slightly shorter than Trinity, and she held herself with a tight energy that buzzed close to the surface. She was compelling, and Trinity was drawn to her. She offered Laila her hand again. "It was very nice to meet you. I hope to see you again."

Trinity watched as Laila turned, walked across the room, and with one last glance over her shoulder at Trinity, left the building. She smiled to herself for a moment until what she'd just done started to sink in.

She hadn't just teased a cute girl. She'd baited someone whose immediate goal was to expose Trinity on behalf of Archer Securities.

Fuck.

By the time the door swished shut behind her, Laila had her phone out and was dialing Max.

"Hollister Investigations, Justin speaking. How can we be of service today?" Justin had a natural way about him that put people at ease and drew them out.

At this moment, however, Laila didn't want to be put at ease. She smelled blood in the water and couldn't wait to sink her teeth in. She needed Max to help her get there. She took a deep breath before speaking. All those phone manners she practiced were primarily for Justin's benefit. It would suck if she blew it now.

"Justin, hey. It's Laila."

"Oh hi! How's the investigation going? We sure miss you around here. Max has been insufferable the last few days."

"Is that Laila? Give me the phone." Max's voice came through the line as a distant growl.

"Keep your pants on. I'm talking to her right now," Justin scolded. Max huffed, but didn't demand the phone again. The two of them had an interesting working dynamic. They were like siblings, vicious toward one another, but equally ferocious in the defense of the other. For her part, Laila stayed well and clear of their arguments. She didn't need that kind of drama.

"Actually, Justin, I need to speak to Max. I'm chasing a lead and need her help." Laila watched for a break in traffic and then sprinted across the road to where her car was parked.

"Okay, boss. Here she is." Justin sounded as chipper as a Disney character.

"Told you to give me the phone," Max said, her voice slightly muffled. Then, "What's up?"

Trinity pressed the button on her fob to unlock the door. As she climbed in and started the car, she said, "I have a name for you. I want a full bio by the time I get to the office, and I mean *everything*. I'm on my way now." She read Trinity's information from the card, including her job title at Archer. "Ten minutes, Max."

"Got it." Max disconnected before Laila could go through her usual good-job spiel.

Laila pulled into the lot outside Hollister fifteen minutes later. Max's sporty red roadster was in its usual spot next to hers, and Justin's bicycle was chained to the rack just outside the glass doors that led into her building.

She engaged the alarm on her car and hit the lobby at a sprint. Trinity Washington had handed her the golden ticket, and all she had to do was cash it in. However, knowing something and being able to prove it were rarely the same thing. When she got this close to solving a puzzle, the rest of the world fell into a blur, and she couldn't wait to wrap her brain around the win. For her, it was the ultimate high.

She pushed the call button for the elevator about fifty times and stared at the indicator arrow. It was pinned at the top floor and moved in a slow arc across the indicator as the car descended. After it paused for the third time, she mumbled "Fuck it!" under her breath and hit the stairs.

Her office was only five flights up, but it was enough to make her breathe a little bit harder by the time she cleared the door to the stairwell. The door to her office stood open, and Max waited for her there, legs crossed at the ankles as she leaned against the frame. She had her iPad in her hands and a smirk on her face.

"You're late."

Laila took the iPad as she passed by on her way into the office. She tossed a greeting to Justin without slowing. Max kept pace.

"Tell me everything." Laila glanced at the main profile page. It told her what she already knew. Trinity was in her mid-twenties, black, stunning to look at, and employed by Archer Securities as a computer support specialist.

Rather than sit in her swivel chair, she leaned against the front of the desk. She tended to think better when vertical. Max stood equidistance between the door, which she'd closed when they entered the room, and the desk.

With her feet shoulder width apart, hands clasped behind her back, Max somehow managed to look both relaxed and coiled at the same time.

"Trinity Washington, no middle name. She lives in a respectable part of the Rancho Verde district." Max recited her address. "Raised by a single parent, Ornella Washington, from Jamaica. Ornella owned a small bakery downtown until two years ago. Trinity works from home in IT services for Archer Securities, but I suspect you know that part. She started there nine years ago and has received glowing evaluations from her supervisor since."

Laila swiped the screen for the next page. It was blank. She tried again. Still nothing. Surely Max hadn't stopped looking so easily. Where was her credit history? Employment and education data? Hell, it wasn't uncommon for Max to include when a person lost her virginity and to whom. So, where was the rest of the information on Trinity Washington? She looked at Max, exasperated. She shouldn't have to ask.

"What else?" She pushed a stack of bridal magazines to one side as she took her seat behind her desk. A row of garment bags hung on a rolling clothing rack to her right. Clearly, Sia had dropped by with a little wedding homework for Laila.

"That's it."

"What?" With that little information, Trinity might as well have been a ghost.

"She doesn't have an online presence. She lives in her childhood home, which signed over from Ornella to Trinity via a quitclaim deed around the same time that Ornella sold her business.

"Trinity gets paid electronically and pays her monthly bills the same way, such as they are. She doesn't hold any credit cards. Doesn't own a car. Doesn't have a cable bill. If she has a cell phone, it's a burner, because I can't find a record of one. The house has phone and Internet, both billed to Ornella. Beyond that, she pays her monthly utilities, and that's it."

"Seriously?" Laila was stunned. Nothing about this made sense. Once, a wealthy, young tech CEO had hired them to find his estranged father. As part of that investigation, they'd researched homeless people with larger digital footprints than Trinity Washington.

"I searched all the regular social media outlets, Facebook, Twitter, Instagram. Nothing. Same for all major retailers. She doesn't belong to a single loyalty program." Max looked at her, one eyebrow arched. "Are you sure she's real?"

"Oh, she's real. And I'm pretty sure she's responsible for the losses at Archer."

"Well, that's interesting."

"Education?" Laila didn't reserve much hope for a useful answer. If Max knew about it, she would have shared by now.

"Nothing past high school, no. She graduated from Jefferson with mediocre grades. She didn't participate in any sports or clubs."

Laila tapped her desk, wheels spinning. "Have you ever come across anything like this before?"

Max stood a little straighter, shoulders squared up. "I have. Nothing this extensive, though."

Laila waited. There were parts of Max's history that she was very guarded about, and Laila had learned not to push.

"I would expect to see something like this for a spook. But even then, those profiles generally include more information. This looks like someone took a giant eraser to her history, as if she's been rubbed out of existence. It's... unsettling."

This couldn't be where the investigation ended, so close to cracking it open, but unable to bridge the information gap. She had no doubt, especially after Max's report, that Trinity was the answer to the questions she'd been asking. But if she was this effective at removing herself from... everything, then how in the world would Laila tie her to the losses at Archer?

She couldn't accept that it might not be possible.

"Okay." Laila returned the iPad to Max. "Keep looking. Let me know if you find anything."

Max took the iPad with a tight nod that didn't make Laila feel good about her chances for learning more. Without a word, Max turned and left.

Laila picked up her phone. She needed to check in with Sia before she lost herself to this completely. Then she would decide how to proceed.

CHAPTER 9

"Your mom is adjusting well, Trinity." The charge nurse assigned to Ornella spoke in a calm, reassuring tone. Her smile was just sympathetic enough to set Trinity on edge.

Carol shifted in her seat next to Trinity, her wide hips just a smidge too much for the sleek office chairs. "She's allowed to bake, right? Without that, Ornella isn't Ornella," Carol said, so earnest in inquiring about her friend despite the still-healing wound on her arm.

For her part, Trinity was glad she asked. Ornella might have forgotten all about her daughter, her friends, and her whole life after she moved away from Jamaica at the age of sixteen, but she would never forget her need to be in the kitchen. That was engrained in her, set deep in her personal code and indelible against the ravages of Alzheimer's. When she stopped baking, she would likely die very soon after.

"Oh yes. She's become a favorite among the staff and clients alike. She's quite talented."

Prior to sitting down in this cheerful little office with the equally cheerful charge nurse, Trinity and Carol had visited with Ornella. She hadn't recognized either of them, but she had asked politely about the bandage around Carol's arm. She was heartbreakingly concerned about Carol's health while being completely oblivious to the cause of the injury.

Trinity closed her eyes and took a deep breath. These people were good. They cared about the patients here.

She could tell that in the way they smiled, in the polished gleam of the windows and floors, and in the warm sounds of laughter and community that surrounded them. Ornella was safe and cared for.

Knowing all that should have made this easier, but it didn't. Trinity hoped that, with time, the sharp edge would fade away, leaving behind only the dull ache of loss rather than the overwhelming wave of grief that enveloped her.

Ornella, were she able to, would tell Trinity to stop with all the fuss and get on with living life. There was no point dwelling on things that can't be changed. For Ornella, Trinity was trying, and would try harder.

In her lap, Trinity held a brown paper grocery bag with the top folded over. She gripped it in both hands, squeezing hard enough to crinkle the paper and wear it down until it was soft to the touch. Carol placed a calming hand on her arm for a moment and offered her an understanding smile. Trinity gave her a tight nod.

"Will you make sure she gets this?" Trinity stood and thrust the bag out toward the nurse. That bag held items that were intrinsically linked to her memories of her mother. "It's her apron and pie pans and a few other things."

The nurse nodded. "Of course." The look in her eye said she doubted Ornella would know the difference, and Trinity swallowed the urge to argue.

Ornella would recognize these things. She would. Even when she remembered nothing else, she remembered the feel of the apron as it rested against her neck, the heft of the glass bakeware as she lifted it out of the oven, the carriage of the wooden rolling pin as she rolled out pie crust.

Trinity nodded again, an embarrassingly curt motion that would have resulted in a serious scolding from Ornella.

If Ornella was able to remember that Trinity was hers to scold.

"Would you like to see her one last time before you go?" The nurse stood. Their allotted fifteen minutes was clearly over.

Trinity looked past the nurse, through the glass wall that led to a community room where the patients were gathered. Ornella sat on the couch between two other women. The three were chatting and laughing and carrying on as if they were lifelong friends. She shook her head. "No. I don't think so. Carol?"

"No. We should get going."

The nurse escorted them out. It was a secure facility and required an electronic fob to exit through the main door. That feature made the building feel just a little bit prison-like, but Trinity couldn't deny the need. She would be unimpressed to learn that Ornella had gone off alone for an unsupervised midnight stroll.

Trinity turned to look at Ornella one last time before stepping out into the bright sunshine. It was a beautiful, cheery day, a stark counterpoint to Trinity's heavy and dark mood.

She walked with Carol to Ornella's ancient Volvo wagon. It was a 1960s-era beast that ran on diesel and good intentions. Ornella had bought it used from a retired postmaster a year after coming to the United States. She'd kept it, maintained it, and driven it right up until Trinity had parked it in their detached garage two years ago. She'd padlocked the door and hidden the key. It had been the only safe thing to do at the time.

Trinity had no idea what to do with it, or the house, without Ornella. Yvonne was pushing hard for Trinity to join her in Costa Rica, suggesting that Graciela would benefit from having a mentor close by. And she'd also mentioned, not so subtly, how nice it would be to have someone there to warm her bed when her boyfriend, Adam, was off saving some endangered plankton. Trinity wasn't sure how she felt about that. Essentially, Yvonne had said she saw Trinity as good enough to fill in, but not good enough for full time. It wasn't new, Yvonne's attitude toward Trinity in relation to Adam, but she'd never said it quite so boldly before.

Trinity unlocked the car, climbed in, and stretched across to unlock the passenger door for Carol. The Volvo was slow to start, having sat long enough for the engine to cool. Trinity gave the engine a moment to warm up before she shifted into gear and pulled out of the lot.

"Sure is strange, the way things work out," Carol said; her whole body sagged with the announcement.

"Sure is." Trinity wished for a distraction, but the road was long, wide, and free of traffic, save them. The only thing to do was talk to Carol. "What will you do now?"

In the past, Carol had talked about going back to Jamaica.

"I don't know. My own kids are spread all over the planet, and I miss home something fierce. But I also feel in my bones like I should be here for a spell longer."

Trinity glanced out the window as the blacktop rolled slowly by. She'd never been much of a driver, preferring the bus or even her bike. It was odd to sit on this side of the car.

"What about you, Trinity? Will you keep the house?"

Trinity took another deep breath. "I've been asking myself that same question."

"What else is there for you?"

"Everything." Trinity didn't know what that entailed exactly, but she repeated the answer more firmly, "Everything."

No matter how hard Laila scratched, she never got any deeper than surface level. She *knew* Trinity Washington was responsible for the shortages at Archer, but every thread she pulled simply evaporated into nothing. This was not how puzzles were supposed to work. When she pulled, the mystery should have unraveled.

Instead, Laila was close to unraveling.

With her tongue in cheek response about *housekeeping*, Trinity had taunted Laila. She'd said it playfully, laying down the challenge. Similar to a child playing Marco Polo in the dead of night, she'd dared Laila to find her.

God help her, Laila had tried.

Ivar, her forensic accountant, had scoured the accounts. While he'd been able to sort out the particulars of which financial nuggets were legitimate business and which ones were fraudulent, tantamount to embezzlement, he hadn't been able to determine where anything went after it left Archer's systems.

He'd brought in a computer guy. Best in the business, Ivar had assured her. Considering the standards Ivar held himself to when it came to work, she counted his endorsement as highly valuable. He had come up similarly empty handed. He'd traced a few financial transactions to the international border, but refused to go beyond that point. Apparently, some institutions enforced their banking security stridently enough to frighten him off.

And so Laila had been left with a Robin-Hood-shaped specter who was siphoning money away from Archer and dispersing it, as far as Laila could tell, to the financially needy. Trinity had teased Laila that day at Open Doors because she could. She was that good, and she knew it. Unless she confessed, which was exceptionally unlikely, she was untouchable. There wasn't a damn thing Laila could do about it.

Rather than making Laila angry, she was intrigued. She'd never come up against a wall such as this before. That made Trinity unique, and to Laila, that was irresistible. She was like the cobra swaying to the lyrical flute music, desperate to strike but too enchanted to do so. Trinity was cast as the snake charmer.

After far too many days in a row, Laila was no closer to proving her theory. It was as if she was trapped in an insane loop, and she wasn't sure if she was chasing Trinity or the other way around. All signs indicated that Trinity was quietly dangerous, with the ability to destroy lives, and Laila had no idea what she'd do if she ever caught her.

That was how Laila found herself standing on the sidewalk outside of Trinity's squatty Portland style home in this quiet Rancho Verde neighborhood. She'd been there, leaned up against a stop sign, for at least twenty minutes. No one had gone in or out of the house, and no lights were visible from this vantage point. It was possible that Trinity wasn't home, but that seemed unlikely given her work schedule at Archer.

Her phone buzzed, alerting her to a text message. It was from Sia.

Gabe asked about you. I gave him your number. You're welcome.

She texted back, unsure who Gabe was or why he needed her number.

Gabe? WTF Sia.

Moments later, her phone buzzed twice, one right after the other. The first message was from an unknown number. The other from Sia.

Gabe! The hottie in the pool at my engagement party. You asked about him. Recently single. Workaholic. Looks smokin' in a Speedo. How can you possibly forget about that?

The other message, the unknown number, was presumably Gabe. Laila ignored it for a moment.

Working!!!!!!!

After she hit send, she flipped over to the other new message.

Are you stalking me, Ms Hollister?

That got her attention. Laila straightened up and glanced around. Nothing had changed. Before she could respond, another message from the same number came through.

Should I call the police and report you for lurking? Or would you like to come inside?

As soon as Laila finished reading, the front door to Trinity's house opened. Trinity stepped out onto the porch and smiled at Laila. Her head was tilted to one side, and her dark braids flowed down over her shoulders, red highlights shining in the early morning light.

Laila stared at her for a moment, considering. How long had Trinity known she was here? How long had she waited to send the message and invite her inside? She was toying with Laila again, and her lack of control over the situation had Laila a little spun. She was used to seeing certain things with laser clarity. Human nuance, no, but clear actions on paper, yes. In this scenario, Trinity held all of the advantages. Laila was stepping into her world, guard down and flat-footed. It didn't feel good.

She squared up her shoulders and set her phone to silent. The buzz of another text message would distract her, and with someone like Trinity, Laila couldn't afford unnecessary distraction.

While Laila dithered, Trinity continued to smile. She arched one eyebrow and gestured for Trinity to join her. With her hand outstretched, she was like a siren calling to a sailor in the fog-filled early morning, and Laila was helpless against her pull.

Trinity turned and re-entered the house. The door remained open, and Laila finally found her senses. She'd wanted to talk to Trinity again since they had met at Open Doors. Why was she hesitating now, when an invitation had clearly been issued?

She walked swiftly from her place at the curb, across Trinity's brick walk, and up the few steps to the porch. At the doorway, she hesitated to give her eyes a chance to adjust. The interior of Trinity's house wasn't as dark as it looked from the exterior. The sun cast a wide swath of light across the living room. With a quick, fortifying breath, Laila stepped inside.

"Close the door, would you?" Trinity's voice came from some undetermined part of the house.

Laila complied and then said, "Where are you?"

"Follow the hall."

There was a short hall on Laila's right, just past a set of stairs. She moved in that direction and found Trinity in the first open door she came to. She sat at a computer station with a headset around her neck.

"Hi, Laila." She spoke simply, all pretense and teasing gone from her tone. It reminded Laila of the one genuine moment of their previous conversation, when Trinity had said she didn't think Laila was rude. Like this, Trinity was almost warm.

Laila stood awkwardly in the open door. She shifted her weight and said, "Hello."

"Come in." Trinity gestured to a chair sat opposite her, covered with a stack of magazines, including *Popular Mechanics*, *Code*, and *Maxim*. "Those can go on the floor."

There were several other similar stacks nearby, and Laila carefully transferred the magazines. She didn't know why, but it was important to not disturb Trinity's home more than necessary.

"Thanks." She sat on the edge of the seat, just as awkward and uncomfortable as she had been standing.

Trinity nodded. "It took you longer than I expected."

Laila blinked. "What do you mean?"

"I thought you'd be here a week ago, banging down my door."

"I wanted to, but that's hard to justify without proof."

"You have proof now?" Trinity looked amused, interested, but not worried.

"No." Laila shook her head.

"You decided to come shake the tree and see what falls out?"

"No, not that. I know nothing will fall. It would have by now if it was going to." Laila stretched out the metaphor Trinity used, but it got twisted up between her mind and her mouth, and she wasn't sure if it made any sense at all. "I mean, you're too good for that."

Trinity stared at her, her expression impassive. "Why are you here, Laila?"

"I don't know."

Trinity quirked an eyebrow. "Would you like something to drink?" As she spoke, she twirled in her chair, opened a dorm-room sized refrigerator, and pulled out a bottle of fizzy water. She held it out to Laila with a one-sided smile.

"Sure. Thanks." Laila started to get up, but Trinity motioned for her to stay put. She tossed the drink, and Laila caught it easily.

For something to do, Laila twisted the top off and took a long drink. After she'd swallowed, it clicked that it was the brand she usually bought, IZZE. She looked at the bottle, with its simple, almost retro logo, an idea taking root at the back of her brain. She shifted her focus to Trinity.

"That's your brand, right?" Trinity asked, that amused lilt that Laila couldn't quite read coloring her tone again.

"How did you..."

"You can learn all sorts of stuff on the Internet."

"You looked me up?" The realization hit Laila like a wall.

"Seems only fair, doesn't it?" Trinity asked mildly.

"Wow." Laila stood, drawn inexplicably nearer to Trinity. "What else did you learn?"

"Not much." Trinity clicked a few buttons on her computer and turned the screen to give Laila a better view. A slideshow popped up, featuring details from Laila's life.

The first photo showed an exterior view of Hollister Investigations. It was located downtown in an old multi-level warehouse that had been converted to office space during a gentrification initiative several years ago. They'd updated and modernized some aspects of the building and left others alone. The result was an eclectic mix of technology that gave the location a funky, hip vibe.

Next came a picture of Laila, standing in the lobby. She was staring at the old-school elevator with the metal fencing that covered the opening when the elevator was in use elsewhere. Presumably, it was to keep people from falling down the shaft. In Laila's opinion, anyone dumb enough to walk into an open elevator shaft deserved to fall down it. That was natural selection at work in the modern era.

There was a photo of Laila and Sia entering a dress boutique. Sia had that unnatural glow that was associated with brides-to-be. Laila looked sulky and suspicious. The window of the shop featured vintage wedding dresses that made Laila feel constricted and choked just from looking at them.

After the fifth or sixth photo—Laila in her apartment, running on her treadmill wearing only a sports bra and really short shorts, sweat dripping from her forehead—she'd had enough. "You can stop now."

Trinity hit a button and the slideshow dissolved from the screen.

"Where did you get those?"

"I didn't take them, if that's what you're worried about."

"No, I just..." She shook her head. "I didn't realize exactly how good you are."

Trinity curled her upper lip in a mild sneer. She waved her hand dismissively. "That was nothing."

"What else can you do?" Laila leaned on the desk, excited.

Trinity shrugged. "Anything."

"Anything?"

"Yeah." Trinity nodded, her smile a little smug.

"Prove it."

Trinity's fingers flew over her keyboard. In seconds, window after window opened on her monitor, each with a new layer of information about Laila, including a copy of the lease for Hollister Investigations, Laila's bank balance, and her movie rental history from Amazon Prime, including some porn titles that she'd rather forget about.

An idea swelled in Laila's mind, brilliant and bright and impossible to ignore. Without pausing to consider it, she blurted, "Come to work for me."

The words, once spoken aloud, buzzed in the air, taking on a life of their own.

Trinity stopped typing and stared at Laila. "You're kidding."

"I don't do kidding." Being able to joke with someone required a level of emotional nuance that she was simply incapable of.

"Then you've clearly lost your mind."

Laila's mind raced, calculating the angles and the implications of what she'd said. All points led back to the same place. "I'm serious. This is a legitimate proposal."

Trinity melted back into her chair, a salacious grin on her face. "Is it now? Tell me all the lurid details."

Laila's face flushed with heat. Fuck. Trinity made her blush. She couldn't remember the last time she'd done that. "No, not like that." She sputtered indignantly, and Trinity's smile grew.

Before Laila could continue, Trinity held up one finger and sat upright, the picture of professionalism. She tapped a button on her keyboard as she slipped her headphones into place.

"Hi, Vonnie," Trinity greeted her caller and then paused, presumably listening. After a moment she said, "That's great. Can I call you back in a minute? I'm with someone." Then with a genuine smile and a nod, Trinity tapped her keyboard again and removed her headset completely. She set it on the desk in front of her.

Laila licked her lips. "You're good," she said, trying to get through this before Trinity could twist her up again. "I mean, you're really good. My guy couldn't even come close to tracing your work. And what you just did there..." Laila shook her head. She didn't have the right words to describe it.

"Laila, is this a ham-fisted attempt to tease a confession out of me? Because, I gotta tell you, it's not going to work."

"No. I'm done trying to link you to my investigation at Archer. That file is officially closed as of three this afternoon."

"Your uncle accepted that?"

Trinity's reference to Samar as her uncle was another example of how deeply she'd looked into Laila. Then again, it had probably taken Trinity longer to boot up her computer than it did for her to find that information.

"Yes. I assured him that we've rooted out all sources of the losses and that they won't reappear."

"Did you?"

Laila shrugged. "You know we didn't. But if this meeting goes well, you'll do it for me."

"I'm listening."

"You come to work for me, for Hollister Investigations. Put yourself on the right side of the law for a change."

The impenetrable, unreadable veil covered Trinity's face again, her expression giving away nothing. Reading facial cues and body language was difficult for Laila, but she knew when someone was shutting down.

"Laws are arbitrary rules created by powerful men to suit their own needs. They rarely match up with what's right."

That was interesting. Laila liked rules. They were clear and concise. Even when they were convoluted, they still made sense. They provided her with a set of parameters to work in. "I..." She paused. She needed to get this right.

After a deep breath, she tried again, this time taking a different tack. "I suck at people. They don't say what they really mean, and they get mad when I do. They are confusing and frustrating, and I just don't think the way they do. Rules and laws make my life livable. They are the lines on the road that you stay between when driving. I've never thought of them as anything other than helpful."

"Laws are stupid. *You* are better than that."

"Can you give me an example?"

"I can give you thousands."

For the next ten minutes, Trinity spoke without stopping. She talked about rape victims, immigration, banking practices, taxation for corporations, the middle class, voters' rights... She was passionate and convincing, and Laila's head spun with the barrage of information. When Trinity finished, she sat back with a huff. Her eyes flashed in challenge, and Laila was awed.

"This is exactly why you need to come work for me. We're really good at what we do. The best, really. You've done your research; you know it's true. With you, we'd be even better, completely unparalleled. I doubt this makes a difference, but we offer an excellent benefits package, and I'll double what Archer pays you."

After a long pause, Trinity said, "Why?"

"Why?" Stupidly, Laila was unprepared for that question. It never occurred to her that she'd have to explain why Hollister was awesome.

"Why would I want to give up what I have to work for your goodie two shoes investigation firm?"

"This job at Archer isn't the norm. That was a favor to Uncle Samar. We help people, Trinity. Real people with real problems."

"Go on."

"We had a client whose husband hid all their assets overseas and then left her. She went from the penthouse to welfare. We helped her expose her ex."

Trinity picked up her headset. "Not interested."

"Wait. We've exposed corporate cover-ups and forced accountability. We do pro-bono work for the domestic violence shelter on Wabash. We recover funds for elderly people who've been scammed. We do good work, Trinity. Far better than helping spoiled execs who don't know how to use their computers."

Somewhere around Wabash, Trinity removed her headset again. She listened until Laila ran out of steam and then said, "Triple."

"Huh?"

"You said double my salary. I want triple."

Laila did the quick math. It was manageable and wouldn't be difficult at all if having Trinity on staff paid the dividends Laila was banking on. "Two and a half times, with a generous bonus structure."

"You know this is a terrible idea, right?"

Laila knew no such thing. "No, it's perfection."

"What are the conditions?"

"You cease and desist all activity at Archer, both above and below board. Quit your job and extract your other... interests."

"What else?"

Laila shook her head. "That's all I care about."

Trinity sighed. "Open Doors relies on those donations."

"I've discussed that with Uncle Samar. He's approved an ongoing campaign of support. They're working with the board for Open Doors to coordinate a full media blitz."

"If you're messing with me, you know I'll bury you." Trinity leveled her threat in a light, breezy tone. She might as well have been talking about the state of her flower garden or a book she'd read recently.

"I have no doubt," Laila said solemnly.

"Then it looks like we have reached an accord."

"Yeah?" Laila sat back, pleased with the outcome.

"Yeah."

"There's one other thing." Laila hoped the next point wouldn't prove to be a deal breaker for Trinity. "There's only three of us, four with you. Because we're such a small team, we all need to be in the same location. You wouldn't be able to work from home."

Trinity shrugged. "Okay."

Wow. The reason Ivar remained a consultant was his refusal to budge on this issue. In her experience, people who worked from home weren't quick to change it. "That was easy."

"Things change," Trinity said, her expression guarded once again.

"What changed for you?"

Trinity gave her a stare that made Laila shrink back into herself. Then she sighed. "I don't know you well enough to explain all that, Laila. Can you just be satisfied with knowing that I don't need to work from home anymore?"

"Yeah. Okay."

They discussed a few more details, established an official start date, and Trinity asked a rapid fire succession of questions about the benefits package Laila had mentioned. When Trinity was finally satisfied, Laila shook her hand and left.

On her walk back to her car, she reflected on the past few weeks. Of all the possible outcomes to her investigation, this was not even on her list of possibilities. Trinity Washington had surprised her over and over. Strangely, she looked forward to being surprised for many years to come.

About Jove Belle

Jove Belle lives in Vancouver, Washington with her family. Her books include *Cake*, *The Job*, *Uncommon Romance*, *Love and Devotion*, *Indelible*, *Chaps*, *Split the Aces*, and *Edge of Darkness*.

CONNECT WITH JOVE:

Website: www.jovebelle.com

.

DAUGHTER OF BAAL

BY GILL MCKNIGHT

THE ARRIVAL

"You know, Jones, much as I love the slicky city thing, there is something to be said for the rustic idyll. Oh, to be an English peasant, haymaking and wassailing all over this green and pleasant land." Lady Margo Quince-Patrick gazed dreamily out the window of her Bentley Speed Six tourer. "A simple but exemplary life. Roaming over the rolling hills with lambs a gambolling, geese a flocking, and cows...cows..."

"A cudding, ma'am?" Jones supplied. She flicked a quick glance to the rear view mirror.

Her employer, Lady Margo, sighed, clearly enchanted by the barley fields and neat farmland passing by. She certainly looked the perfect country lady in her Lewis tweeds, tailored to the latest cut by Saville Row. The delicate Persian pearls at her throat and earlobes set the ensemble off beautifully.

"I hear the laughter in your voice," she said. "You're incorrigible. I suppose, compared to your United States, this is all very tame."

Jones took in the landscape flitting by. It had its charm, but it was all so tiny—so fenced in and toy-like. "On the bright side there are no bandits, marauding Injun's, or rattlesnakes, ma'am," she said.

"Oh, you'll find snakes aplenty where we're going. My uncle Wesley is especially slippery. Despite its surroundings, Clamp House is far from bucolic. You'll definitely have your eyes opened. I think London has been too sweet on you, Jones. It's time you saw the underbelly of English aristocracy, and Uncle Wesley's leaves grooves in the ground."

"I'm sure to be agog, ma'am."

"The only decent Clamps are my cousins, Betsy, who's seventeen but really not much more than a child, and of course, Melisandrine, and she'll be heading for Scotland once she's married. Perry will want them to reside in London of course, but his father will demand they spend the first year of their marriage on the home estate in Argyll."

"Yes, ma'am."

"Poor Perry. There'll be no one from his family there. He's the only one not in the army. Even his father, Lord Gladbeck, can't get away from the Somaliland campaign to attend the wedding. And his mother is dead these past ten years." She tutted at the perceived injustice. Then, "Oh dear, we're almost there." Lady Margo sighed. "And to think, if it wasn't for this beastly family wedding, we would be on-board the Queen Mary on our merry way to your old stomping ground."

"New York? Hardly, ma'am. You'd need to go much farther south-west to find anything I've stomped on." Jones turned right, and the mink coloured Bentley sailed through the imposing gateway into the grounds of Clamp Park.

The tall iron gates were flanked by impressive stone pillars, each crested with the Clamp family coat of arms—a cartouche bearing an emblazoned sun poised over crossed palm fronds, supported on either side by rearing crocodiles. The heraldry clearly indicated that the family fortune had been made in the Middle East and Africa.

Jones drove on through the parkland, flatter and less pretty than the surrounding countryside, though the open acres and wooded areas provided for a reasonably sized deer park before the more formal gardens began. The Bentley rounded the final curve of the half-mile driveway, and Clamp House finally appeared. After the suspense-building drive up, the house itself was a disappointment. It was an ugly, squat building at odds with the grounds in which it stood. Its Palladian facade was built in the latter part of the previous century, with little architectural merit. The proportions were wrong, and the addition of crenulated ramparts at some later date only added to the cramped, brooding feel of the place. Not even the huge marquee dominating the front lawn could lift the gloom. The house glowered at the visitor, and despite the gay bunting that zig-zagged overhead from tree to tree, twirling in the June breeze like a thousand welcoming handkerchiefs, the overall effect was disagreeable.

Jones swung the car into a majestic, gravel-crunching halt before the granite steps, and she was out of her seat to open the rear door for her illustrious passenger.

"Ma'am," she murmured smoothly and offered her hand.

A slender leg, tapering down to a dainty ankle and a stylish lady's leather brogue first emerged from the vehicle, soon followed by the rest of Lady Margo in her tweeds and pearls. A cloche hat in pleated bronze silk adorned her platinum bob. She looked a delight, and Jones very much approved.

Above them, the impressive oak front door opened, and a solemn faced butler emerged. No doubt, he had seen the Bentley's approach from some vantage point or other. He cleared his throat and began to descend the steps when—

"Quincy!" The door burst open, startling him, and a young girl flew past him almost toppling him over. "Quincy, you're the last to arrive. I've been waiting for you all day!"

"Betsy! How wonder—oof!"

Lady Margo, or Quincy to friends and family of a certain age and demeanour, was caught up in an enthusiastic hug that pinned her arms to her sides and set her elegant hat askew over one eyebrow.

Jones suppressed a small smile and removed herself to the rear of the vehicle to begin to unpack the weekend luggage.

"All the old fogeys came yesterday or earlier this morning. Gosh, it's good to see you. You look as spritzer as ever, Quincy. Oh, sorry. Did I squeeze too hard?"

Margo gently unravelled herself from the hug and corrected the tilt of her hat. "Not at all. Your hugs are soft as eiderdown and twice as warm, just like always." She gave Betsy a brilliant smile, and the girl blushed wildly, right up to the roots of her auburn hair. "And I'll wager all the old fogeys galloped over here in time for lunch," Margo continued. "While we took it easy and had a picnic along the way."

"What fun. I wish I had been there with you instead of stuck here greeting boring guests." Betsy threw a surreptitious glance at Jones, who tapped the peak of her chauffeur cap politely. It made her blush even more violently. Jones pretended not to notice and went back to work.

She was used to the undisguised curiosity of Lady Margo's friends and acquaintances. Which only heightened once they realised she was female as well as American Indian.

She had met Betsy before at another family gathering, though the girl had been several years younger. They had played cricket together on the lawn in an impromptu staff versus "the family" game to celebrate Armistice day. She remembered Betsy had a mean right arm. It had been a fun afternoon, but Betsy was no longer a child. Now her attention was keener and a little more cumbrous.

"How are things," Margo linked arms and skilfully redirected Betsy towards the stairs. There was a twinkle in her sea-foam green eyes as she sauntered past that let Jones know the moment had not gone unnoticed. Lady Margo quite liked the effect her tall, stately Navajo "personal aide cum chauffeur" had on her set. Ladies in britches caused enough of a sensation, but chauffeur britches with knee length black leather boots? London town was already atwitter, and to be sure, Lady Margo would have her fair share of disapproval from the older, staider guests over the weekend—and she would enjoy every minute of it.

Jones became aware of the butler poised at her elbow, waiting to grab the bags and return to the house. Contrary to his young mistress, his beady, birdlike eyes shone with disapproval at her exoticism. Jones was used to this, too. Above stairs, the curious rich could afford to prod and poke. Below stairs, they pinched.

A faint whiff of whiskey drifted off him. She didn't drink herself, so her nose was sensitive to the smell of alcohol on others. It was an unpleasant, sour smell, and she concluded the man imbibed regularly. She straightened to her full height of six foot, which gave her considerable advantage over him. She kept her face cool and hard edged. He grudgingly moved back a pace, giving her more room to manoeuvre, but not before he exchanged a scornful look of his own.

"Forcep," Betsy addressed him in passing, suddenly becoming a lady of the manor. "See to Lady Margo's things. She's in the Peacock room."

"Yes, Miss Betsy." Forcep took this as an opportunity to lean in and try to snatch a bag from near Jones feet. Weekend luggage to Lady Margo amounted to a small mountain of leather and brass, monogrammed Louis Vuitton, and none of it was light. With satisfaction she watched as Forcep reddened and grunted as he tried to move the small trunk she had easily lifted clear of the boot and set by the rear fender. She left the last of the luggage before him, dusted down her hands and closed the Bentley's boot. Her part of the job was done; he could see to the rest. She hoped the Peacock room was up many, many flights of stairs.

"The garages are around the back, beside the stable block," he muttered. "Mrs Mallory will show you to your quarters. Go on through to the kitchens; you'll find her there."

Without a backward look, she slid behind the steering wheel and threw the chauffeur cap onto the seat beside her. Her ink-black hair tumbled down her back in a thick plait. She wore it that way when in uniform, but itched to release her hair from its confines now. It had been a long and tiring drive despite the picnic interlude which had been very pleasant. A bubbling brook in a field of wildflowers and meadow grass, a Harrods picnic hamper on a tartan blanket, and Lady Margo, hat and jacket discarded, sipping sparkling cider and nibbling on a watercress sandwich.

In moments such as that, Jones let down her guard. Her cap and jacket had also been discarded, and a ginger beer substituted for the cider. They had lain, relaxed on the blanket and chatted amicably, and Jones remembered why she had accepted the bizarre job proposal in the first place. Lady Margo had charm and humour, mixed through with a certain vulnerability. In her own aristocratic way, she was as exotic to Jones as Jones had been to her.

Circling to the back of the house, she slid the huge motorcar silently towards the stables and the large garaging facilities adjacent. As she drew parallel to the main stable block, a flicker of movement caught her eye. A large chestnut brood mare was being rhythmically groomed by an equally well-oiled stable lad. The sweat from his effort shone on the well-tanned shoulders and biceps popping up from his baggy dungarees. Little wisps of sun-bleached hair escaped from an old flat cap. Dust motes leapt and danced around this sun-lit scene; it looked to be hot, sticky, and tiresome work. Jones was grateful for the cool breeze rolling through the Bentley's open windows and the buttery leather of her seat. The sophisticated luxury of the car reflected her new life well. She had travelled worlds and liked the one she lived in now.

It was a short stroll from the garages, through a small herb garden to the open kitchen door. With her chauffeur jacket unbuttoned and a small travel bag over her shoulder, Jones entered the unique sweltering hell of an English manor house kitchen in June. The heat hit her like a slap in the face. Not as warm as New Mexico but welcome. Its swirling heat was full of steam, aromas, and frantic human voices. About a dozen aproned staff were running round in a state of pandemonium that could only indicate a professional kitchen or a mortar attack.

Overseeing this mania was a mountain of a woman in starched white. She trumpeted out instruction and admonishment in equal measure. In one fist, she held a huge bowl of cream clutched to her bosom. Her other was wrapped around a whisk, which she occasionally shook vigorously at some ne'er-do-well. Her staff scuttled around like agitated beetles, and it took Jones a moment of quiet observation to understand that this was a synchronised performance in which every player knew her role by heart.

She also surmised this must be Mrs Mallory, head cook of Clamp House. All the rest of the hoo-ha must be preparations for the wedding. Mrs Mallory looked as if she thrived on the challenge; her staff did not. They were wilting like day-old lilies.

Pushing into the fuggy blanket of heat and cooking odours, Jones approached the matriarch de cuisine and said, "Mrs Mallory? I was told you could direct me to me my room. I'm with Lady Quince-Patrick's party."

"Party! Party! Don't tell me there's more than one of 'em. I was distinctly told Lady Margo would be unaccompanied. I can't go changing all the dinner arrangements now. It's bad enough as it is, what with people sticking their noses in left, right, and centre, without unexpected guests popping up everywhere like...like...prairie dogs!"

"It's still a party of one; no changes there. I'm the staff," Jones said calmly. Mrs Mallory looked her up and down, taking in all she needed to know in one glance.

"Are you now." Then she turned and hollered to one of the girls over by the huge cooking range. "Sarah, show..." She turned back to Jones, "I'm sorry but I've forgotten your name already."

"I never gave it. It's Jones."

"Show Mr Jones to his room." Mrs Mallory completed her instructions, not registering the gender of her guest correctly. This was another anomaly Jones was familiar with. It didn't matter to her; it would merely be tedious later on when Mrs Mallory finally realised her mistake and either apologised for or huffed over it.

Sarah approached, wiping her hands on her apron and looking relieved at having a distraction. She was young and sassy and already had a gleam in her eye on seeing her charge. Jones kept her face an impassive mask, though Sarah's hip sway of a walk was hard to ignore.

"Follow me." Sarah's voice had a cheeky lilt. Her pretty face glowed from the kitchen heat, and her eyes sparkled flirtatiously as she led Jones out through the bedlam into the cool, tiled back hall. "The staff quarters are in the attics, so we have to take the rear stairwell. You don't mind the rear, do you?" It was a suggestive, silly question. House staff would use no other stairway. Jones ignored the blatant flirtation and nodded, letting Sarah take the lead.

"Is it always so manic?" she asked, watching Sarah's undulating rump as she ascended the narrow staircase a few steps ahead of her.

"We've got this bleedin' wedding, ain't we? And Cook's got herself in a right old pickle," Sarah answered over her shoulder. "Doesn't help that one of the guests is a celebrity chef and keeps pushing his snooty French nose in. Has her in a proper spin, he does." Her backside mamboed its way up the narrow stairway, inches from Jones's face. Sarah knew more about sauce than Mrs Mallory had ever taught her.

"How many staff are there here?"

"About twenty, including the groundsmen and stable hands. I'm full time in the kitchen with Whimsy and Gladys. Though Whimsy sometimes helps with the housekeeping, cos between you and me, she's useless for aught but pot scrubbing," she said. "Today, we got several women come in from the village to help out. Good thing too, what with John taken ill. He had to go to the hospital this morning—oh, and there's Mr Forcep. He's the butler, but you probably met him already. Leery old boozer!" She snorted in derision. She was puffing now. Not as fit as she was spirited, Jones thought.

"Blow me down. I swear these stairs get steeper."

"I wouldn't fancy running up and down these several times a day. Especially not after a stint in the kitchen. That looked like hot work," Jones said. "Do all the house staff room up here?"

Sarah shook her head. "Only the junior staff and visitors like yourself are up here. Mr Forcep, Mrs Mallory, and Miss Bloom, the Housekeeper, are on the floor below."

She led Jones down a gloomy corridor. "That's my room there." Her fingers trailed across the brown, chipped paintwork of a closed door. "You're further on down, on my side." Here she flicked Jones a sly sideways glance.

She swung open the guest door to a cramped but scrupulously clean little bedroom and stood back so Jones could enter first. It had a small washbasin in one corner, a narrow bed with fresh but worn bed linen, and a wardrobe of dark wood.

"The bathroom is third on the left." Sarah came into the room after her. "Need any help unpacking?" Their eyes locked—Sarah's brazen; Jones's bemused.

"I've only got this bag." Jones swung it off her shoulder and dropped it onto the bed with a thump. The rusty bed springs squeaked convulsively. Sarah started at the suggestively squeaking bed, then turned her gaze sharply onto Jones, and for the first time, seemingly took her in. Jones knew the effect she had. Her black uniform jacket lay unbuttoned against a crisp linen shirt, startlingly white against a dark column of throat. Her chauffeur jodhpurs stretched taut over her thighs and were tucked into soft black leather boots. Her Navajo heritage gave her a dangerous, sexy broodiness that pulsed from her and was stifling in the little room. She watched as her gender hit home and a deep blush scorched the young maid's cheeks. Sarah glanced away, as hot and bothered as if she'd stayed in the kitchen after all.

"Well then, I'll leave you to sort it out on your own," she said tartly. The mischievous look immediately re-entered her eyes. "But never let it be said I didn't offer to help...or raise a finger." With that she flounced out, calling over her shoulder. "There'll be a cup of tea at four o'clock, after the nobs have had theirs."

Bemused, Jones watched her leave. It was refreshing how quickly she had bounced back after she'd discovered her gaffe. Sarah's room was five doors down from hers. That maybe was something worth remembering.

Afternoon Tea

Lady Margo sipped Earl Grey from her china tea cup but waved away the cake plate Betsy lunged in her direction. Beside her, Mrs Ford-Hughes happily helped herself to a second fondant. Mrs Ford-Hughes was a rotund woman who had delivered her esteemed—and unfortunately now deceased—husband of several sons and felt it her duty to indulge herself a little in her widowhood. This involved eating as much as she liked and keeping a firm eye on her many daughters-in-law and grandchildren. She had informed Margo of all this within seconds of her taking the seat next to her. After several comments of feigned interest, Margo felt it time to circulate. After all, there were many other guests to greet, some she had not seen for at least a year, if not more.

Most drifted around the room, idly chatting with each other. Some examined the various antiquities which had been unearthed in some foreign clime and returned to England for scholarly research and then auction. Every room in the house was full of scarabs, fragments of tablets inscribed in hieroglyphics or runic scrawls, statuettes, and votive charms. Two full-size Egyptian mummies, complete with sarcophagi, stood upright in the main hall. One already sold to the current Chancellor of the Exchequer, who at this moment, was having a sherry with an officer of the Coldstream Guards.

"Quincy." Betsy was at her side, looking harried. Her father, Sir Wesley Clamp, had decided to take his afternoon refreshment locked away in his study, leaving Betsy to oversee any remaining introductions, a task she was not best suited to. "May I introduce you to the Reverend Tupper. He's officiating at the wedding."

"How do you do, Reverend Tupper." Margo shook his hand. He was a small, swarthy gentleman with sharp, intelligent eyes and a quick handshake. The palm of his hand was as dry as rough sand, and his greeting clipped.

"I'm very well, thank you, Lady Margo." He gave a small bow and moved away.

"I don't remember him from my last visit. Is he new?" Margo discreetly asked Betsy once the good Reverend was out of earshot. "I thought Reverend Michaels tended your parish?" She had a warm spot for the tender-hearted minister.

"Tupper's a replacement. He's just come in for the service," Betsy informed her. "Reverend Michaels had to go to Chichester to see his poor mother. She took a bad fall at her local library."

"How awful; I do hope she is well. So, who is here? I recognise a few, but some are entirely new to me."

"Like Mrs Ford-Hughes?" Betsy giggled and linked arms as they moved across the drawing room. "Father invited her. Apparently, she's some sort of hob-nob on the museum board."

"Oh dear, don't tell me he's filling up Melisandrine's wedding with business contacts?"

"Between you and me, I think Melisandrine is beyond caring. I've never seen her so disinterested in anything before, especially something where she's supposed to be the centre of attention."

Her cousin Melisandrine had always displayed a prodigious, if dubious, talent for drama and the arts in general. Surely her own wedding would be a wonderful opportunity to take centre stage?

"How unusual," Margo said.

Betsy steered her towards a suave, foreign looking young man with an engaging smile and oiled slicked black hair.

"Alexandro, may I present my cousin Lady Margo Quince-Patrick," Betsy said, with a twitter of excitement in her voice. It seemed Jones was not Betsy's only weekend crush. "Margo, this is Señor Checa. He's come all the way from South America to be Perry's best man."

Alexandro raised Margo's hand to his mouth and brushed his lips across her knuckles.

"Enchanted," he murmured in a voice as smooth as melting molasses. His gaze never left hers, and she felt the definite pull of his magnetism. Señor Checa had charm and knew how to use it. Margo smiled divinely, the smile she reserved for socially awkward moments, and carefully removed her hand from his grasp.

"It's a pleasure to meet a good friend of Perry's. And where *is* the man of the moment?" she asked.

Simultaneously, both Betsy and Alexandro turned towards the sideboard where Perry Gladbeck stood refilling his crystal whiskey glass. Perry was tall and blond and exceptionally good looking. The brilliant afternoon sun poured through the west window and shone on the masculine column of his throat where his Adam's apple gently bobbed as he downed his drink in one swallow. A faint sheen of perspiration dampened his forehead, causing a golden lock of hair to curl in a pleasing, rakish manner. As if aware he was under scrutiny, he turned towards his onlookers and gave a charming smile that could have graced the face of a Renaissance angel.

"Quincy! Well, I'll be damned." He strode over and gave Margo an overeager hug, enveloping her in a fug of whiskey fumes and stale cigar smoke. "When did you arrive? Alexandro, this is Margo, Melisandrine's cousin and an old pal of mine from way back when. Eh, Margo? Remember that year we all went to Cowes for the yachting and you fell in?" He talked non-stop, not seeming to need an answer to any of his questions.

Margo smiled tightly. "That was Jane Fortescue who fell in at Cowes, not me," she corrected. Beside her, Betsy sighed quietly. A conversation with Perry took a lot of patience, and poor Betsy was stuck with him as a brother-in-law. Lord only knew what Melisandrine had seen in him. News of their Christmas engagement had shocked Margo, and now she was as confused as ever as to what they saw in each other. She couldn't think of two more mismatched people.

"We've just been introduced." Alexandro took the opportunity to cast Margo another scorching look. She decided that once his natural flirtatiousness abated, he could be good fun. She would wager that behind the searing glances lay an intelligent humour and dry wit, unlike Perry who seemed a trifle put out at the attention she was garnering from his good friend.

"And what about St. Moritz? Are you for St. Moritz this winter?" he continued, brashly assaulting the conversation, though his attention had strayed to the drinks tray again. "Can I get you a drink? What will you have, Margo?"

"I'm thinking of the Caribbean this winter. And I'll finish my tea, thank you."

"Pish pash." He made a face at her teacup. "I'll get you a gin."

"You need to meet with the Leakeys, Margo." Betsy gently drew her away. "And you're seated opposite Timothy Arbuthnot at dinner this evening, so it's best to say hello now."

Margo gratefully followed her, pleased at Betsy's quick thinking. The Leakeys and the Arbuthnots were the most dreadful bores, but anything was better than Perry when he was on a toot.

"Good gracious, Betsy. It's not even four o'clock, and he's ossified. He's like a man in the depths of despair. Whatever's happening?"

"You wait 'til you see the bride," Betsy said glumly. "I swear, Margo, this is a rum do if ever there was one. No one is happy. Perry has been zozzled since before he got here. Father is in such a stink because of a sale that fell through, I can barely look at him sideways, and as for Melisandrine... Well, see for yourself!"

The door opened to a chorus of welcoming coos and trills as Melisandrine Clamp, the bride-to-be, entered the drawing room. Her afternoon dress of cream silk floated around her slim, waif-like figure as she drifted across the floor. Melisandrine never failed to look as if she'd been born into the wrong century by about two thousand years. A faint, rueful smile played upon her lips, and Margo fully expected her to announce a tragedy of worldly proportions like some ancient actress in an amphitheatre. She duly greeted her guests. Perry, who should have been among the first to meet her, was ensconced in some heated debate with Alexandro and had not even noticed his bride's entrance.

Then Melisandrine was before her, a vision of impalpable loveliness.

"Darling, Margo." She reached for her with outstretched arms and pulled Margo into an embrace as warm and welcoming as a cobweb. "So wonderful to see you." Melisandrine stepped back and gazed deeply into Margo's eyes. "I must talk to you as soon as possible."

"Of course." Margo was so disconcerted by the intensity of the stare that, after Perry arrived to claim Melisandrine and they moved off, she realised she had not congratulated them both on their upcoming nuptials.

"See what I mean?" Betsy hissed in her ear. "It's as if *she's* in a stupor, and *he's* upset about something."

To be frank, Perry was always drunk, and Margo saw little difference in Melisandrine's outward demeanour. It was only the intensity of that gaze that had discombobulated her. She had the distinct impression Melisandrine was in trouble. And it was more than the nerves of a jittery bride.

KITCHEN GOSSIP

With her shirt sleeves rolled up, Jones plunged her strong forearms elbow deep into the bucket of warm, sudsy water. Jones relished the sweat-inducing labour of washing the Bentley. She trusted no other to not scratch the paintwork so took the chore upon herself.

Her ritual was nearing its end. The huge car shone. Not one mote of dust attached to its gleaming surface. The soft mink colour with its buttercream leather interior, the inherent luxury inside and out, to her mind, complemented Lady Margo perfectly. And when that throaty engine purred... Oh my.

"She's a beauty, ain't she?" The stable lad had wandered in from next door.

"Yes, she is." Jones wiped her hands dry on a towel.

"Is it the new Bentley?" The stable lad came further into the garage, and Jones realized she was talking to a young woman rather than a lad. It amused her to have been on the other end of a gender confusion. It caused her to elaborate more than she normally would.

"Yeah. Speed Six tourer. She's the straight six cylinder with a half-litre upgrade through an added manifold."

"What's the top speed?"

"I can get up to seventy miles an hour if there's a fire."

"Wow."

"And you are?" Jones asked.

"Wentworth. I manage the stables in that I do most everything around here to do with horses. You're Jones, ain't ya? I heard about you already."

"Yeah, I am. So, stable work can't be bad," Jones said casually. In her experience, service staff usually found the jobs they preferred and stayed with them for a lifetime.

"I love horses, always have done. I'm lucky to be working with some of the finest horse flesh in the county." Wentworth inadvertently verified her ideas.

"Wentworth?" A soft call came from the stables. Wentworth flushed.

"Excuse me," she said and withdrew.

Intrigued, Jones followed at a discreet distance as far as the doorway that joined the two buildings and witnessed a tender moment between Wentworth and a young maid, one she recognised from the kitchens but had, as yet, no name for.

"I've got to work late tonight," the young lass said, clasping Wentworth's hands in her own. "The news on John isn't good, and Mrs M is in a fearful fluster."

"Is it that French twit again?" Wentworth asked.

Her paramour nodded.

"And do they know what's wrong with John?"

"No. But it seems to be very serious."

"If you have to work late, then I'll wait and walk you home. You can find me here, all right?" Wentworth leaned in and stole a chaste kiss that set both of their cheeks ablaze. "I love you, Whimsy Bell."

Sarah had mentioned a maid called Whimsy. Jones smiled at the sweetness of the kiss and was about to withdraw when the Palomino in the stall beside the couple began to dance and snort in alarm. This drew Wentworth's attention away. Jones moved further into the stable block to see what was wrong. She knew the sound of a distressed horse, and this animal was far from happy.

"I better get back. It's nearly tea time," Whimsy said. She spied Jones and ducked her head, quickly turning back the way she had come.

"What is it?" Jones came to stand by Wentworth at the stall door.

"I can't see anything, but something's spooked her." Wentworth shot the bolt and carefully brought the animal out. She walked her out into the paddock, examining every step the mare took. "She's moving along okay."

Jones watched them disappear into the sunlight before turning her attention back to the dark shadows of the stall. She took a step in. It was cool and quiet and ought to have been a restful place for the mare. A few empty canvas bags and several traces hung on the wall. The floor was covered in clean straw. The stall had been mucked out recently. Wentworth was right. There was nothing that seemed untoward. Jones was about to go when a rustle from the straw pushed into the far corner alerted her to another presence. She picked up a rake and cautiously approached. A gentle probe with the handle revealed a rat. It was long and sleek and looked dead, as in stiff-as-a-board dead. Yet Jones knew she had heard it rustling only a moment ago. She prodded it again but it lay still. It was definitely dead. Rats didn't play possum. Satisfied she had heard the death throes of a rat, Jones turned to go. It was not her job to dispose of vermin.

"I found a dead rat in her stall," she told Wentworth.

"Forcep's been poisoning them again. I already told him he shouldn't." Wentworth's face darkened. "We've plenty of cats for the vermin. I hate poison lying around a place. I'm always worried it will get into the feed."

With the Bentley washed and polished, Jones's work as chauffeur was done for the day. She left Wentworth fussing over her mare and headed for the kitchens for afternoon tea with the house staff.

"Ah. *Miss* Jones," Mrs Mallory greeted her. The gleam in her eye was accusatory, as if she had been deliberately misled in assuming Jones was a man. Behind her Sarah smirked and gave Jones a conspiratorial wink.

"Jones alone will do," Jones said affably and slid into a seat at the long central table. She had little time for the myopia of the Mrs Mallorys of this world. And though she sounded agreeable, there was enough firmness to her tone for "Jones alone" to stick. There was no *Miss* Jones in her life.

Her tea was poured without any further comment, and a plate of bread and butter passed over.

"Whimsy says you were out washing the car?" Sarah took the seat opposite, and Whimsy, one chair down, burned scarlet as if Sarah had exposed her somehow.

Jones nodded. "I do that every time we arrive."

"Can you work on the engine too?" Sarah asked.

Jones nodded. "I can work the mechanics."

"Work the mechanics." Sarah giggled. "I love your accent."

"We don't get many Americans down this way." Mrs Mallory spoke from her position at the end of the table. "Oh, there's always a few as guests at parties and what-not, but rarely downstairs with us."

"You're the first one," Sarah said.

"This is good tea." Jones sought to turn the conversation away from her.

Mrs Mallory looked pleased. So pleased, in fact, that she offered further introductions. "Sarah you already met. This here is Whimsy, and beside her is Gladys. We had John, but he took ill, and Mr Forcep will be along shortly. Miss Bloom is off having her appendix out." She sniffed as if she'd little time for such frivolity as appendixes.

"How long are you here for?" Sarah asked Jones.

"Lady Margo is leaving for New York early next week, so I imagine we'll be away sharpish on Monday morning." Jones obliged her with a more involved answer than the shrug she usually gave anyone asking after Lady Margo's movements.

"New York." Sarah sighed. "I'd love to see New York."

Gladys snorted into her tea cup.

"What's that supposed to mean?" Sarah turned on her.

"Only that you want to go everywhere." Gladys came back at her. "It was France when that chef arrived earlier this week. Then Argentina. Ow. Stop pinching me."

"Behave yourselves," Mrs Mallory scolded.

"She pinched me," Gladys whined and rubbed her upper arm. Jones noted no one had any sympathy. Perhaps Gladys always whined?

"Have many of the guests come from far away?" Jones asked idly. She hadn't much interest but wanted to keep the conversation rolling. She'd been in other situations where the staff were so elderly or oppressed that taking tea with them was like pulling her lungs slowly out her ears. That wasn't the case here. This lot seemed a lively bunch, and she wanted her weekend to be entertaining enough to pass quickly. Lady Margo was not alone; Jones itched to go Stateside too.

"They've come in from France, Scotland. Even Argentina." Sarah went all dreamy. "Señor Alexandro Checa arrived on Wednesday with the groom's party." She practically cooed.

"Oh, catch yourself on, Sarah Duggins." Mrs Mallory scolded. "The groom's lot are from Argyll. The Gladbecks of Bute," she explained. Jones shrugged. The name meant nothing to her.

"The Earl of Gladbeck is worth a fortune."

"Sarah," Mrs Mallory warned.

"Well, they are." Sarah huffed. "We all know the marriage is about money. Perry Gladbeck will be a millionaire when he becomes the next Earl." She winked slyly at Jones. So slyly that no one noticed.

"Don't let Mr Forcep catch you uttering things like that," Gladys said.

"What. You think Miss Melisandrine has any real interest in Perry Gladbeck?" Sarah snorted. "He's wet and daft as a brush with it," Sarah continued defiantly. "Now if the gorgeous Señor had some money, I'd wager she'd marry him in a blink. He's the berries."

Gladys looked like she agreed, though she said, "He's naught but a gigolo. Mr Forcep says he is."

This caught Jones's ear. A gigolo at a society party such as this was paramount to dropping a piranha in the baptismal font. Who had invited him?

"Now that definitely is enough, both of you." Mrs Mallory slapped the table, and all came to order.

"I hear one of your staff fell ill this morning?" Jones redirected the conversation in the hope of quelling the thunder in Mrs Mallory's face.

"Ah, yes. Poor John." She perked up at having a sad story to tell. "John Anders is the footman. He took awful bad this morning."

"I bet it's his guts because of *you know who*."

"Hold yer tongue, girl." Mrs Mallory snapped at Sarah.

"It wasn't just his guts. He said he felt queer all over," Whimsy spoke up for the first time since Jones had sat down. Her voice was subdued and filled with genuine concern. She accidently caught Jones's eye and blushed furiously. Jones gave her a level, reassuring smile. If she and Wentworth were having a secret romance, it was none of her business and she could easily forget all she had seen in the stables.

"Ooh. Get you all brave and outspoken," Sarah teased her, and Whimsy flushed further.

"Leave her alone." Mrs Mallory tutted. "What did John say to you, Whimsy? You must have been the last person he talked to before he collapsed."

"No. That was Gladys."

"Just that he was rotten." Gladys was eager to add her tuppence worth. "Said he felt dizzy and sweaty, and he'd prickles all over and said everything tasted funny, and he thought he would spew."

"Told you. Poison!" Sarah said, triumphantly. "I found one of the yard cats dead this morning. Stiff as a stick it was." Then she leaned over the table towards Mrs Mallory and, in an effort not to be overheard—though by whom Jones wasn't sure because everyone at the table was riveted—hissed. "He's been at it again with the rat poison." And she made a motion of a shaky hand spilling something all over the table top.

"Hush now!" No sooner had Mrs Mallory spoken than footsteps could be heard approaching down the hallway, and Forcep entered the kitchen.

"Would you like some tea, Mr Forcep," Mrs Mallory said, all cheer and false smiles.

"Good afternoon, Mrs Mallory. Yes, I would love a cup, thank you." His words were slightly slurred, and he had a glass-eyed look about him.

It was obvious he'd had a drink. Jones could smell the sourness of it from across the table, combined with the God-awful mints he'd been sucking to cover the tell-tale stench. He gave a cool but courteous nod to everyone seated and took his place at the end of the table facing Mrs Mallory. Whimsy stood to serve him his tea and bread and butter. His hand trembled as he raised the cup to his lips, and he slopped tea all over the table top.

"Gladys, go get a clean dish towel." Mrs Mallory tutted at the mess. Gladys scraped her chair back and sulked from the room.

"What's this about John?" Forcep asked bluntly. So, he had overheard something of the conversation from the hallway and was now using it to draw attention away from his own clumsiness. Jones observed him closely and got a hard stare back. She could see the itch on his tongue to say something. He was a nasty drunk, and he did not like her. Not that she cared. If he took one step out of line, she'd ram his head down the nearest gopher hole. Or the nearest indigenous equivalent to it.

"Nothing," Mrs Mallory said. "There's been no word from the hospital; that's all we were saying."

No one so much as breathed the word poison, Jones noted. So the boozy old fool had power over them all. One word and the offender would probably be packing a suitcase and swinging it down the driveway.

If the footman had been indisposed by rat poison, then things might just change around here. She liked the idea of Forcep legging it all the way down to those impressive gateposts and out into the real world. That would sober him up.

"Madame." A little Frenchman arrived like a force of nature, almost taking the door off its hinges. Forcep staggered to his feet as quickly as his lack of sobriety would allow.

"Monsieur Lefurgey. Are you lost, sir?" he asked.

"Madame," Lefurgey continued as if Forcep had not uttered a word and the staff were not on their tea break. "I 'ave a list of my requirements for the savarins I will bake and the puits d'amor *and*, of course, my famous meringue de glas." He waved a piece of paper in the air with authority.

Mrs Mallory reddened. "I don't know what's on that list, Moosewer Lefergie, but I will send one of the girls down to the village store to see what they have for you. Even though we are short staffed and heavily burdened already." She glowered and made no move to take the list. Sarah reached over and plucked it from Lefurgey's fingers and passed it along.

"We'll do everything we can to comply, Monsieur." Forcep was oily as fish with his reply.

With a look of affront, Lefurgey glared at him and answered, "See that you do. I 'ave promised these delights to Miss Melisandrine to 'ave with café after the marriage. She will *not* be disappointed! I will not 'ave it!" And with that he marched off.

"He's mad," Sarah said bluntly. "And he sweats like a pig."

Jones raised her eyebrows. "I take it that's the famous French chef?"

"Famous French nuisance," Mrs Mallory muttered. "Look at this. Three dozen eggs. Who needs three dozen eggs for some fancy pants buns?"

"Now, now, Mrs Mallory. He's a friend of Miss Melisandrine and a guest of Sir Wesley," Forcep said.

"And what's a *mocha*?" She frowned at the paper. "It says mocha cream. He must have spelled it wrong? Why can't he give me a list in English?"

Jones rose and took her cup and plate to the sink. In seconds, Sarah was beside her taking them out of her hands. "Let me do that. You're as good as a guest too. We've got to treat you special."

The rest of the staff rose from the table and had begun to go back to their chores when Whimsy's shrill cry came from the scullery. She came running back into the kitchen.

"It's Gladys," she cried. "Gladys is lying on the floor."

Jones moved fast and was the first to reach her, closely followed by Sarah, who was also spry on her feet.

"She's breathing, but it's laboured." Jones quickly diagnosed. She pulled back one of Gladys's eyelids to verify that she was, in fact, conscious but slow to react. "Can you hear me, Gladys?"

Gladys gave her a slow blink in response.

"Can you talk? Can you tell me what happened? Did you fall?"

There was another blink, but this one was slow and sluggish, and her eyes rolled back in their sockets. Gladys passed out.

"We need an ambulance," Jones said.

"Whimsy's calling for one right now." Mrs Mallory wrung her hands. "Oh, this is terrible. Terrible." Forcep stood off to the side, his face a sickly white. He looked as if he might slide down the wall at any moment.

"Are you going to faint?" Jones asked him and got such a look of scorn that she had to bite her tongue to stop from ordering him out. *Let him fall flat on his face. Prejudiced pig.*

"Oh calamity! What will we do for this evening?" Mrs Mallory fretted aloud. "Gladys was going to stand in for John on the serving staff."

"I can help out if you want." Jones volunteered. "I know what to do at high table."

"Would you?" Mrs Mallory sounded suspicious and relieved all in one. Forcep was about to open his mouth, a veto etched all over his face, when Mrs Mallory went on, "It would be a blessing if you could. It's too late to send down for another village girl, and none of them have the training for the silver service."

"I have," Jones informed her quietly. "I'll need to attend to Lady Margo first, of course, but I'll be free after that."

There was something wrong here. Two members of staff succumbing in one day to a mysterious illness, and Forcep looking like he was either the next victim or a very guilty perpetrator? Jones wanted to get to the bottom of it. She gave the butler a dark stare. He was hiding something, and she was going to smoke him out like the ugly, little termite he was, hiding in the big house and slowly munching his way through everything.

The Well

Margo stood on the west wing of the veranda and watched the ambulance sedately leave the grounds using the rear gates. She was perplexed at the sight.

"Another blasted catastrophe in the kitchen." The explanation came from behind her.

She spun around. "Sir Wesley!"

He approached to kiss her sedately on the cheek. "Welcome, Margo, my dear. Lovely to see you again. I'm afraid our felicitous weekend is beleaguered by one mishap after another."

"An ambulance is slightly more than a mishap."

"There's a bout of something or other running through the staff quarters. As long as it stays there, we may just about be able to press on with this wedding."

Margo glanced over to where the huge marquee billowed on the lawn like an underdone meringue. "At least you have decent weather," she concluded with a wry grin.

Sir Wesley barked out a laugh. "You always see the bright side."

"Rather that, than the curse side. Do you still have that brutish thing in the house?" she asked, remembering that Betsy had mentioned a big deal had just fallen through on him.

"The idol? I have a special home for it now."

"It's sold?" This was good news. Sir Wesley's expeditions to the Middle East threw up interesting objects d'art that he either bequeathed to the nation through various museums or sold on to private collectors. He had often joked with Margo about one particular find that proved harder than most to dislodge.

"Perhaps," he said. "Though the supposed curse seems to have affected the wedding preparations. First we lose the good vicar, then the damned staff!" He laughed again, but it sounded strained. "Nevermind. It might lend to the allure of the piece."

"How enigmatic," Margo joked back. Sir Wesley frequently dressed up his finds with rumours of strange powers of ancient mysticism. He was too much the showman not to let this little flurry in the wedding arrangements go unmentioned. The "allure" he referred to could make an item more saleable, especially for collectors who wanted the mysteriously unquantifiable laced with a soupçon of danger.

Privately, Margo thought the mental state of the bride and groom should take up his attention, rather than making money on his mishaps, but Sir Wesley was first and foremost a man of business.

"If you'll excuse me, I think it's time I mingled with my guests." He smiled and withdrew. Margo watched him leave and wondered just how many of his guests had been brought in specifically to browse the ancient wonders that decorated his house—all with a price tag, of course. From what she could see, not many were friends of Perry or Melisandrine. In fact, most of the guests were of another generation entirely, and were all well leathered in the wallet department. She imagined Sir Wesley had manoeuvred it that way. Why waste a wedding invite when there was business to be done?

"There you are, Margo." Melisandrine moved out of the shadows and joined her by the veranda railings. "I've missed you. It seems like ages since we last talked."

"Yes. Last September, before I left for the Continent."

"Do you still keep that marvellous driver of yours?"

"Jones? Oh yes. I couldn't do without her." Margo smiled. Most of her conversations with female friends opened along these lines. Jones fascinated her people.

"It must be delightful to have such a...an association."

Margo frowned at the clumsy choice of words. Usually Melisandrine was adroit. "Oh, she's more than that. She's a truly valued aide and companion."

"Of course she is." Melisandrine accompanied this with a penetrating stare that made Margo very uneasy. She did not fully understand what Melisandrine's intentions were.

"A lot has happened since we last met," Margo said, changing tack. "I was so surprised...and pleased," she hastened to add, "when I heard about you and Perry becoming engaged."

Truth was, she had nearly fallen off her chair at the breakfast table when she'd read the announcement in *The Times*. Perry was idle and dangerously so—mostly to himself—whereas Melisandrine was equally idle, but at least she dawdled in the arts and was a member of several societies. She kept herself sane with gallery openings and exhibition visits and sponsoring raw, new talent. She spent her summers in Paris at the Louvre and on the left bank of the Seine. She visited the Borghese in Rome and the Uffizi in Florence for her own inspiration.

Then she would return home and daub dreadful sludge upon a poor unsuspecting canvas on some hilltop or other around the estate. Soon, she would be daubing away on the Isles of Bute, Margo suspected.

"Margo." Melisandrine's voice dropped to a whisper. An urgent whisper. "I need to talk to you."

"Yes?" Margo took a step back, surprised by the fervor of the request.

"It is a very private thing I must say." She looked around her furtively. "It is about," she hesitated, "the well."

"Yes?" Margo wracked her brains to recall any previous discourse about a well and could find none, so it must have been some time ago.

Melisandrine stared at her queerly. "I would like to go down to the well with you," she said.

"You have a well? Here, on the grounds?" This was news to Margo. "Is it a new feature?"

"I'm referring to the *Well of Loneliness*." Melisandrine all but hissed.

"Not if we go together." Margo tried to cheer Melisandrine up with a bright smile. "Do we need pennies to make a wish?"

DRESSING FOR DINNER

"Gosh, Jones. Talk about the blushing bride." Margo brushed rouge across the curve of her cheek. "You'd hardly think she wanted to get married. I've never seen anyone so blue. I know Melisandrine is very...well...what's the word?"

"Aureate, ma'am?" Jones was bent over Margo's shingle bob hairdo, fingering the platinum tips to follow her jawline perfectly.

"As in golden and arty?"

"She does gild the lily."

"Um." Margo pondered this. "Well, she writes poetry, I suppose. And one summer she dallied with abstract watercolours—awful, sludgy brown things. She made me take one home." Margo shivered. "I think you are too kind with the artistic allusion, Jones."

"Art is in the eye of the beholder, ma'am." Satisfied with the hair, she lifted two lipsticks from the dressing table. "Raspberry Rogue or Black Cupid?"

Margo looked up from blending her grey eye shadow out from her kohl eyeliner. The smoky colours emphasised the soft green of her eyes. She examined both lipsticks and sighed. "What do you think, Jones? I'm so caught up with Melisandrine's woes I'm not sure if I should be a vamp or put on the Ritz tonight?"

"Why not Ritz it up, ma'am. It's always best to up the ante at these sort of dos." Jones set down the Black Cupid and applied the Raspberry Rogue to Margo's softly pouted lips. She held out a tissue for Margo to tamp her mouth and seal in the colour and shape. Margo inspected Jones work in the mirror.

"A perfect Cupid's bow. You really are excellent with the lipstick. You're the artistic one."

"All it requires is a steady hand, ma'am."

"Well that's much more useful than Melisandrine's awful poetry. Did I tell you she was trying to get me to go down to a well and probably read some to me?" Her eyes, as fresh and crisp as springtime lawns, darkened to toad green at the thought.

"A well?" Jones moved to the armoire and took down the Schiaparelli wild-silk evening dress hanging there. It shimmered in her hands like spun gold.

"Yes. She said something about being lonely, and she wanted to go down to this well." Margo stepped into the dress, and Jones drew it up over her. It shivered along Margo's body. Then Jones fastened the pearl button at the nape of the neck before making sure the dress draped in soft petaled folds that exposed Margo's spine to just above the soft flair of her hips.

"Did she refer to it as *The Well of Loneliness* by any chance, ma'am?"

"I don't know where it is. Loneliness might well be a place in Scotland. They have a Loch Ness, I'm sure of that." Margo fussed over a stray curl at her temple. "But if she means loneliness—as on one's own, then what's the point of me tagging along? It's not as if I even *like* poetry *or* garden ornaments."

"Indeed, ma'am." Jones managed to keep a straight face. When she'd first met Lady Margo Quince-Patrick, she'd assumed the sexual naivety was an artifice. Now she knew better and found it a remarkable quality. It was refreshing that one so seemingly worldly should be so self-effacing about her own sexual attractiveness. Lady Margo had not so much a moral code as a gap in her education. It made her vulnerable and alluring all at the same time. Her good looks and greater fortune meant sharks were constantly circling, and Jones had harpooned many a hot-blooded admirer before they got close enough to bite.

"I'm surprised at Perry's choice for a best man." Margo continued her chatter. "I'd have thought one of his brothers would have fit the bill. But I suppose they're all away at war, shooting the unsuspecting, and Alexandro seems such a good friend."

"Señor Checa seems to be a favourite with everybody," Jones said dryly. This was one fish she'd be keeping an eye on.

"Oh, he's definitely swoon worthy." Margo missed the acerbity in Jones tone. "Tall and dark and handsome—the straight out of a crystal ball type. Impeccable dresser, exotic ancestry." She sighed. "Mysterious with a scintilla of danger."

"Only a scintilla, ma'am?" Jones quirked an eyebrow.

"You don't like the sound of him. Do you, Jones?"

"I have no opinion either way, ma'am. Shoes?"

"The Perugias, I think." Margo pointed at a pair of delicate evening shoes with gold buckles and a modest heel. She sat down by the dresser and lifted first one slender foot and then the other while Jones knelt and slipped on the fashionable footwear.

"I've heard there may be good reason for the bride-to-be to want some 'me time' by the garden ornaments." Jones steered the conversation away from the oily Señor Checa. She opened the traveling jewellery box and presented it for Lady Margo's deliberation.

"Oh? What's the jam in the kitchen?" She lifted out the drop diamond earrings.

"That this is more a money match than the meeting of two hearts. It seems the young lady's father is the driving force behind the affiliation." Jones drew out the matching necklace, placed it around Margo's neck, and closed the clasp so that the heavy, deep cut diamond nestled gently in her décolletage.

"Sir Wesley is a force of nature when it comes to having his own way. I can't see Melisandrine withstanding him. I'm not so sure about his finances, though. He always seems to be rolling in molasses. Those expeditions of his aren't cheap, and the National Museum can't fund them the way they used to, so he must bankroll himself. Though a deal he desperately wanted fell through recently."

"Does he sell all his finds when he returns from an expedition?"

"He's meant to bequeath the real treasures to the museum; that was the original deal. That's why he got the funding in the first place. But there's a lot more competition these days, and I'm not so sure what happens now that the museum backing is drying up."

"So he sells privately?"

"He does. Mostly to universities and centres of anthropological research, not so much to the private collectors. That's frowned upon in the circles he moves in. He's supposed to be an anthropologist not a tomb looter."

"But you suspect he sells to whomever he wants?"

"You bet your bottom dollar and a bucket of gin, I do." Margo stood to inspect her completed ensemble in the full length mirror. "He'd sell to the highest bidder, should it be the devil himself. No doubt about it."

Jones stood slightly behind and to her left. Her hair was loose, and she had removed her uniform in favour of a plain dark shirt and loose, high-waisted trousers. This was her usual dress when she was not driving her employer about, but rather acting as a personal aide. They made a striking pair, she noted candidly. After all, she was a tall, dark, and handsome foreigner—straight out of a crystal ball, and with exotic ancestry. A woman with more than a scintilla of danger—and beside her—a petite, effervescent, society lady.

"I think we've done rather well, Jones." The light in her eyes spoke volumes. She saw it, too. The irony of the crossover from her former description.

Jones bowed her head in acknowledgment and went to open the door. As she passed the bed, she lifted up the matching wrap and handbag that belonged to the Schiaparelli. She draped the wrap artfully across Margo's shoulder and handed over the beaded bag.

"Don't wait up for me, Jones. I'll see you in the morning."

"Have a wonderful evening, ma'am."

"Oh, don't worry. I won't. The whole thing will be murder."

A STABLE AFFAIR

The evening was cool but pleasant. Jones drew deeply on her cigarette Turque, savouring the sweet, sun-cured tobacco. It was her custom to take a stroll and have a smoke after setting Lady Margo up for the evening. Even though she was promised to Mrs Mallory for the evening meal, there was still time to indulge in this ritual. It was her time and hers alone.

A smoke, a think, an evaluation of the day passed. Her grandfather, Shiprock Joe, had always impressed upon her the need for a warrior to take stock of the day and to plan tomorrow while smoking his favourite pipe. She had no pipe; she had Ottoman cigarettes. Still, the aromatic pull of smoke into her lungs allowed her mind to relax and wander.

Not knowing the layout of Clamp House, she retraced her steps to the garage and stable block. It would do no harm to check up on the Bentley, and she was pleased to see the gleam of its fenders in the dying daylight. It was a truly beautiful vehicle.

From the corner of her eye, she saw a shadow flit by in the stall that had housed the skittish horse. The animal was long gone, so the strange play of light and shade caught her attention.

Wary now, she stubbed her cigarette out against the wall. Stealthily, she inched through the door of the neighbouring stall. She could hear boots shuffling against straw underfoot. The intruder was behaving just as stealthily as her but was not quite as good at it. Someone was in there, and it was not Wentworth for Jones had already seen her in the lower paddock. There came a rustling noise which Jones struggled to identify before her attention was seized by another set of footsteps approaching.

"Alexandro?" The whisper was loud. Too loud. "I thought I saw you come down here."

"Perry?" Followed by an angry, "Shush."

It didn't subdue the new arrival. "God, it stinks. Did you know I was allergic to horses? Atchoo!"

"Will you shut up? That girl will be by here in a minute." Alexandro sounded frustrated.

"The stable girl? She'll be piddling about down by the paddocks for ages yet. Why are you loitering in here? What on earth are you up to? Are you being a naughty boy?" Perry Gladbeck spoke in an unpleasant slurred whine.

"Perry, for the last time, will you please lower your voice."

"Stop complaining and kiss me, you rugged beast."

This caught Jones by surprise. There came a moment of hard, heated breathing, which she took to be Alexandro complying with the request. This was not the sort of gigolo Jones had expected. Alexandro was very multi-faceted.

"What was that noise?" Alexandro broke the kiss to ask anxiously.

"I heard nothing."

"Shush. The stable girl is returning. Go now. Go on, go!" Alexandro ordered Perry out of the stall.

There was silence for a short while after Perry's departure, and then the rustling resumed, followed by a frustrated sigh. Jones frowned. What was Alexandro doing in there? Eventually, he gave up and slithered out of the stall at the crunch of footsteps along the gravel path.

Jones reached in her pocket for her cigarette pack and tapped out a new one. She casually strolled out into the main standing and struck a match, checking out the lay of the land. Sarah was taking clothes in from the washing line. Alexandro marched stiffly towards the gardens and the deer park beyond, and Perry Gladbeck was nowhere to be seen.

"Evening," she called softly when Wentworth trudged up the paddock path. She looked surprised to see her there. Jones offered her a cigarette which was gratefully accepted but not immediately lit.

"Cheers." Wentworth pushed it behind her ear. "Watch how you put it out, won't you." She indicated the burning tip of Jones's own cigarette.

"Of course." Jones nodded. "I'll be very careful."

Wentworth moved off, and Jones took the opportunity to duck into the stall Alexandro had vacated. Nothing seemed amiss from her earlier visit. The dead rat had been removed. This time, she paid attention to the canvas bags hanging on the wall. When she scrunched them in her hands, they made the same rustling noise that had confounded her before. So, Alexandro had been examining the bags? These bags were empty. What had he been looking for?

POLITE DINNER CONVERSATION

Margo loitered on the way to the dining room. The guests had to pass through the hallway, which had been cleverly and stylishly designed to display many of Sir Wesley's objects d'art. She suspected it was, in effect, a tasteful shopping experience for Sir Wesley's possible clients searching the black-market for antiquities. She understood it to be a very lucrative business.

"That one's mine." Betsy came up behind her and indicated a bronze, about the size of a fist, that displayed a crude carving of a monkey's head. "He gave it to me for my sixteenth birthday. He says he'll never sell it, but I'm not allowed to remove it from the display either."

"Where's the fun in that?" Margo asked.

Betsy shrugged. "Father never thinks of fun. He gave a statue of a rhinoceros to Melisandrine once, but she said she'd rather have horsefeathers than his Judas pieces of silver." She giggled.

They moved towards the dining room and took their places at the table. Margo was pleased to be seated with Alexandro on one side; however, Reverend Tupper on her right hand did not enthuse her.

Melisandrine sat opposite, already too familiar with the wine, which Margo knew depressed her. Beside her, Perry had the same problem with his wine glass, in that it emptied too soon. He showed scant interest in his bride-to-be and seemed to be enjoying the conversation all around him.

Engaged in idle chatter with Alexandro, who proved to be charming, Margo was surprised when the soup arrived and was served from her right. The wrist emerging from a crisp white shirt cuff and black jacket was decorated by a thin silver and turquoise bracelet. The skin was dark and exotic, and the scent of the server was one she knew well. A spicy, morish scent, deep and dark and mysterious like its wearer.

"Jones!" She looked up in astonishment. "What on earth?"

"There was a mishap downstairs with the staffing for tonight's dinner, and I thought it best to step in and help," Jones said quietly.

Margo picked up on the tone. A mishap to Jones was a disaster to many others. Something was up, and she itched to know what. That would come later. For all her solemnity, Jones was a vibrant raconteur. She nodded slightly, and Jones duly withdrew.

Dinner was a delicious but dragged out affair. The only spot of interest came when Jones appeared to serve the fish, then the main course of veal, and finally dessert. Monsieur Lefurgey did not seem enamoured with any of it and excused himself from the dining table several times only to return with a face like blue cheese. Bad blue cheese.

"I just adore all the items I find dotted around your home, Sir Wesley," Mrs Ford-Hughes said. She was a gushing guest. Everything was wonderful; everything was charming, interesting, or delightful.

"Idols of false worship." The Reverend Tupper wiped his mouth with his napkin. "There is no place for them in a civilised society."

"Many people are interested in the past, Reverend." Sir Wesley sounded defensive. "In fact, private collecting has become a very fashionable pastime."

"Not in a Christian household," Tupper replied.

"But surely, as these are pagan gods, and decrepit at that, it can't be that objectionable?" Margo asked. His eyes turned flint hard, and she wondered what line she had crossed.

"There is no true home for artefacts such as these in this country," he said.

"Not even in museums or universities?" Margo was surprised.

"They do not belong in England. England is a Christian land."

"But surely for the sake of scholarship? When I was at St. Hilda's, Oxford, we studied—"

"'The Lord said, I shall forbid a woman to teach or to exercise authority over a man; rather, she is to remain quiet.' Timothy one, verse three." His snapped response seemed to be his definitive answer, and Margo was disinclined to engage him further. He was an odd little man, and she had no time for people who hid their hate behind the bible.

"People are passionate about religious idols one way or another," Alexandro murmured. "If they could only put as much effort into civility."

"I totally agree. No middle ground to be found." Margo shrugged and rewarded his charm with a smile. Around them, the conversation flowed.

"Well, as you know, I am on the board at the Museum of Natural History, and even I would not like some of these things under my roof." Mrs Ford-Hughes laughed.

"Aren't some of them cursed?" A gentleman dressed in the uniform of the Coldstream Guards asked.

"Oh, yes. And they are the most collectable." Sir Wesley warmed to the subject. "In the main hall, you will see things extracted from Northern Africa, especially Egypt. The Nile is a very fertile hunting ground."

"I've got my eye on one of those mummies," another gentlemen Margo recognised as the Chancellor of the Exchequer called across.

"Excellent choice," Sir Wesley replied. "I keep my Babylonian collection in the library. I'll show you all after dinner."

"It's all loot. Pillaged from the womb of mother earth," Melisandrine exclaimed.

"My daughter does not approve of my business interests." Sir Wesley laughed. He seemed to like the dash of drama Melisandrine supplied. It did whet the appetite of the curious, Margo noted.

"You have destroyed my seclusion with that objectionable..." Melisandrine, for once, was lost for words, then said, "Sheela na gig. I can't write anymore with that thing looking at me."

Perry snorted into his glass. He was absolutely blotto. In contrast, the guests on either side of her had barely touched their glasses. Like them, she was pacing herself. She was tired after her day's travel and knew it was to be a long night before she'd make it to bed.

"Sheela na gig?" she asked, forcing herself to focus on the conversation. "That's not from Africa or even Arabia."

"Melisandrine is upset that I have given the grotto over to my latest find. A fantastic piece," Sir Wesley said. "None other than a Phoenician god."

"Which one?" someone asked.

"And is this one cursed? Miss Melisandrine seems to think so?" This drew some laughter, and Melisandrine sulked.

"I tell you what. Why don't we go and see for ourselves?"

It was the last thing Margo wanted, but the suggestion was met with a chorus of approvals. Everyone seemed up for a nighttime adventure.

THE CURSE STRIKES

The evening air was balmy, a welcome change from the opulent stuffiness of the dining room. Even with the French windows open, the room was too hot. Margo rejoiced at the breeze caressing her skin. Her head felt light from what little wine she had imbibed. Above her, the moon was full and filled her with a sense of excitement despite her tiredness.

Alexandro appeared at her elbow and casually linked arms with her, as if they were lifelong companions. "Please, let me escort you, Lady Margo," he said. "Are you interested in such things? Do you collect?"

Margo, at first surprised at the gesture, melted against the bulge of his bicep. "Of course not. I'm interested in the history behind them. In their anthropological value. But in my opinion, they are not commodities to be bought and sold on the open market. These are indicators to our joint history as mankind and need another type of reverence."

His handsome smile widened, and they walked across the lawn, skirting the white canvas walls of the marquee and on towards the copse of trees that marked the boundary of the formal gardens and the start of the deer park.

"Alexandro?" Perry called over. "Come and join us." He was walking with Melisandrine, but they were several paces apart.

"I'm escorting Lady Margo across the grass," he answered. His impatience, though well-hidden, was still discernible to Margo's ear. Or perhaps it was the stiffening of his shoulder at the request.

"Oh dear, the ground is so uneven." Mrs Ford-Hughes grabbed at Margo's other arm, and she found herself in an ungainly stretch between the good widow and her suave admirer. The lawn was not so much uneven as Mrs Ford-Hughes had imbibed a little too much and was unsteady on her feet. Reluctantly, Margo slid her hand free from the warm nook of Alexandro's arm and gave full attention to keeping Mrs Ford-Hughes upright. A task that put considerable strain on her own balance.

"Alexandro! Come here. See what I've got for you," Perry called over. His tone mewling and petty. Freed from his obligation of escorting Margo, Alexandro peeled away.

From the corner of her eye, Margo could see the flash of a silver hip flask. Alexandro did not look impressed.

"I didn't realise it was such a distance," Mrs Ford-Hughes complained. "Really. Sir Wesley should have warned us. Do you buy this stuff, dear?" Margo was surprised at being asked more or less the same question twice.

"No. I've no interest in it that way," she said.

"Me neither. It must be a 'man thing.'"

Margo wondered if Sir Wesley had been pressuring the widow to buy from him.

Up ahead, he led them forward with a quick resume of what they were about to behold. "Baal was a warrior god and also the thunder and rain god of the Phoenicians. He was a supreme deity. He had many names: Baal-gad, Baal-hamon, Baal-tamur—"

"Ba'al-ze'bub," Reverend Tupper interrupted.

"Yes. Let's not forget how low the Old Testament has cast him." Sir Wesley had a bitter twist to his mouth.

"The Phoenicians were a sophisticated civilisation with a marvellous maritime tradition and trade routes thought to go as far as Ireland."

"But the licentiousness of their Baal worship brought them into disrepute with the Israelites," Tupper added.

"The Israelites turned to Baal worship many times. In fact, there was outright competition between the two religions," Sir Wesley answered. "Imagine the world today if Baal had emerged as the victor?"

Tupper shuddered.

"We'd all be dancing around naked in church." Perry giggled. "Sunday mornings would be a lot more interesting." He looked around for approval but got none.

"Baal worship was more than nude frivolities. It was particularly bloodthirsty," Alexandro said. "They had child sacrifice and danced naked with snakes." He quirked an eyebrow at Perry. "Want to go to church now?"

"So Baal lost the religious war and became Beelzebub, the fallen angel?" Margo asked. She was intrigued.

Sir Wesley smiled at her, perhaps relieved to have a sensible listener. "He has many fallen names too. The Lord of the Flies, Prince of Demons, even Lucifer himself."

"Unthinkable." Mrs Ford-Hughes broke away from Margo and made a new allegiance with the Reverend as if hanging onto Margo somehow contaminated her.

"And the other fallen angels, are they the other Phoenician gods? Do all the displaced deities become demons in the Christian faith?" Margo asked, pleased to be free of her excess burden and gladly wishing Mrs Ford-Hughes onto the vicar.

"That is my personal hypothesis, Lady Margo. Much as the winners of war rewrite history, so do the new religions vilify the old while standing on their shoulders."

"Atrocious," Tupper muttered.

They approached the opening to the grotto, marked by a stone archway and flagged by yew trees.

"I had this stonework brought over from the old chapel." Sir Wesley patted the pocked limestone approvingly. "Lovely workmanship. Look at the fluting."

Margo had the impression he did this deliberately to annoy Tupper even more, and it worked judging by the furious tutting of the reverend.

The moonlight shone eerily over the weathered stone, casting long shadows of dark upon dark. The breeze died away, leaving the air fetid and still. The grove had a heavy, noxious odour, as if something had died in the undergrowth. The fun had evaporated away, and they found themselves in the dark before a gateway to some heathen thing.

"Well, get on with it, man." The officer from the Coldstream Guards was brusque.

"Yes. What's inside?" Timothy Arbuthnot followed his lead.

"Is Baal in there, then?" someone from the back of the crowd asked.

In answer to their questions, Sir Wesley became every bit the showman. Margo speculated he had much practice at this while raising funds for his adventures before various boards and committees. With his arm raised to show the way, he bowed genteelly and allowed his guests to crowd into the grove.

Margo hung back, not wishing to be caught up in the squeeze, when a dark presence at her elbow made her jump.

"Jones!" Her hand fluttered to her breast. "You startled me."

"Sorry, ma'am. There was no other way to be circumspect. I thought you should know that of the two service staff struck low today, one has died in hospital. The footman, John Anders."

"Oh dear. Any idea what happened to the poor boy?"

"They will conduct an investigation in the morning. Apparently he died from respiratory failure." Jones indicated the entryway to the grove. "The way seems clear now."

Perry staggered and clutched Alexandro to prevent from falling over. They both stumbled and fell to the ground. Perry rolled about shrieking with laughter while Alexandro struggled to his feet and brushed himself down with sharp, flustered movements.

"Oh Perry, do grow up," Melisandrine said and walked on. Alexandro followed her without a backward glance.

Perry finally righted himself and burst into a fit of giggles. "Come on, Quincy," he called, offering her his hand. "We'll miss the show!" He looked all around at his feet and then pounced on something. "Ah. There it is." And lifted the hipflask in a mock salute.

"I'd rather you escort me." She offered her arm to Jones. "Otherwise it could all get very tedious."

"Ma'am." Jones took her elbow and led her into the grotto.

It was a circular affair, deliberately engineered with mature yew and cypress all around, giving a sense of gloom and malevolence. Probably built in the early Victorian era to house some folly or other, but whatever that had been was now been replaced by a stone alter. Torches flared on either side, setting the stage for what, to Margo, was becoming distasteful theatrics.

On top of the alter, illuminated by the torches, stood a stone idol about four foot tall. The carved detail was softened by age and the flickering light, but the grotesqueness of the features still managed to impress upon the mind of the beholder. The thing oozed malice, mouth agape, eyes wild and fierce. A snapping, snarling thing. In one hand, it held a trident, and in the other what looked to be an orb of flame.

"'And the children of Israel turned from the commandments of the Lord God and made molten images of calves and placed them in a grove and worshipped Baal.' Kings two, verses eleven to thirteen," Tupper declared loudly, and Mrs Ford-Hughes quickly disentangled from him in order to cross herself several times.

"But this idol is female?" Margo pointed out what, to her, was blatantly obvious.

"And bloody ugly," Perry said.

"Was Baal represented as both sexes?" Margo asked, ignoring the interruption.

"No. Baal's consort was Astarte," Sir Wesley said.

"So, this is Astarte?"

"No, Lady Margo. Nor is it Baal. Baal, you will find in the British Museum of Natural History. This..." He turned with obvious pleasure towards the idol. "This is Jezebaal, daughter of Baal."

"Well, she's still bloody ugly," Perry stated. "You're telling me, you went all the way to Arabia to dig up this brutish thing? What's it worth?"

"You said it was cursed?" Alexandro asked.

Everyone seemed intent on ignoring Perry and his effrontery. He sulked and took a swig from his flask.

"Oh yes. Jezebaal is the goddess of vengeance and ill-will. It is said, she could strike a man down with a thought."

"She could strike a man down with just a look from that crook eye of hers, I'll wager. And what's more—" Perry broke off midsentence. His eyes rolled back in his skull, and he clutched at his chest before spilling backwards onto the ground at Alexandro's feet.

"For God's sake Perry, get up," Alexandro said, anger and exasperation clouding his voice. "You're embarrassing yourself. You always go that one step too far."

Perry lay unmoving.

"Tell him to damn well get up," the Coldstream officer said. "This is tosh. I'm going." And he turned for the house with several other guests at his heels.

"Perry, this is not funny. No one is amused." Melisandrine joined Alexandro in condemnation, though Betsy stood giggling near the back, proving Perry had entertained at least one individual.

Jones let go of Margo and knelt by the recumbent man and lifted his wrist to feel for a pulse. She tried again, this time at the carotid pulse in his neck.

Alexandro dropped to one knee beside her. "What's the matter?" he asked in concern.

"He's dead," Jones replied.

Mrs Ford-Hughes let out a gasp of horror, quickly echoed by the remaining guests.

"No! It can't be." Melisandrine grabbed at her father's arm for support. He looked on, his face white and grim.

"'And I will execute great vengeance upon them furiously, and they shall know that I am the Lord.' Ezekiel verse twenty-one," the Reverend Tupper brayed.

"That is hardly helpful." Lady Margo berated him.

Those bystanders that were left began backing away.

"We'll need to call the police." Jones met Lady Margo's gaze and held it.

"Betsy?" Margo moved to the young girl who stood frozen, transfixed by Perry's prone body. "Betsy, can you run to the house and have Forcep, or somebody sensible, call for the police, please?"

The request rattled Betsy out of her horrified stupor. "Cripes, yes!" She turned and fled without another word.

"Reverend Tupper," Margo turned her attention on him. "We'll need everyone to return to the house. Could you have cook organise refreshments? I'm sure some people are in shock and will need tea."

"Yes, yes, of course I shall." He began to corral the remaining guests across the lawn.

Margo crouched down beside Jones. "Can you see anything unusual," she murmured discretely for Jones's ear only. Her answer was a furtive shake of the head.

"I can't believe it," Alexandro kept repeating. He had shaken off the Reverend's hand and refused to move.

Melisandrine gently pulled him away to a respectful distance. Her face was wet with tears and frozen in shock.

"It has to be a dream," he told her.

There came a huffing and puffing across the lawn, and two of the groundsmen appeared, followed at a distance by Forcep.

"The police?" Sir Wesley barked at him as soon as he appeared.

"On their way, sir." Forcep and his party stood, looking down at the body. "I brought some men to stand guard and allow the rest of the party to return to the drawing room. Mrs Mallory is brewing tea."

"Good idea," Sir Wesley told him.

"Some of the guests have already gathered, and there is great hysteria among the ladies. People are asking if they are cursed," Forcep said.

"Alexandro, kindly escort Lady Margo and my daughter back to the house. Send the police over as soon as they arrive, you hear me?" Sir Wesley snapped. "I need to stay here. I have no inclination to go back and soothe ruffled feathers."

"Of course, Sir Wesley." White-faced, Alexandro gathered his charges.

"I'll remain here and keep an eye on things, ma'am," Jones murmured as Margo prepared to go. It would have been too morbid for Margo herself to demand to stay.

As gracefully as she could, Margo took one arm of the shivering Melisandrine, while Alexandro supported her on the other side. Between them, they headed back to the house with the erstwhile bride.

Not as it Seems

Sir Wesley lit a cheroot and exhaled a shaky plume of smoke. Jones noted the tremor of his hands. The groundsmen faded back into the shadows, shuffling and ill at ease, and she didn't blame them one bit. The torchlight flickered over the grimacing visage of the idol, making it even more obscene.

"It's all a bloody nonsense," Forcep muttered to one of the men. "Ugly goblin of a thing can't kill nobody. *And* it's meant to be worth a mint."

"Ought to be locked up somewhere safe if it's worth something. Lying about out here in the wind and rain won't do it no good," the man answered.

Forcep snorted. "Except, he's been trying to get a buyer for years. What's the point of going to Africa or Arabia or wherever and not bringing back gold or diamonds, eh? Now that makes bloody sense." The other men nodded in agreement. "I'd rather hit it with a hammer than have it in the garden," Forcep said.

"Careful now, it's supposed to be cursed. Look at 'im there, all flaked out on the grass. Bet he had something to say and look where it got 'im," one of the men said.

"He always had something to say, and it was always bloody ridiculous." Forcep sniffed derisively.

"Forcep." Sir Wesley's call from the other side of the grove broke up the muttered conversation.

"Sir?" Forcep approached him, all deference.

"Go back to the house and see what the devil is keeping the police. Call again if you have to."

Forcep bowed and removed himself but had barely taken two steps when voices could be heard approaching from the manor house. "I think they are here now, milord," he said. "And Dr Lowry's with them."

"Thank God for that."

Doctor Lowry appeared, accompanied by a police officer and two others to act as stretcher bearers.

"I can't seem to avoid Clamp Park today." He barked out a greeting and vigorously shook Sir Wesley's hand. "Officer Sims came along with me." He indicated a police officer with a tad more brass on his sleeve than the other two. The officer saluted Sir Wesley and was immediately ignored.

"This is awful, James. The groom dying on the eve of his wedding. And Melisandrine is in a terrible way. You'll need to look in on her." Sir Wesley spoke openly to the doctor, and Jones noted how they held each other in high regard and behaved as friends.

Dr Lowry knelt to examine the body. A quick check to ensure the man was actually dead, and he indicated for the stretcher bearers to cart him off.

The clearing was emptying as people followed the stretcher out. Jones flattened herself back into the cypress and quietly listened to Sir Wesley and the doctor talk.

"Lord Gladbeck's son." Dr Lowry watched the stretcher depart, dusting down his hands on a handkerchief. "It's a rum thing. This curse malarkey will ruin you yet, Wesley."

Sir Wesley gritted his teeth and offered the doctor a cheroot, which he took.

"I'll pop in on Melisandrine on my way out," Dr Lowry continued after his first inhalation. "I've a busy morning ahead of me as it is, dissecting your staff, never mind a guest. What are you feeding them, for God's sake?"

"Jesus, James, watch what you say! That boy was to be my son-in-law," Sir Wesley said, obviously put out.

Dr Lowry exchanged a dark look with him. "Well, he's the third person to die in Clamp Park this weekend. The kitchen maid, Gladys Smith? She didn't make it."

Sir Wesley puffed in annoyance. "First John and now this. Any idea what the hell happened to them?"

"Poison of some sort, I'll wager. But it will take time to find out if it's food poisoning, which is most likely, or something else."

"And Perry?"

"Heart attack candidate if ever there was one. I don't think that boy's been sober since he was thirteen. Gladbeck had no time for him, and it bloody well shows. A ruin of a youngster, and not one word of sense out of him in all the years I've known him." The doctor was obviously not a man to mince his words, and Jones appreciated his candidness. It was a talent underrepresented in the English upper classes as far as she was concerned.

"Good God, man. He fell over like a piece of lumber."

"Well, he always did have wood for brains. You don't think there's anything in this curse, do you?"

Sir Wesley snorted out a laugh. "Just five thousand pounds if I can get some fool to buy it."

A discreet cough from the doorway alerted both men that Officer Sims was still hovering and anxious to begin his own enquiries.

"Damned but I need a drink now." Sir Wesley peeled away. "Let's adjourn to my study," he told Sims. "James, join us after you've seen to Melisandrine if you feel in need of a nightcap."

Dr Lowry shook his head. "Too much on tomorrow. I should have been attending a wedding," he said grimly, "but now I'll be working all day in the morgue."

MY LADY'S NIGHTCAP

Jones brought Margo a brandy to her room.

"I was just about to ring down for one, but I know the whole house is in uproar." She gratefully took a sip. "Lord, Jones, what a palaver. Have you any ideas?"

"Hard to say, ma'am." Jones unzipped the Schiaparelli. The silk fabric fell away in a gossamer of cobwebs. "It's interesting that the doctor talks about poisoning with regards to the servants, yet is so blasé about a heart condition for young Gladbeck."

"Run a bath for me, would you. I'm so tense."

The bathroom was en suite, and Jones soon had it filling up with steam as piping hot water gushed into the enamel bathtub. She added bath salts, and the fragrance of white grapefruit and lotus blossom filled the air.

Margo took her hand and stepped delicately into the tub. With a soft moan, she slid down and let the hot water envelope her.

Jones set the snifter of brandy to hand and retired to the bedroom.

"Did you notice that Monsieur Lefurgey was absent from the grotto?" Margo called from the tub. "In fact, he was in and out all through dinner. You'd have thought his chair was on fire."

"I did notice, ma'am. Apparently he has made several sweeps of the kitchens before he begins to bake tomorrow,"

Jones called back from where she was setting out Margos nightclothes. "Mrs Mallory, the cook, is full of anxiety."

"There will be little need for his delicacies now," Margo said. "Poor Perry."

"A small victory for Mrs Mallory. The kitchen staff resented Lefurgey's intrusion. At the same time, they suspect the butler has been careless with rat poison," Jones said.

"Good grief. What do you think?"

"Lefurgey had plenty of opportunity, and Forcep is a drunk. At the moment, it's a coin toss."

"As for Melisandrine." Margo's voice continued to float in from the bathroom accompanied by the odd splash. "She was in a dreadful state. Alexandro and I could barely keep her upright."

"How did the young gentleman take it?" She stood by the tub with a huge bath towel at the ready.

Margo arose Venus-like from the water, and Jones enfolded her in the soft towel. "He seemed at a complete loss. Almost as vacant as Melisandrine. He kept repeating that he couldn't believe it."

Now dry, Margo slipped on the silk kimono Jones held open for her. "In fact, at one point, I thought that he would fall over, and I'd have both of them to drag across the lawn."

"Genuine or overacting?" Jones pulled back the bed clothes.

Margo thought about this. "Genuine, I think. After all, he was the best man. They had to be good friends."

"Maybe even more than that," Jones said. She took back the kimono and left Margo to slip on her nightdress while she attended to straightening the bathroom.

"Whatever do—" Margo began. Then, "You don't mean—"

Jones came back to the room. "I saw them in the stables. They were very good friends indeed."

"No wonder it hit Alexandro hard." Margo slumped on the edge of the bed, apparently confounded by this revelation. "It explains why he was best man over one of Perry's brothers. Except, why was Perry getting married at all? And did Melisandrine know?"

An Extra Sausage

Jones left Lady Margo to contemplate the vagaries of the heart and returned to the kitchen. By now, the hour was late, and only a single lamp shone. It haloed Mrs Mallory and Forcep sitting at the table with a bottle of cooking sherry between them. They both looked up as she entered.

"Oh. It's you," Mrs Mallory sounded disappointed.

"Who were you expecting?" Jones asked.

"I thought Sir Wesley might come and tell us what to do with all this food. It's not like there's going to be a wedding now, and we've a ton of stuff that will go to waste." She blew her nose wetly into a hanky. Jones could see she had been crying for some time.

Forcep took a healthy gulp of his sherry and glowered at the table, disinterested in the conversation and, from the look on his face, lost in his own glum thoughts.

"Sir Wesley's in his study with the police," she told Mrs Mallory. "He may come along yet." But she doubted surplus food was on his lordship's mind at the moment. "I think I'll go along to bed."

Neither of them spoke as she closed the door on them and headed for the servant's stairway up to the attics.

She was tired. It had been a long drive down and a busy, if macabre, day, and Jones was looking forward to sleeping in what she hoped was a comfortable bed.

A door clicked open as she passed, and Sarah peeped out.

"I thought it was you," she said. She flitted a nervous glance up and down the corridor. All was still. "You're up late. What do you do for that lady of yours at this hour?" she asked cheekily.

Jones stepped forward out of the shadows. At six foot, she towered over Sarah, who gasped and backed slowly into her room. Jones followed and closed the door quietly behind her.

The next morning, relaxed and refreshed after a cold shower, Jones was pleased to receive an extra sausage on her breakfast plate, delivered with a knowing wink from Sarah.

The mood downstairs was otherwise sombre.

"What are we going to do with all this food!" Mrs Mallory's lament had not changed, so Jones assumed Sir Wesley hadn't visited the kitchen last night. Whimsy walked about, red-eyed, with a permanent wet sniff and damp hanky. And the village help had been postponed indefinitely, though several boxes containing Monsieur Lefurgey's ingredients had been delivered that morning.

"And has he even come down to see them? Has he, by heck!" Mrs Mallory glared at the boxes cluttering up her workspace.

As Lady Margo would not call for her for at least another hour, Jones excused herself after a hearty breakfast and left to take a cigarette in the fresh morning air.

It was her ladyship's habit to sleep late, and for Jones, this was a favoured part of the day when she had time to see to her own needs and any other minor duties.

The mist rolling in from the deer park began to dissipate under the growing heat of the day. The foggy outline of trees and fencing began to emerge and take shape, as if the estate was once again being put to order after the upheaval of yesterday. The events at the grotto had taken on the proportions of a bad dream.

Jones lit her cigarette and drew in a lungful of smoke. She idly strolled towards the kitchen garden with its trim box hedges and orderly vegetable beds. Beyond this was the ladies' garden full of blousy blooms and heady fragrances as designed by Miss Melisandrine. It was a very restful place with various seating areas and arbours, and Jones was circumnavigating a very pretty pergola when the toe of her boot hit something hard. She looked down to see another boot. This one attached to a foot extruding from a particularly large hibiscus. Forcep lay flat out beside the shrub. He was spread-eagled, wide-eyed, and dead.

IN THE LADY GARDEN

"I can't believe we're in lockdown." Margo was aghast at the news. "They're practically imprisoning us."

"I'm afraid Officer Sims had put his foot down. At least until his superior arrives from London. It seems multiple murders are too much for the local constabulary, and they need a firm hand to help solve the case. Or in this case, cases." Jones pushed the final pin in Margo's bobbed hair.

"And you found him?"

"Yes. He was in the ladies' garden, probably having his first snifter of the day."

"Did you see a bottle, or whatever it was he was drinking?"

Jones frowned. "No. And there wasn't much time to check. One of the groundsmen came along, and I had to get things moving. If I was found rifling the fellows pockets, I'd have been in more than a spot of bother."

Margo reflected on the truth of this. She had seen it time and time again. Jones was so obviously a foreigner and had to fly far above the suspicion that would always be levelled at her.

"Who's there now? Could we slip back and investigate for ourselves? I think I would cry if we were locked up here all week and missed out on America," Margo said. The very thought of it made her feel panicked.

"I agree entirely, ma'am. Though I can't see them stopping you from making your sailing. But there is a difference between being invited for the weekend and being unable to leave."

"To the lady garden! I have to see this for myself, Jones." Margo sprung to her feet.

Sir Wesley and Dr Lowry stood to the side as two uniformed policemen supervised by Officer Sims hoisted Forcep's remains onto a stretcher and took him off.

"You really know how to ruin a man's weekend of golf, Clamp," Dr Lowry barked out, plainly unaware of Margo approaching from behind. She left Jones free to wander about and have a snoop.

"First a damned wedding, then the groom dies and the wedding is off, then *three* dead servants. *Three*. It's damned carelessness, man," the doctor declared. "Either that or you truly are cursed and need to stop playing these bloody stupid games."

Sir Wesley's cheeks bloomed an ugly red, and he snapped. "For God's sake, watch what you say. This isn't a game. People are dead! Can you even begin to tell me what the hell killed my servants?"

"Definitely a poison of some sort, but until I get the results from the toxicology department of Kings Hospital, you're as much in the dark as I am." He turned and saw Margo. "Ah, Lady Margo. Should you be out here?" He swapped a look with Sir Wesley.

"I've come to find out if it's true that we're stuck at Clamp House until this ghastly affair is over." Margo choose a tone that took no prisoners. She was annoyed at the lockdown.

"Officer Sims seems to think it's for the best," Sir Wesley said. The officer, on hearing his name, came over. He was young and rank with inexperience. Margo sensed his promotion was recent, and he was eager to prove himself.

"Milady," he said cordially enough. "We do need to keep everyone on the premises until the officers from Scotland Yard arrive."

"Everyone?" Margo raised her eyebrows. "Even members of the Cabinet?" She referred to the chancellor who had bought the ugly Egyptian mummy.

Sims reddened. "The chancellor left last night, ma'am. He had urgent government business to attend to."

"And I saw that young major from the Coldstream Guards leave this morning, directly after breakfast. Was that with your blessing too?" she asked.

"He had to get back on duty." Sims was having a hard time with these questions.

"I see," Margo said, making it obvious she didn't. "And what about those of us with tickets for the Queen Mary? I'm booked for America; does that count for any special favours?"

Sims's gaze slid past her and fixed on Jones, who was ambling about the garden with her hands casually crossed behind her back. The quick assessment Sims made shone through; here was a suspect if ever there was one.

"And who are you?" he asked in a suddenly imperious voice. Sir Wesley rolled his eyes, and Dr Lowry smirked and moved away. His part in the proceedings was done.

"I can vouch for my own staff, officer," Margo said primly.

Sims made the mistake of ignoring her. "I'm sorry, but I was talking to this fellow here, ma'am." He turned back to Jones and repeated, "Who are you?"

"Jones. Lady Margo's chauffeur and personal aide," Jones replied monotone.

"And where were you last night?" Sims tried to sound professional, but his voice was too light, too young for the hard touch he was trying to convey.

"Putting Lady Margo to bed."

This halted Sims in his tracks. He blinked owlishly at Lady Margo and back to Jones. Dr Lowry sniggered.

"Don't be alarmed, Officer," Margo said. A small smile played around her mouth. "Jones is acting exactly as I'd expect any female member of my staff to."

"Oh. I see. Well...well, I'll want to have him—her—present for future questioning."

"Why? I've already vouched for her?"

"I'm sure there'll be more questions when my colleagues from the Yard arrive." He was trying to save face and offering up a possible suspect was one way of doing that. A lazy, careless way, and Margo fumed at it. She wrapped her cardigan tighter around her, feigning a chill.

"Well, with your powers of observation, I'm sure I'm completely safe." With that she strode away. Jones followed close at her heels.

Once they were out of earshot, she let loose. "Colleagues from the Yard! What a cheeky young whelp. I've a good mind to call his superiors and have him hauled over the coals."

"Would that help us leave any sooner, ma'am?"

"Probably not."

"Isn't that the objective?"

Margo sighed. "You're right as usual, Jones. We're stuck here with baby-faced Officer Plod in charge, and we can only hope his replacement has some common sense and doesn't want to stick everything on you." Then she perked up as a delicious idea raced through her mind. She snapped her fingers. "I have it! We'll investigate for ourselves. Cut straight to the chase and get out of here."

"Well done, ma'am. A brilliant idea." Jones reached inside her jacket. "Especially as I found this in the garden not far from where Forcep fell." The silver of a hipflask winked from under her coat.

BETSY COMES THROUGH

"But that's so unfair." Betsy's voice rang strong and true with unrequited justice. "Jones would never do anything wrong." She fixed Jones with a forlorn, wide-eyed stare filled with unexpressed—and probably misunderstood—emotion, and Jones shuffled slightly on the Feraghan Sarouk carpet at the intensity of the look.

"I'm afraid that's the way of the world, Betsy. Jones does not look like us, she is 'other' so therefore must be treated with deplorable suspicion by those less intelligent than ourselves, like Officer Sims," Margo told her. "There's more sensitivity in a river pebble than in that man's brain."

"I'm going to complain—" But before Betsy could threaten hot coals and superiors, Whimsy came into the room and curtsied.

"There a call for Sir Wesley, miss," she said. "It's the Reverend Michaels, but I can't find His Lordship."

"I'll take it in here, Whimsy."

Margo gave Jones a small, conspiratorial nod, and Jones left the room. Whimsy returned, holding the candlestick phone on its extendable cord at arm's length as if it might bite.

"Reverend Michaels?" Betsy said into the receiver, the earpiece glued to her temple. "It's Betsy Clamp here. Father is visiting with Dr Lowry at the hospital. May I help you?"

Margo drifted to the window and left Betsy to have a private conversation. She ran her mind over the current situation. A wedding weekend and the groom perishes, possibly because of a heart attack. Sad, but nothing criminal there. Except that three servants of the house hosting the weekend were dead in mysterious circumstances. Two most likely by poison, the third, still a mystery, as yet.

The hipflask was important. Forcep had most likely purloined it at the scene of Perry's death. Had it any relation to his own demise?

"Margo," Betsy called over to her. "Reverend Michaels would like a quick word." She handed over the receiver and earpiece.

"Hello?" Margo said. "So good to hear from you, Robin."

A good friend, Reverend Robin Michaels repeated his upset at the terrible news leaking out of Clamp House all the way down to Chichester where he nursed his poor mother. Yes, she was doing okay but maybe had hit her head as she insisted she was pushed from the top of the library steps by a ghost, a woman in black? He was glad his good friend John Tupper had managed to step in at the last minute to perform the nuptials. And then he began apologising all over again as, of course, that was a moot point now Perry Gladbeck had passed on. So very, very sad.

"I've met Reverend Tupper. He seems nice," Margo lied, but she wanted to turn the conversation away from the maudlin. Betsy had already updated him with the upsetting details of the past twenty-four hours.

"I've known John since we attended St Paul's Theological College together in 1911. He's been a firm favourite of mother's since then. Every spring, he spends a week with us and does all the awkward jobs in the garden like tying up the beanstalks, trimming the trees, pruning mother's Morletti roses. He's got the height for that. Mother calls him Little John and me Robin Hood."

They both chuckled at that, Robin Michaels was definitely a Robin Hood in the manner with which he looked after his flock at Clamp Park and beyond. Margo finished up by fervently wishing a speedy recovery for Mrs Michaels before handing back the phone.

"We need to begin to detective," Betsy told her, now that they could talk quite frankly. "And I'm all for helping. I can be your 'man in the shadows'. I know all about this house and its grounds. All the secret places where someone might hide to do dastardly things."

"Thank you, Betsy. I do believe I may need someone in the shadows."

"I won't let anyone hurt poor Jones. Not one hair on her wonderful head."

"Yes. Well, none of us want to see that."

"So, what can I do?"

"Oh. You're ready to start?" Margo wracked her brains. "Could you return to the grotto in daylight and see if there are any clues about. Anything out of place, for instance?"

Betsy leapt to her feet. "I'm on it!"

FANCY FRENCH STUFF

Jones drifted back to the kitchens where Sarah sidled up to her.

"Is it true you're stuck here?" she asked.

"Seems so."

Sarah gave a sexy, dimpled smile. "One door shuts and another opens. At least, for you it does," she said.

"What am I to do with all this French stuff?" Mrs Mallory was fussing over Monsieur Lefurgey's boxes. "There's no room in the larder." She pulled out a hanky and patted her eyes. "Oh my, poor John and Gladys. And now Mr Forcep. It's like we're cursed."

"I blame that ugly statue in the garden," Sarah said.

"Hush, girl. Don't even mention that heinous thing in my kitchen. Lord only knows what will happen to all of us." Mrs Mallory buried her face in her hanky and wailed. Sarah grinned wickedly and dropped a wink at Jones.

"I'm going to collect the eggs," Whimsy said quietly. She lifted a wicker basket and exited the backdoor.

"More like snuck off for a sly moment with her beau," Sarah murmured so only Jones could hear.

So Sarah knew about Whimsy and Wentworth? Jones's thoughts were interrupted by a scream from outside. She bolted for the door just as Wentworth streaked past towards the sound of the cry. It was coming from somewhere near the kitchen gardens.

They arrived together at the chicken coops to find Whimsy in a state of distress.

"What is it, my love?" Wentworth gathered her in her arms, all the while gazing around for the cause of the alarm. Whimsy pointed inside the chicken run with a trembling finger.

"In there," she whispered.

Cautiously, Jones entered the coop. The chickens ran to the other end. None seemed injured.

"What am I looking for," she asked.

"Over in the corner," Whimsy cried. "Be careful!"

Jones saw it at once. It's bright green body was coiled up into a tight and terrifying knot. Uncoiled, she guessed the snake would stretch out to over five feet. She carefully stepped back.

"It's a green mamba," she said.

"A what?" Sarah asked, straining to see.

Mrs Mallory and a few of the groundsmen showed up. It seemed the whole household was on tenterhooks for the next emergency.

"A highly venomous snake. Keep back." She ushered them all backwards by several paces and then reached for a garden spade perched near the doorway to the coop. There was something about the snake that rested uneasily with her. Taking time to observe it for several minutes, she slowly approached and gave it a gentle prod with the blade of the spade. There was no movement. She tried again, cautious of an ambush. These snakes were known to play dead, only to then lunge at their prey. She had travelled enough to be aware this was a vicious predator.

"It's dead. Definitely dead." She lifted the vivid green body on the flat of the spade. It drooped in lustrous green coils on either side. Its body was round and plump. Slowly she began to back out of the chicken coop.

Sarah squealed and ran back, dragging a screaming Mrs Mallory with her. Everyone gave Jones room to manoeuvre the beast out.

"It's evil looking, that," one of the groundsmen said when Jones had deposited the dead snake on the ground. Mrs Mallory visibly sagged, and Sarah had to hold her upright.

"Best to get her back to the kitchen," Jones said. Turning to Whimsy, she asked, "It was lying there when you opened the coop? You didn't see it move?"

"No. Not a twitch." Whimsy was still very pale.

"The chickens look fine," Wentworth pointed out.

"I think it went in there to hunt all right, but something else killed it instead. Remember that rat I saw in the horse stall?"

Wentworth nodded. "The poisoned rat."

"Maybe this fella ate it?" Jones said. "And the horse disturbed it? That horse was very nervous, and rightly so if a brute like this was in there with it. Did you clean out the rat later? It was gone the next time I looked."

Wentworth frowned. "No, I forgot about it. Are you saying this snake has been eating poisoned rats, and that's what killed it?"

"Yes. And I wager that when Dr Lowry's lab report comes back, we'll find John, Gladys, Forcep, and Gladbeck all died because of snake bites," Jones said.

"What? It can kill you that quick?" one of the groundsmen asked.

"Yes. The green mamba venom can kill a man in under thirty minutes. The bite doesn't always hurt at first. It's followed by dizziness, convulsions, and finally respiratory failure. All coming on very fast. It's one of the deadliest snakes in Africa. The real question is where the hell did it come from?"

THE DOCTOR CONFERS

Later in the afternoon, Dr Lowry called along with a grim-looking Officer Sims. They made a special request for Jones to join them in the drawing room, along with the remaining guests. Margo noted the party had thinned out even more. Sims's request for people to stay had largely gone ignored. No one wanted to loiter in a house of death.

Margo was surprised to see Alexandro join the group. He sat quietly in the corner, his upset still clearly visible. Sir Wesley had disapproved for any of his daughters to be present, so they hadn't been called down. It was to a small group that Dr Lowry delivered his news.

"Snake bite!" Sir Wesley looked horrified. There were gasps of dismay from around the room. "Here? In Hampshire?" he said in disbelief.

"Oh my goodness," Mrs Ford-Hughes clutched her breast and looked fit to faint.

From the corner of her eye, Margo saw Alexandro start and grow pale. His reaction was similar to the majority of people in the room but somehow felt more keenly. Perhaps because he assumed a similar fate had befallen Perry?

"Yes." Dr Lowry was grave. "John Anders had a bite on the back of his calf, and Gladys on the upper arm. There was slight swelling but nothing too drastic. The venom worked very rapidly."

"'The nursing child will play by the hole of the cobra, and the crawling child will put his hand on the viper's den.' Job two." Reverend Tupper crossed himself and sadly shook his head.

Dr Lowry promptly turned his back on him and turned to Jones. "The specimen you sent down to my office. You say you found it in the chicken coop?"

"The house maid found it when she went to collect eggs, sir," Jones answered.

"Good thing it was dead, or we'd no doubt have another fatality on our hands," Dr Lowry said. "I've sent it up to the zoological gardens in London. They'll tell us if your guess was right about the rat poison."

"You seem to know a lot about these snakes." Officer Sims stepped up. He stood a little too close to Jones before he realised her height dominated him, and he took a step back. His attitude was stiff and defensive. To Margo, it was obvious he wanted Jones to be guilty. It was a personal thing now, and that would blind him to the truth if they weren't careful.

"I've travelled to eastern Africa and know a little about green mambas." Jones kept her tone polite and cool.

"Enough to keep one as a pet?" Sims pressed.

Sir Wesley snorted. "No one keeps a green mamba as a pet. Captivity makes them meaner. Don't be ridiculous, man." Sims reddened and seemed to hold Jones responsible for his embarrassment.

"I hear John collapsed outside, but Gladys was in the house when she was bitten," Margo said. She had to make them move on from hovering over Jones. They needed to dissect what little information they did have. "Could a snake that size move between the kitchens and the grounds so freely?"

"Well, they're damned sneaky things." Sir Wesley poured himself a stiff whiskey and proffered the decanter to the doctor and Margo. Both refused.

"What about Perry? Was he envenomed?" Margo asked.

"That's the damnedest thing, and really why we are gathered here," Dr Lowry said. "The report states he died of cyanide poisoning."

This was met by silence.

"You mean he was murdered." Margo finally spoke.

"The Lord sayest—" the Reverend began but Dr Lowry spoke over him.

"It's a hard thing to accidently do," Dr Lowry said. "Poison yourself with cyanide."

"How the hell did he ingest it?" Sir Wesley asked.

Dr Lowry shrugged. "In the amounts found in his system, it would have knocked him flat in anything from five to fifteen minutes."

"We were outdoors all that time," Sir Wesley pointed out. "When could he have been poisoned?"

"The hipflask," Margo said. "Except that Alexandro was drinking from it too?" Alexandro started at his name being used. It pulled him out of his stupor, but he still looked dazed. Margo wondered if the doctor had given him any medications for shock as he had for Melisandrine.

"What hipflask?" Officer Sims demanded.

"I found a hipflask near where they found the body of the butler. I wondered if it might be the one Perry drank from last night, so I sent it down to the police station." Margo thought it best not to mention Jones's part in the recovery. She also didn't mention that she'd had part of the contents sent up to London to a private laboratory for analysis. From the dull flush on Sims's face, she guessed the flask had lain unheeded somewhere at his station. The evidence degrading hour by hour.

"I'll need to see that." Dr Lowry growled, none too pleased at the oversight.

"So, you're telling me, three of my servants died from a venomous snakebite by some African snake, and we have no idea how it got here?" Sir Wesley said. "And that Perry Gladbeck was poisoned, deliberately or not, by cyanide? How the hell do I tell Lord Gladbeck that!"

The incredulity in his voice echoed the sentiments of the room. While many were relieved by the conclusion of the servants' mysterious deaths, the cyanide threw up a whole new spate of uncertainty. Especially frustrating for those wanting to leave for home. This was still a murder investigation, and those remaining were still under lockdown. Everyone seemed to erupt at once with discontent.

"Dash it all, I have to get back to work."

"This is a rum deal, Clamp."

"I am needed in Paris. Paris needs my pastries." Monsieur Lefurgey actually stamped his foot.

"And I am neglecting my parishioners," Reverend Tupper piped up.

Sir Wesley pinned Sims with a beady eye. "You seem to be rather unpopular, Sims. What have you to say to these good people?"

Sims was on the spot. His Adam's apple bobbed. "I understand that this is a very unfortunate occurrence, but it you can just bear with me for one more—"

He was interrupted by a further chorus of discontent.

"My wife wants to see her children."

"How long are we to be stuck here?"

"I've been talking to my lawyer, and you can't do this!"

Margo almost felt sorry for the young officer until she saw the gleam in Jones's eye. She was laughing at his predicament, and she deserved to laugh at his pomposity as she was the real victim of it. With a discrete nod, Margo indicated they should retire from the pending brouhaha. They moved quietly towards the door, which Jones opened for her, and left just as the good doctor tried to calm nerves.

"I think, under the circumstances, one more day would not annoy. After all, it is rather late to set off for London, and the last train has already gone," he said. "Can we all agree to wait until I get the last set of lab reports before you disperse far and wide? I mean, some of you have come down from Scotland or even France." Here he indicated Monsieur Lefurgey, who was huffing and puffing in a corner seat.

Margo rolled her eyes as Jones gently shut the door behind them.

MORE FRENCH STUFF

Lunch was a small and sombre affair. Margo sat with Sir Wesley and Dr Lowry, who had stayed on for a bite to eat. Most of the guests dined in their rooms.

"Sir?" Whimsy stood by Sir Wesley's elbow and spoke quietly. "You're needed upstairs immediately."

"What now." He threw his knife and fork down in disgust.

Whimsy burned scarlet, and Margo felt sorry for the girl. "It's Moosewer Lefurgey," she whispered. "He's dead."

Dr Lowry's cutlery clattered onto the plate. He glared at Sir Wesley.

"What? It's not my bloody fault!" Sir Wesley cried.

Margo followed hot on the men's heels up to the first floor.

"Must you, Lady Margo," Dr Lowry asked wearily.

"Yes. I'm afraid I must," she answered tartly and barged on into the French chef's room. His body lay in the bed. The smell was ghastly even though someone had opened all the windows.

"Oh, good Lord!" She pinched her nostrils. Sir Wesley did the same and turned green about the gills.

"At least this one is no mystery," Dr Lowry said. "Death by diarrhoea."

BACK TO THE GROTTO

"I thought I would swoon, Jones. The smell was horrendous. Needless to say, lunch was ruined."

"Not the best way to go, ma'am." Jones agreed. "Mrs Mallory insists it was the mocha." A dry smile played around her lips.

"Betsy wants to meet us out here," Margo said. "I've had her do a bit of snooping of her own, and she's come up trumps."

They walked through the formal lawns towards the clump of yew and cypress that marked the grotto.

"How tall do you think these roses are, Jones?" Margo asked.

Jones cast a glance and said, "I'm six foot, so I'd say these are closer to eight, maybe even nine feet?"

"Mmm." This would have been Margo's guess too. Before she could comment further, Jones asked her a question.

"How long do you think it will be before Officer Sims turns his attention on Señor Checa?" Jones asked.

"Because he's a foreigner too?"

"Because if the cyanide *was* in the hip flask, then Señor Checa must have pretended to share it with Gladbeck. Otherwise he'd be dead too. Did you see him actually drink from it?"

Margo hesitated in her step. "Gosh. I never thought of that. I'm not sure."

"When do you get the lab result, ma'am?"

"I'm to call later this afternoon. I guess we'll find out then."

They resumed their walk, casually watching as a group of groundsmen slowly lowered the huge and unused marquee.

Margo sighed. "Poor Melisandrine. This is how she'll be remembered, you know. As the girl whose bridegroom died on the eve of the wedding."

"Do you think she'll be terribly upset?"

"No. She'll probably write a sonnet about it and then put it behind her."

Betsy greeted them as they entered the cool shade of the grotto. "Gosh. Isn't this exciting?"

Margo now had a chance to examine the Jezebaal icon in better light. It did not improve any in daylight. "My, what an ugly thing."

"Hush, Quincy," Betsy all but whispered. "Look what happened to Perry."

"I think you'll find that was far from supernatural," Margo said. "The poor boy was murdered, Betsy. Poisoned, to be exact."

Betsy gasped. "By that ghastly snake." She shuddered. "I've never seen such an evil thing. I'm glad it's dead and out of the house. To think we were sleeping while it slithered around the place."

Margo shook her head. "By cyanide poisoning to be exact. The snake had nothing to do with it."

There had been much to-do about the snake once it had been removed from the coop and placed in a box for transport to Dr Lowry's office. Everyone from the house, upstairs and down, had come to take a look. Some had even dared to try to touch, but Jones warned them off.

"Murder! Poor Perry." Betsy lamented. "Melisandrine hasn't come out of her room. She refuses to eat, just sits around reading all day." Privately, Margo thought that was Melisandrine's usual daytime routine.

"So," she asked. "What have you found for us?"

"This bag." Betsy's hands fluttered with excitement as she unfolded a brightly patterned carpetbag. "It was stuffed away under the trees at the back of the altar. It's full of weird voodoo stuff." She thrust it into Margo's hands.

Intrigued, Margo carefully opened the rough handmade bag. Inside she found a small roll of carpet, folded over to fit comfortably. Opened out, it was only a few feet square and was brightly woven wool in the Arabic style. It was wrapped around a large bottle of water. Lying loose at the bottom of the bag was a small army compass.

"Good grief, Jones," Margo said. "What does it mean?"

Jones laid the small rug on the ground. "It's a sajjãda, ma'am, or prayer mat." She pointed to the vibrant and intricate design. "See the mihrab at the top of the central block of pattern? That should point to Mecca when prayer commences. I'll wager the compass is to help the owner find north."

"You mean, it's Muslim? Someone here is praying secretly to Mecca? But why hide it?"

"Unless they are praying to that awful creature." Betsy nodded at the state. "Praying to the daughter of Baal?"

"I sincerely hope not." Margo cast it a wary glance. It was unnervingly spooky with its hollowed eyes and gaping mouth.

Something clanged at the bottom of the bag and Jones withdrew a silver hipflask. She held it up for Margo to see.

"Another one?"

"Seems so, ma'am. I wonder what the significance is?" She packed the bag away and returned it to Betsy. "Maybe it's best to leave it back where you found it?"

"It doesn't enlighten us much for the moment," Margo said, "but it is interesting that someone felt the need to hide it. I think we may have a guest who is not what they seem, Jones."

Another Strange Night

Sarah had small, high breasts with pert, dark coloured nipples that strained for attention. Jones took her time and let Sarah writhe under her. Her body was sinewy and tight from a life of domestic labour, a smaller and more fragile version of Jones's own, with its hard muscles and burnt butter skin. She slid across Sarah's belly and breasts and pushed her thigh between Sarah's to apply a slow, delicious pressure. Sarah groaned in her ear and then nipped her earlobe. She was almost as rough in her post-coitus play as she was fucking. Jones had the scratches all down her back to prove it.

"I'll be sad when you go," Sarah said.

Jones disentangled herself and stretched. There was no answer to that. She sat naked on the edge of the bed and looked around a room similar to her own, except this had a few more personal items. A blurred photograph of Sarah's mother. A colourful shawl thrown over a chair to make it homier and, beside that, a small posy of yellow flowers on a table. The only anomaly was a pair of expensive silk stockings draped over the wardrobe door. A luxury usually outside the wages of a house maid. Before she could ponder this any further, Sarah poked her with her bare foot and asked coyly, "Do you service your lady like this?"

"No."

Sarah shrugged. The curt answer was off-putting as intended. "I was just being nosey." She defended herself and pulled the blanket up over her chest.

There was an awkward silence for a moment, then Jones lifted the battered bible from the bedside table. It was the last thing she expected to see in the brazen Sarah's room.

"All the servants have one," Sarah said, as if reading her mind. "It belongs to the house."

Idly, Jones flicked through it.

"What do you worship?" Sarah asked.

Jones frowned. "What do you mean?"

"I mean do you worship buffalo or mountains or what?"

"I'm a Baptist, but I don't bother with it. Can I hold on to this for a while?" She indicated the bible.

"I thought you didn't bother?"

"This one's interesting," she said and lowered herself across Sarah's warm body.

Later that night, Jones prowled. Her own room was comfortless, and her mind was active, a bad combination. She needed to get outside into the night air to think.

After sex with Sarah, she thrummed with excess energy. The moon was bright, and the tip of her cigarette pulsed red and hot with each inhalation. Other than that, there was no other light. The sky was moonless, and clouds hid the stars. She decided to circuit the house. The vast lawns at the front stretched on down to the grotto and then on to the deer park. The marquee had gone, leaving no sign of the wedding celebrations that should have taken place. All that was left was a circle of dark, flattened grass.

Jones turned another corner towards the west wing of the house and noted Margo's bedroom light was still on.

She frowned. Margo was a deep sleeper and usually conked out as soon as her head hit the pillow. Why was she still awake? Was she unwell?

Jones stomped out her cigarette and went back inside.

Outside the Peacock room, she gently tapped on the door. "Ma'am?" she said in a hushed tone so as not to disturb anyone else residing in the other guest suites.

"Oh, Jones." The plaintive cry came from inside. "Jones, I need help. But be careful. Very, very careful."

Jones turned the handle, and the door swung slowly open on the Peacock room. Margo sat huddled on the bed, her arms wrapped around her knees. She was haloed by the pool of light from the bedside lamp. She raised a finger to her lips, her eyes wide with fear.

"Ma'am?" Jones inquired quietly.

"Shush. Something is in here with me. I heard it slithering in the bathroom, and then it came in here." She looked around anxiously.

Jones stood very still, straining to listen. The clock on the mantel ticked. The drip of a faulty tap coming from the bathroom. And a rustle behind her—out in the corridor. Jones cautiously turned her head and met Sarah's guilty gaze.

"I followed you," she said bluntly, though quietly enough. "What's wrong?" There was a nervousness to her voice. As if she knew she had gotten into something too deep.

"There may be a second snake in Lady Margo's room," Jones said. Sarah paled. "I'll need your help." Jones held her gaze to let her know this was a serious statement.

"Who are you talking too?" Margo whispered hoarsely from the bedroom.

"The maid, Sarah, is here," Jones told her. From the corner of her eye, a slash of vivid green undulated under the dressing table. It was a slender specimen that she estimated to be about six feet long.

"Send her for help," Margo hissed, unaware of the proximity of the creature.

"There's no time for that," Jones told her. Then she turned to Sarah and said, "When I go into the room, I want you to follow me and peel off to the left. Get on the bed with Lady Margo and grab one of the blankets. I'll need to make a sack of some kind. Got that?"

Sarah swallowed hard and nodded. She had a determined tilt to her chin, and Jones knew she had good backup.

Jones took several careful steps into the room. There was a whisk as Sarah rushed past, followed by the creak of the bed as she leapt onto it beside Margo. Jones kept her gaze fixed on the mamba. It retracted slightly at the movements, though Jones knew this was due more to the vibration of their feet than it actually seeing them.

She took a few more steps away from the door towards the window, and the snake's head moved slightly along with her. Its tongue flicked the air, tasting her scent. There came a rustling from the bed as Margo and Sarah pulled free the blanket.

"What do you want us to do with it?" Margo whispered.

"Hand it over to me, carefully. No fast movements." A snake this size was capable of launching an attack from several feet away. She did not want to alarm it any more than she was already doing. She stretched out her hand, and the blanket was pressed into it.

"Okay. Here's the hard part," she said. "I'm going to throw this over the snake. It should grow still for a moment, then it will try and wriggle free. In that moment, I want you to take a side each and help me bundle it up. Make sure not to let it see the light, or it will struggle harder."

"Oh my goodness." Margo sounded faint.

"I need you both to be certain about this. It's pretty docile at the moment. We don't want an angry snake free in this room. Okay?"

"Can't we just ask Sir Wesley to come and shoot it?" Sarah's voice was weak with fear.

Jones shook her head. "I've no idea how it got in here, and if we lose sight of it, Lord only knows where it might pop up next. This is the only chance we have, and we need to act now. Are you ready?"

There was no answer, so she assumed they were nodding behind her back. "On the count of three. All you have to do is help me tuck in the loose ends; I'll be the one holding the snake, not you. Okay?"

"Okay."

"Yes."

She got proper answers this time.

"One. Two. Three—" She threw the blanket in a wide arc and covered the snake completely. Immediately, she dived for where she knew the head to be and gripped it as tightly as she could through the layers of fabric. She prayed it would effectively deaden any fanged attack to her hands.

Margo and Sarah appeared either side and began furiously bundling the now writhing body deeper into the folds of the blanket making a crude sack.

"Give me the curtain sash," Jones ordered Sarah. "You go and get Sir Wesley," she told Margo.

The snake was whipping about ferociously now, and it took all her strength to hold the folds of the blanket together. Sarah ran for the window and tore down the sash so hard the entire curtain fell to the floor. She brought the sash over to Jones and helped her tie the neck of the bag they had made as tightly as possible. Jones lifted the heavy parcel and dumped it in the bath and switched the light off, plunging the room into darkness.

"Oh my sweet Jesus." Sarah sagged at the knees.

"The dark will calm it down," Jones said and placed a hand on Sarah's back. "Are you okay?"

"I feel sick." She turned into Jones's arms and laid her head on her chest.

"There, there." She awkwardly patted Sarah's back.

"Where is it?" Sir Wesley appeared with a pistol. Margo was hard on his heels. She gave Jones a curious look as Sarah slipped from her arms.

"In the tub." She pointed to the blanket, now innocently still. "There's no need to kill it, sir. I think it's a specimen the zoological gardens would be pleased to have."

"Damned if they will!" He let off several shots into the bath tub. A first the blanket jerked and writhed and blood stains began to appear. On the sixth bullet, the blanket became still.

Margo and Sarah stood with their hands over their ears, deafened by the noise of a Browning handgun blasting off in a tiled bathroom. Jones kept her face impassive. Once the shooting stopped, she turned away to the bedroom. Margo followed her out, ashen faced.

"Are you all right, ma'am?" Jones asked. "I think you'll need another room."

"I think I need a cigarette. Have you any on you, Jones?"

They went outside where the dull pewter of day laced the eastern sky. Side by side, cigarette in hand, they strolled across the lawn in no particular direction and with no particular conversation. It was chilly, and Margo shivered in her shawl.

"We should return to the house, ma'am," Jones said.

Margo hauled on her cigarette. "I'm fine, Jones. It's just the shock. That thing was vile; though, I'm sorry Sir Wesley shot it."

A movement over by the grotto caught Jones's eye. She touched Margo's hand and indicated the incident with a tip of her head. Quietly, they sank down behind a rose bush and sat hunched, peering through the foliage to see Alexandro Checa emerge from the grotto and walk briskly towards the rear of the house.

THE JIGSAW

The next morning saw a mass evacuation of Clamp House. The remaining guests refused point blank to stay in a house overrun by snakes. There was nothing Officer Sims could do to stop them. The threat of litigation was flung in his face with such force he almost carried the bags to the waiting vehicles himself.

Jones helped heft luggage into the rows of private cars and taxis that lined the drive. She spun around and bumped into Reverend Tupper, who, although declaring his intention to stay, insisted in getting in the way of everyone trying to ease the debacle.

"Reverend." Jones stood back respectfully and let him past, which he did with incredible coldness. She surmised he was as ungracious to foreigners as he was to women. Jones rubbed her ribs. She also surmised the Reverend had a very big bible in his pocket.

"Jones," Margo appeared at her elbow as she was hoisting a particularly heavy portmanteau. "I need a word with you when you are done here. I'll be in the orangery."

Jones joined her minutes later. "Ma'am?"

Margo hand her a piece of paper. "It's the report from the lab in London about the contents of the hip flask. It came in this morning's post."

Jones skimmed the letter. "Cyanide." She wasn't surprised.

"So where does that leave Alexandro?" Margo asked.

"In jail, I don't doubt," Jones answered. "We have maybe a four-hour head start on Dr Lowry with this news. Once Officer Sims sees this, he'll arrest Señor Checa for murder. It will seem obvious that he added the poison before handing the flask back to Gladbeck for the last time."

"Yes. Nice and neat. Except that Alexandro looked genuinely shocked."

"That will make little inroads with Officer Sims's reasoning. I understand the Scotland Yard detectives will be here in a matter of hours. Sims will be anxious to show the investigation has moved on. Plus, it wraps up Forcep's death nicely. He stole the hip flask and sealed his own fate."

"And the snake?" Margo paced up and down the tiled path through the mature Navel orange and Kaffir lime trees. "No one seems to realise how strange it is for two such snakes to be loose around the house and grounds."

"It is very convenient for the snakes to have dispatched Gladys and John. No work for Sims to do there." Jones stifled a snort of disapproval. The snake she had captured had been a mature adult and not the kind of thing to prowl happily around a house unnoticed. Not even a house this size. As far as she was concerned, it had been placed in Lady Margo's room deliberately.

"So, we have Perry and Forcep killed by the same method, though Forcep was not the target. Monsieur Lefurgey... Well, he hardly fits the pattern, but he's dead all the same. We have a mysterious bag of Muslim prayer items hidden in the grotto behind that awful statue, and two people dead from venomous snakes, and I mean how many more can there be?" She looked around her nervously.

"I think just the two, ma'am."

"Oh? Why is that?"

"Because, I remember seeing two canvas sacks tied up a horse stall in the stables. The horse was in a terrible way, but it didn't occur to me at the time that it was anything more than rats annoying it."

"Let's go see, Jones."

Out in the hallway, Jones cannoned into Reverend Tupper again. He was looking everywhere but where he was going.

"Excuse me," she apologised and got a glare in answer.

Ignoring him, she went after Lady Margo, who had reached the back gardens by now.

The sacks had gone, and the mare stood at ease, staring back at Jones and Margo with the same curiosity they levelled at her stall.

"Wentworth," Jones called. "Where did the canvas sacks go?" she asked when Wentworth appeared.

At first she looked confused, then the fog lifted and she said, "I think Sarah took 'em. At least, I'm sure I saw her walking back through the kitchen gardens the other night with them folded under her arm."

Margo and Jones exchanged a look of surprise. Jones took off for the kitchens with Margo right behind her.

"Sarah," Jones called from the back door to the kitchens. Sarah looked up, her face flushed and sweaty from the cooking range. She smiled on seeing Jones and came over, wiping her hands on her apron. Then she noticed Margo just behind Jones, and the smile fell away.

"Could we have a word with you in the garden?" Jones asked and walked away without waiting for an answer. Margo walked beside Sarah. Neither spoke.

"Sarah, what is your connection with Señor Checa," Jones asked once they had reached a quiet spot.

Sarah visibly started. "What do you mean?" She tried to sound accusatory. Margo looked intrigued.

"I saw you near the stables the night you were meant to rendezvous with him, but Mr Gladbeck turned up before you. What was in those canvas sacks? Señor Checa was extraordinarily interested in them." Jones was stern; she knew how intimidating that could be.

"You're mad. I never—"

"Sarah," Margo interrupted gently. "Señor Checa is about to be arrested for the murder of Mr Gladbeck. We don't think he did it, but he will have a very hard time convincing the law otherwise. If you know anything that might help him, you better speak up now."

Sarah seemed to sag. "Señor Checa found me a few months ago. He asked me to keep an eye on what was going on downstairs and meet him for a 'report' each evening. He was particularly interested in Lefurgey. I've no idea what was in the sacks. He told me to bring 'em to him last night, and I did. He gave me five bob and some nice stockings."

"And what exactly were you to report on?" Margo asked.

Sarah signed. "Whoever came to see his Lordship," she said in defeat. "A lot of people come and go to buy those ugly knick-knacks of his. Señor Checa wanted to know all about that, and especially if anyone was took down to the grotto to see the creepy statue down there." Her head snapped up. "But I'm keeping them stockings! Is that all, ma'am? I need to get back to work."

"Yes. On you go." Margo dismissed her.

Sarah spun on her heel but not without a smile for Jones. They watched her head back to the kitchen.

"You know, Jones, I think that girl is inordinately fond of you."

"You do, ma'am?" Jones feigned surprise.

"So, Alexandro had the maid spying on Sir Wesley?" Margo said. "How bizarre."

"I think we need to pay Señor Checa a visit, ma'am."

SEÑOR CHECA COMES CLEAN

Alexandro was in the hallway. In handcuffs.

"It's so unfair!" Betsy greeted Margo and Jones as they entered. "I know he didn't do it. I just know. Alexandro adored Perry; they were the best of friends."

They were more than the best of friends, but Jones didn't see the need to reveal that.

"Just a moment, Officer." Margo halted Sims in his tracks. "There is more to this than meets the eye."

"What do you mean?" Sir Wesley snapped. He and Dr Lowry stood to the side, glaring at Checa as if they'd like to give him a good thrashing.

Off to the left, the Reverend Tupper tutted disapprovingly. His luggage was stacked beside him. Mrs Ford-Hughes loitered by the door; her luggage had already been deposited in the vehicle that was to take her to the station, but she lingered to watch the proceedings. These were the only guests left after the snake incident, and now they were departing.

"What's going on here?" Melisandrine appeared at the top of the stairs. She stood immobile, as if Artemis herself had descended from Olympus to give judgment on the folly of mankind.

"They're saying Alexandro killed Perry!" Betsy wailed.

"The evidence is there, miss," Officer Sims spoke up. "He put the poison in the hipflask for Mr Gladbeck to drink." He looked at Dr Lowry for support, and the doctor withdrew a silver hipflask from his pocket.

"I'm afraid it's true, Melisandrine," he said. "There was cyanide found in the hipflask."

"Let me see that." Melisandrine floated down the stairs and took the flask from the doctor's hands. "This is not Perry's hipflask," She dismissed it almost immediately and handed it back. "I bought his as an engagement present. It has his initials on it."

Dr Lowry and Sims looked dumbfounded.

"That's my hipflask," Alexandro said.

"So you swapped hipflasks in the dark, eh?" Dr Lowry growled at him.

Alexandro shook his head.

Jones stepped up. "The hipflasks got muddled up in the dark," she said. "And Perry grabbed the wrong one." She turned to Alexandro. "The poison was meant for you; wasn't it?"

He nodded miserably. "And Perry died instead."

"What?" Sims frowned in confusion.

"What the hell do you mean, man?" Sir Wesley said.

"He means someone came to this weekend party with the intention of killing *him*, not Perry," Margo said. She stepped up to stand beside Jones.

"But why?" Dr Lowry asked.

"Tell them," Margo told Alexandro. "This is the time to come clean."

Alexandro sighed. "My name is not Alexandro Checa, and I am not from Argentina. I'm Akeem Bahar, and I work for the Damascus Bureau of Antiquities. We monitor the comings and goings of foreign academics such as

Sir Wesley. Men who run expeditions under an official license but behave in an 'unofficial' manner." He jingled the handcuffs. "Could you remove these, please?"

Sims scowled and didn't move.

"Free the man and let him speak," Sir Wesley told him. Suddenly, he seemed very interested in what Akeem Bahar had to say. Sims grudgingly obliged.

"How did you know?" Akeem asked Margo and Jones. "My mother is Spanish; I don't look typically Arab."

"We found your salāt bag and watched you leave the grotto after Fajr, your dawn prayer," Jones said.

"But what were you doing with a hipflask?" Margo asked. "Muslims don't drink alcohol."

"My hipflask contained water for me to wash my mouth before prayer. I had another larger container in my bag with water for the wudhu ritual. It was not clean enough to drink."

"Wudhu is a ritual washing of the body before prayer," Margo explained to Sims who looked well adrift of the conversation.

"I had to hide who I really was from Sir Wesley," Akeem said.

"And you had his servants spy on him," Margo said.

Sir Wesley bristled. "If you are responsible for John and Gladys, I'll see you hang!"

Sims took a step closer in anticipation.

Akeem shook his head. "You have another guest who is not as they seem."

"Oh, we know that already." Margo gave her attention to the Reverend Tupper. "I think we have a false prophet among us, in fact."

The reverend stiffened, and Jones moved imperceptibly closer to Margo. This man was dangerous.

"I talked to Reverend Michaels, who enthused about his good friend John Tupper. Little John he called you. Little John who towered over him and was able to reach the highest Morletti roses in the garden." Everyone took in Reverend Tupper's small stature. "What did you do with the real John Tupper when you took over his identity?" she asked.

"Little John is just a nickname. A joke." Tupper spluttered. "Surely you know that?"

"But you misquoted from the bible on several occasions," Jones said. "I checked, and each time you were close but wrong. Also, you are meant to be a Methodist minister, but I saw you cross yourself. You seem to be very confused regarding your particular form of Christianity."

Tupper's face crumpled into a sneer, and he pawed at his inside jacket pocket.

"Are you looking for this?" Jones held up the khanjar, a wickedly curved Arabian dagger.

Tupper spat at her and made a run for the door. Sims tackled him to the floor with great gusto.

"Finally." Dr Lowry crowed. "A decent piece of police work."

"Would someone tell me what the hell is happening here?" Sir Wesley bellowed as Sims cuffed Tupper and dragged him to his feet.

"Infidel!" Tupper screamed. "You come to our country and pillage and loot from the gods! This will not go unpunished. Jezebaal will smite you to dust."

Akeem stepped forward. "Sir Wesley, in my country there are many who still follow the old path. The statue you 'unofficially' removed is of a maleficent goddess still worshiped in the more far-flung regions." He pointed at Tupper. "This man travelled here in order to steal the icon back and punish you while he was at it. I can only think he recognised me and tried to kill me, but unfortunately Perry fell victim." His face clouded, and he looked as though he was going to cry.

"Did that bastard bring those snakes into my home?" Sir Wesley seethed.

"I imagine so, milord," Jones answered. "As you know, snakes are a part of the Daughter of Baal worship. They strike at the profane, the unbelievers. I suspect this was Tupper's way of cleansing your household."

"I saw the canvas bags in the stable but was disturbed before I could investigate further. I asked the maid, Sarah to bring them to me later," Akeem admitted. "They were both empty when I found them. He'd set the snakes loose. One for the household staff, and one for Lady Margo when he realised she was beginning to put the pieces together."

Sir Wesley lunged to strangle Tupper, and only Dr Lowry pulling him away kept things calm.

"I fear I had an annoying point of view expressed as early as dinner on the first night. That marked me out for special treatment. And yet, Tupper was not working alone," Margo said. "Someone needed to get the Reverend Michaels out of the way for his impersonation to go forward. Someone had to push Mrs Michaels down the steps of her local library to incapacitate her and have Robin Michaels go home to nurse his mother."

She pointed at Mrs Ford-Hughes, who stood ashen by the front door. "Mrs Michaels insists she saw a ghost before she was pushed. A woman in black. That was you, wasn't it Mrs Ford-Hughes? *You* have worked on the board of the museum for several years and helped sponsor Sir Wesley's expeditions, and also, I fear, his black-market dealings. *You* were the spy for the other side. You knew what he had smuggled in from abroad and could report back to your masters. Especially when he brought home the Daughter of Baal. How long have you been in thrall to Baal worship?"

Mrs Ford-Hughes took a step back. "I... I..." She turned and ran out across the lawn, making for the grotto.

"For a portly woman, she has a fair turn of speed." Dr Lowry noted.

"Let me take care of this." Betsy picked up the small bronze monkey head and hoisted it deftly at the fleeing Mrs Ford-Hughes. It hit her on the back of the head, bowling her forward, flat-faced onto the lawn, in the exact circle of flattened grass left by the marquee. She lay there, motionless.

"Oh, well done, Betsy," Margo said. "You still have a marvellous right arm."

Jones and Dr Lowry politely applauded.

"There's another one for you, Sims," Sir Wesley said with a gleam in his eye for his youngest daughter.

"And finally, Monsieur Lefurgey," Margo said. "My only loose thread."

"I think I can help you there," Dr Lowry said. "Monsieur Lefurgey was a victim of his own cooking. The lab reported the cause of death as mycetism. That's mushroom poisoning to you and me. It started a few days ago, possibly while he was in France. Calls to his home have proved that he was poorly before he left. That's pretty usual for a slow poison action."

"It might be why the poor man was so delusional and oddly behaved while he was here," Margo said.

Dr Lowry shrugged. "Well, he was French."

"Good God, what a weekend," Sir Wesley watched as one of Sims's officers cuffed Mrs Ford-Hughes and led her to join Tupper in the back of the police car. He turned to his companions. "If this doesn't sell that statue on, then nothing will. No one can deny the curse now!"

"Sir Wesley, that is very black-hearted of you." Margo was aghast. "Several people have died, including your practical son-in-law."

Sir Wesley sobered. "I agree. I suggest we all have a spot of lunch while Sims here writes it all down in his report." Sims looked a little shell-shocked at the unfolding of the last half hour.

"I shall be in my room," Melisandrine announced. "I feel my muse urging me to write an epic poem about all of this. Fallen idols swallowed whole by the sands of time. The heart as empty as the tomb it despoils." She was wafting up the stairwell as she spoke, her hands forming dreamlike phantasms in the air as her words fell like fairy kisses on the heads below. "Send up a tray."

Jones blinked. "At least it's not a watercolour, ma'am," she murmured.

"Praise Baal for that," Margo muttered back.

AMERICA BOUND

Jones strolled along the promenade deck, enjoying the sea breeze. Her dark hair was loose, and the wind billowed the white cotton shirt she was wearing. Her grey twill pants raised many an eyebrow. But she strode on, ignoring the promenaders and their disapproval.

In one hand, she balanced a silver tray with a Long Island Tea sweating prettily. Tucked under the other arm was a precious three-day-old *Times* newspaper.

She found Lady Margo resting on a lounger on the First class sun deck and presented her spoils. Margo was very appreciative.

"Do sit with me a moment, Jones, and keep the juice-joint Johnnies at bay." She indicated a knot of young men loitering by the ships rail nearby, throwing surreptitious looks her way. "Such dreadfully bad flirts. I've just ordered some lemon tea for you."

Jones obligingly took a seat on the lounger next to Margo's. "Thank you, ma'am." She glared at the juice-joint Johnnies, and they melted away.

Margo unfolded the newspaper and became engrossed, leaving Jones to enjoy her tea and the panorama of a sunny Atlantic.

"Good grief, Jones! Have you seen this?" Margo said, looking up from the paper.

"What ma'am?"

"Sir Wesley Clamp, the esteemed anthropologist and explorer, has met a tragic death at his home in Hampshire. According to dispatches, Sir Wesley was organising the removal of a large stone statue on his grounds, which had been sold abroad, when a rope snapped. It fell on him, crushing him to death instantly. The funeral will take place on Monday 12th—" Margo stopped reading. "Why, Jones, that was yesterday. Oh poor Melisandrine and Betsy. I wish I could have been there for them."

"A sad affair, ma'am." Jones sympathised.

Margo folded the paper and put it away as she reached for her cocktail. "You know, Jones, perhaps that icon was cursed after all."

"It would seem so, ma'am. It would seem so."

About Gill McKnight

Gill McKnight is Irish but spends as much time as possible in Lesbos, Greece, which she considers home. She can often be found traveling back and forth between Greece and Ireland in a rusty old camper van with her rusty wee dog. Gill enjoys writing, roses, and by necessity DIY.

CONNECT WITH GILL:

Website: www.gillmcknight.com

Evolution of an Art Thief

by Jessie Chandler

DEDICATION

This book is dedicated to Ursula Thiebaux, who, as a result of bullying, took her own life at the age of 13.

ACKNOWLEDGEMENTS

I'd like to thank Astrid and Jae of Ylva for taking on this collection. Jove Belle, thank you for your editing wizardry. Also for your cover-making prowess.

To my first readers, Lori L. Lake, Judy Kerr, DJ Schuette, and Devin Abraham, thank you for everything. You're my backbone.

I played footloose and fancy-free with established dates of some places and organizations within the story. One of these is the Museum of Jewish Heritage, which actually opened in 2003. If you have a chance to Google the Museum and The Garden of Stones, do it. It's amazing.

Lastly, thank you Betty Ann—you're my love and my light. Your patience as I peck out words and form them into something sort of readable is nothing short of extraordinary.

Foreward

If you're an LGBTQ teen, or any teen who's being bullied, please, *please* know it gets better. Check out the It Gets Better project: **www.itgetsbetter.org**. Reach out to family, to an elder, to a school counselor. Tell them what's going on and who the perpetrators are. It might feel like you're alone in dealing with this, but you're not.

If you're a parent, a sister, a brother, a friend of someone who you think is being bullied, talk to them. Check out the It Gets Better project together. It'll provide ideas on how to help and how to cope.

We are losing way too many kids way too early. We need to step up, speak up, and speak loud.

CHAPTER 1

"Mikala Ana Flynn, get your caboose in gear. It's almost five thirty."

"Coming, Tubs." I pasted a reluctant smile on my face even though she couldn't see me through the wall dividing the living room from my bedroom.

My grandmother—Tubs to me, Tubby to family, Leah to friends, and Leahlabel Flynn to the rest of the world—was a clock hawk. We were due in an hour to the 2001 Goldsmith Foundation dinner at the Museum of Jewish Heritage near Battery Park. We had plenty of time, but even if we were Johnny-on-the-spot, we were late in her book.

Probably where my father got his sense of punctuality. Ah, crap. Why did my mind have to go there now? The thought of him dropped me right back into a boatload of morose memories, exactly the state my grandmother was trying to shake me out of. I knew she meant well. And I knew she was struggling too. Today was the one-year anniversary of my father's death. Her son's death.

Death?

Oh, hell no. It wasn't just a death. Might as well call it what it was. Murder, plain and simple. Cold-blooded homicide.

And as yet, unsolved.

Three hundred and sixty-five days ago, my fourteen-year-old self walked into the house my father and I had shared in Key West, Florida—the same place we'd lived since I was six.

It looked like a World Wrestling Federation cage match had rolled through the place. Lots of broken glass. Trashed furniture. And blood. So much blood.

I'd freaked the hell out when I found my strong, tall, capable father—an Army officer—sprawled on the kitchen floor, bleeding from a gash in his neck. He'd been a West Point grad and then an airman. After that, he'd transferred into Special Forces. Special Forces, dammit! He trained people to kick ass. How had someone gotten the better of him?

That day, terror had chased itself down my spine and made my legs weak. Even now, a year later, when I thought too hard about it, that exact feeling shot through me like lightning and left me shaking and spacey.

I'd pulled myself together and called for help. Then, I'd desperately tried to stop the unstoppable with a dishtowel. I'd begged my dad to hold on, pleaded with him over and over and over again. Eventually, emergency responders had dragged me away.

Military police had ruled it a burglary gone bad and then promptly closed the case. Even though the place had been tossed, all that was taken was an old puzzle box made by my great-grandfather. Suddenly, my secure world had been blitzed—completely demolished. I was thoroughly confused and pissed off. I hurt so much I couldn't think straight.

My grandmother—my dad's mom—came to Florida from New York and helped sort everything out. She brought me back to Brooklyn—to the house where I'd spent my "formative years," as my dad used to say—from the time I was eighteen months until just after I turned six. But that was another story entirely.

Three hundred sixty-five days was a long time. Yet it was the blink of an eye. What a paradox.

I sighed, rolled off my bed, and tucked my white button-down shirt into my jeans. Under the shirt, I wore a white tank top. As soon as this fiasco was over, I planned to lose a layer. Thanks to years of living in the tropics, I hated being constricted by clothes. Too claustrophobic. Summers in New York City were almost always hot, but the daylong drizzle that fell from the battleship-gray sky upped the humidity and reminded me of everything I'd lost in the Conch Republic.

I trudged into the living room.

Tubs waited by the front door, arms crossed. Where the nickname "Tubby" came from, I had no idea. My grandmother was lean, fit, ready to go—everything but chubby.

She looked me over. "You're damn lucky this isn't a black-tie affair. Jeans? Honestly. Kids these days. At least your shirt is clean."

At five eight and still growing, I could finally look her in the eye. With a one-sided smile that took some effort, I said, "And I buttoned my shirt. Besides, it's not like you're all dressed up."

She wore faded black Dockers, a blue blouse with a bunch of flowers on it, and a well-worn pair of shit kickers. Her reading glasses rested like a permanent growth on top of her head, ready to be whipped off and put to use at a moment's notice. She devoured three newspapers every morning and read fiction like a bookworm on steroids.

"Is this a western-themed evening?" I asked.

"What?"

"The boots."

"Oh, those. No. Figured, if the rain came again, I could stomp through the puddles with you."

I laughed. That woman could always make me smile. She possessed a great sense of humor, and her mind was always busy calculating something or another. Her Romani ancestry had given her dark skin, twinkling deep-chocolate eyes, and salt-and-pepper hair that she wore in a braid halfway down her back.

While I'd inherited Tubs' russet coloring and bone structure, the added olive tinge to my skin came from my Italian mother. Thanks to the two of them, I usually didn't burn in the sun—a really good thing when I'd lived in Florida. The nod my genetics gave to my dad's half-Irish heritage was green eyes and a mess of dark-brown hair that glinted red in the sun.

When I looked back, I realized how amazing Tubs was. She had been a child of the Holocaust, incredibly lucky to have made it out alive. She was a survivor in so many ways. Before I was born, my granddad had been killed in a construction accident while building the World Trade Center's Twin Towers. Tubs had rallied and worked multiple jobs to take care of my dad. She managed to put herself through college and then grad school. She was nothing if not stubborn, a trait we shared in spades.

All that crazy perseverance of hers led to an appointment to the President's Commission on the Holocaust back in the seventies. The Commission did its thing and came to the conclusion that it was high time the US did something to honor victims of the Third Reich. Eventually, the United States Holocaust Memorial Museum in Washington DC was built, and when I was a little kid living with Tubs, we visited every year.

After that, she helped get the ball rolling for Manhattan's Museum of Jewish Heritage. She still worked there as one of the exhibition coordinators, and that's where we were headed today.

"Come on, then." She grabbed my arm and manhandled me out the door. "Time's a-wasting."

We exited the subway at Bowling Green. Battery Park was soggy and quiet as we scurried through the rain toward the Museum of Jewish Heritage. The building was lit up with amber light, softening the sharp edges with the mist that hung heavy in the air. Clouds pressed low to the ground, bringing twilight early and threatening to dump even more rain on our parade.

The damp in the air mixed with scents that are uniquely New York—an unsettling combo of bus exhaust, food aromas, and rotting garbage—were a world away from the sun and salt water of Key West. Once in a while, I had to remind myself that this was my new reality, not a recurring nightmare I'd eventually wake up from.

"Thank you," Tubs called to a man who held open one of the museum's huge glass doors for us. We scooted into the lobby, better known as the Grand Foyer. This was where Tubs would mingle, and I would be bored as hell until we went up to the Events Hall for dinner. There was sure to be plenty of gossip about the Goldsmiths, their foundation, and whatever fancy-schmancy award was being given out tonight.

While she wasn't Jewish, Tubs' family name was Lautari. Her tribe of Romani made the mistake of briefly settling in Poland near Lodz, about seventy-five miles from Warsaw. Her family had been rounded up by Hitler's war machine, and Tubs had been born in the Lodz ghetto. She was the only one in her family of six to make it out alive. Her father bought off a couple of guards and somehow managed to smuggle Tubs out just before mass deportations to the Chelmno concentration camp began.

Whenever I thought about that, I felt physically sick at how close Tubs came to death. I was lucky to be able to escort her to these pain-in-my-ass events. My father sure would have gotten a kick out of the fact that his impatient, moody, restless, and yeah, sometimes reckless kid would do something so civilized. That thought brought me full circle, and I sighed heavily.

Tubs tightened her hand on my arm. "Mikala, would you please find me a beverage?" It was crazy, but somehow she always sensed when my thoughts were headed for the shitter and did her best to distract me from myself.

"Sure," I said. "What do you want?"

A woman I recognized from another city museum said, "The servers have those cute little pink drinks with Hawaiian umbrellas."

"Music to my ears," Tubs said. "Mikala, will you please find me a glass of that pink concoction?" She patted my arm, and I put my hand over hers. We'd been through a lot together, and there wasn't much I wouldn't do for her, no matter my mood.

As I meandered through the sea of overdressed humanity, the roar of voices grew exponentially louder as more people arrived. This was so not my style. It wasn't Tubs' style either, but she got a kick out of bringing highbrow society down a couple of notches by simply being in attendance.

She always told me never to underestimate the power of place and presentation. Thanks to her association with the museum, I'd been able to take the entrance exam to Stuyvesant High School late last summer. By the time we'd gotten back from settling my dad's affairs in Florida, the normal testing window had been closed. I'd scored well, and the school had accepted me. Only later had I found out how hard the place was to get into. Personally, I didn't get what the big deal was, but it made Tubs happy, and *that* mattered to me.

Tuxedo-wearing waiters skillfully navigated through the crowd, holding trays of appetizers and flutes filled with champagne. I didn't see any special little pink drinks, though.

My stomach rumbled, so I snagged a bite-sized turnover from a passing tray. It was pretty good. Next, I grabbed a tiny triangle of bread with a white smear of cream cheese topped by some gelatinous goop that looked like black beads. What the hell. I popped it in my mouth, and just like that, my mouth was filled with the nasty fish guts they rinsed off the dock every morning. I chewed and swallowed in a hurry. So gross. I grabbed a glass of bubbly off a waiter's tray and downed it before he could stop me. He gave me the evil eye, and I faded into the throng before he could do anything about it.

Halfway across the space, I zeroed in on someone carrying a tray of pink beverages with multi-colored paper umbrellas. Bingo. Now I just needed to get from here to there before the server's tray was emptied. I zigzagged and weaved my way around the Goldsmith Foundation donors and groupies who liked to hang around the Goldsmith Foundation donors. Focused on the drink tray, I didn't notice the girl until it was too late.

I tried, unsuccessfully, to sidestep and, of course, plowed right into her. She was shorter than me, with a solid build, which was probably a good thing, or the impact would've sent her flying right out of her black high heels.

"I'm so sorry!" I grabbed her arms to steady her. The pink drinks and their umbrellas disappeared from view. "Shit," I muttered under my breath and refocused on the girl. It took a second to realize that I knew this person in the fancy black dress. Embarrassment bubbled up from the bottom of my stomach, making my cheeks hot and my ears burn. I'd nearly flattened the daughter of the head of the Goldsmith Foundation.

"Kate! Oh my God. I'm so sorry."

The corner of her mouth lifted, and two dimples creased her cheek.

My stomach did a weird flip-flop, a cross between horror and something else. Kate Goldsmith went to Stuyvesant, too.

Last year, we'd been in the same Intro to Bio class. She'd sat a desk ahead of me but had a different lab partner. We hadn't shared more than a periodic hello and goodbye. Even though she didn't seem overly snooty, she ran with a crowd I tried to steer clear of. She was born into money, and I worked for mine. That drew a pretty clear delineation in our social strata.

Kate narrowed her eyes and gave me a sideways look, the half-grin still in place. "Mikala, right? From Bio. You ought to slow down. I think the speed limit is thirty in here."

I laughed. I was so out of my element. Why hadn't I stayed home, where I was safe with my books and Walkman and it didn't matter what embarrassing comments might escape my lips?

I said, "Just call me Flynn. Otherwise you'll sound like my grandmother." I glanced around again. "Speaking of, she sent me on a mission for one of those obnoxious pink beverages people are drinking, and I was hot on the trail when I nearly took you out. Gotta run." I took a step away, and she grabbed my elbow to stop me.

"The ones with the umbrellas?"

"Exactly."

"Come on." She slid her hand down my arm, grabbed my hand, and gave it a tug. "Let's see if we can find that for her."

Fifteen minutes and much giggling later, we'd chased three different waiters through the crowded Grand Foyer and finally caught up with one. We each nabbed a Jersey Girl—stupidest drink name ever—and found Tubs. She'd drifted away from where I'd left her and was talking to a couple of people who looked vaguely familiar.

Tubs lit up when we handed her the glasses. "Why, it's a twofer. Thank you." She looked Kate up and down. "Who's this pretty lady?"

"Kate, meet my grandmother, Leahlabel Flynn. Kate and I go to Stuy together."

"You can call me Tubs," my grandmother said.

Kate shot me a weird look and then said, "Nice to meet you."

"And you as well." Tubs beamed. "It's nice to see Mikala with a friend. It's a rare occurrence."

Oh my God. I loved Tubs, but sometimes I wished she'd keep her mouth shut. My ears got hot again.

Kate said, "You've got a sweet, smart granddaughter."

It was my turn to give *her* a weird look. An entire semester of casual greetings, and in fifteen minutes, she decided I was sweet and smart? Wow.

"I certainly do," Tubs said. "Since I can't check my watch without dumping my beverages, Mikala, can you stop gaping long enough to see the time?"

I closed my mouth and glanced at my watch. "A little after seven."

"Okay. We've still got forty-five minutes before they begin seating. Would you mind running down to my office and grabbing the *Faustian*? If it's not on my desk, it should be on the bookshelf under Petropoulous."

"Yeah, sure." Perfect excuse to get the hell out of Dodge and enjoy some peace and quiet for three seconds.

Tubs handed me her key card and dove back into her conversation.

I gave Kate a quick shrug and rueful grin. "Sorry to run, but..."

She took my arm again and steered me away from Tubs and company. "What's the *Faustian*?"

"It's about art the Nazis looted in World War II."

"I'd love to see it. Can I come with you?"

Come with me? *The* Kate Goldsmith wanted to come somewhere with me? Was the world about to end?

Kate gave my arm a squeeze. "Has anyone ever told you you're cute when you frown?"

What was happening?

"Sure," popped out before my brain had a chance to catch up to my mouth. "I mean no." *Jesus Christ, Flynn.* I tried again. "Sure, you can come, and no, no one's ever told me that."

"Well, they should've. Come on, let's go."

Apparently, Kate not only had a good sense of humor, but she was bossy, too. Of course she was. Her dad was the head of a multi-million-dollar foundation. Probably had to be bossy to make that work.

Man, I was so out of my league. What was I doing? I plowed our way through the foyer. Kate clung to my belt, practically plastered against my back so we didn't get separated. Five hundred people had to be packed in this foyer. The more the space filled, the hotter it became, and the more I wanted out.

The security door at the rear of the Grand Foyer led to a warren of business offices. By the time I passed Tubs' card over the black security box, I was sweating. The box beeped, and the red light turned green. I wrenched the door open, and we slipped inside. The door shut behind us with a thud, and I paused to let the cool air and silence swirl over me.

"Whew." Kate fanned her flushed face with a hand. "I hate these events. We all know Dad appreciates the support, but I'd sure rather be doing anything else."

"Who's we all?"

"My brother Will, my mom, and me."

"Aren't they going to wonder where you are?"

She lifted a shoulder. "I don't care. They probably won't notice unless I'm not at the table when they seat everyone for dinner. Wily Will snitched a whole bunch of those Jersey Girls and is probably puking in the bathroom, and my mom is probably still talking to the award coordinators. Too many 'probablys' for me. I was trying to escape when you ran into me."

"Uh..." I was such an idiot. "Sorry about that."

She glanced at me, her ice-gray eyes penetrating. They kind of reminded me of the storm clouds outside. "Are you kidding?" she said. "You saved me from a slow, painful death. Now, where's that book?"

I led the way through a maze of hallways and found my grandmother's office. Sure enough, the book was on her desk. I grabbed it and turned around.

Kate stood in front of the floor-to-ceiling bookcase, running her finger slowly along the shelf and reading titles aloud. "*Salt Mines and Castles: The Discovery and Restitution of Looted European Art. Nazi Looted Art. Art Treasures and War. Hitler's Art Thief: Hildebrand Gurlitt. The Nazis and the Looting of Europe's Treasures.* Wow. What does your grandmother do?"

I had a general idea, but no clue about the particulars. "She researches art provenance and coordinates exhibitions."

"Provenance?" Kate echoed. She slid the *Faustian* from my hands and turned it around so she could read the cover. "*The Faustian Bargain: The Art World in Nazi Germany.* I knew the Nazis looted art but didn't realize there was an entire library on the subject."

"Yeah." I'd been surrounded by the topic my entire life, so it didn't seem as foreign to me as it might to others.

"Provenance is the history of a piece of art. Ownership is traced back to its origins."

"Who knew I'd actually learn something tonight." Kate looked up from the book.

Her gaze was intense enough to scorch a hole right through me. My stomach flipped again. I blinked in an effort to buffer the connection and occupied myself by retrieving the book from her. "Come on, we better get this to Tubs."

Kate followed me out of the office. "Oh, yeah. Why do you call your grandmother that?"

Boy, she asked a lot of questions. "Don't know. Just always have. Her real nickname is Tubby."

The rest of the short trip back to the Grand Foyer was taken up discussing nicknames. Once we exited the offices, Kate took off to find her parents, and I hunted Tubs down and delivered the book. Before too long, dinner seating began. Hopefully that meant we were at least half done with this fiasco.

"Thank you," I said to the server after he'd removed my plate. All around me, people chowed down on their main entrees. The chicken hadn't been too bad, but the mixed vegetables were mushy. Yuck. I laid my napkin on the table in front of me and wished I could fast-forward time. Although, I had to admit, thinking about Kate Goldsmith was a strangely pleasant distraction.

Now, dessert still needed to be delivered, and somewhere along the way, the award ceremony would begin with the inevitable speeches by too many people who thought they were a lot more entertaining than they were. I blew out a painfully bored sigh.

Tubs paused momentarily in her conversation with an art donor to give my leg a pat. That was something I appreciated about my grandmother. She always checked to make sure I was okay, no matter where we were or what we were doing.

We were seated toward the back, and that made me happy because, when this was over, we could make a quick and easy escape. Waiting for five hundred people to filter out after the presentation had ended was no fun. Idly, I swirled ice in my water goblet and willed the freak show to get on the road.

Someone poked me in the back, startling me out of my attempt at mental telepathy. The poker poked again, and I turned around to see who it was.

"There's that frown I like," Kate said with a smirk. She lightly settled her hands on my shoulders.

Smack me with a feather. Kate Goldsmith was speaking to me again. And touching me. It was almost too much to comprehend.

"Hey," I managed. Yeah. Lame.

She said, "Come on. I know just the place we can go."

"I, uh—"

Tubs elbowed me. In addition to all of her other tricks, she had a weird ability to hear two conversations at the same time and keep track of both. "Go on," she said. "Just come back before nine thirty so you can escort me home." Yet another thing I loved about her. She twisted reality and somehow made doing things with her an honor instead of a chore.

I grinned. "Okay. Thanks, Tubs." Before I thought too much about it and balked, I followed Kate out of the Hall. She led me to a set of fire stairs, and we went down to the

Garden of Stones, my favorite place in the museum. After school sometimes, I'd wait there for Tubs to finish work.

The Garden was finished last year—a memorial to those who perished in the Holocaust and for those who survived. The Garden's creator, Andy Goldsworthy, was a British dude who specialized in combining sculpture with living things. He'd arranged eighteen boulders outside of the museum in a rectangular area that was maybe half the size of a basketball court. It faced the Hudson River. Then, he'd drilled holes in the rocks and planted dwarf oak saplings in them. The trees were still little, but as time went on, they'd grow tall and strong. They were supposed to somehow merge with the rock. It was a pretty cool idea, a reflection of how life could survive in the most unlivable of places.

I trailed Kate down a series of steps to the crushed gravel that made up the base of the memorial. The rain had stopped, but the concrete benches installed along one side of the garden were still puddled with water. A waist-high Plexiglas wall hemmed in the far end, and Kate pulled me through the stones and stopped at the wall.

"I love this place," she said.

"Me too. It's...peaceful, I guess."

"Yeah." She shifted to lean a hip against the Plexi. "You're interesting."

Interesting? Was that good or bad? "What did you expect?"

She looked across the black, open expanse of river. The lights of Liberty State Park and Jersey City, with its jagged landscape of skyscrapers, apartment buildings, and row houses, were softened by fog. It looked kind of like one of those impressionist paintings we learned about in art class.

"You're different than the kids I usually hang out with."

Probably because I didn't have dollar signs after my name. "How so?" My fingers curled around the drippy handrail attached to the wall. I was unsure I wanted to hear the answer.

"You're not trying to one-up anyone here, and you obviously don't care how you look."

Ouch.

"Oh crap. Wait," she backtracked. "No. That didn't come out right." She released what sounded like a frustrated breath and faced me. "What I meant was, you...you do what you want. You don't follow the crowd. I respect that."

Well, jeez. That wasn't so bad. I breathed out a laugh. I'd figured she was going to say that with me she was living dangerously by hanging out with trash from the other side of the river.

"And," she said, "you're kinda...cute."

What the hell? I ripped my focus from the blurry reflection of lights on the water to look at her again. My mouth opened, but I couldn't make anything come out.

"For a girl. You're cute for a girl, I mean."

Holy shit. My heart double-timed. Was she coming on to me? Hadn't she dated one of the lacrosse players last year? I wasn't sure about which team I batted for, but I knew kissing a guy made me want to hurl. Self-consciously, I tucked a few loose strands of hair behind an ear. "Thanks, I think. You're not so bad in that skimpy dress yourself."

The darkness muted the power of her gaze, but I felt its weight anyway. Kate finally released me from her devastatingly intense scrutiny and mirrored my stance, hands resting on the railing, staring off into the distance. "I suppose we should get back."

"Suppose so."

In silence, we backtracked through the garden and up to the Events Hall. At the entrance, Kate stopped.

Inside someone droned on in the midst of a speech. She said, "You made this night bearable. Thank you."

I gave her a roguish grin. "Anything for a damsel in distress. Although, I think I was the one in distress, trying to get my hands on those Jersey Girls. Thank *you*."

"Anytime."

I inhaled, about to ask for her phone or pager number. Just to touch base. Before I could open my mouth, she pressed her finger in the divot in my chin, smiled, and spun around to thread her way between the tables to her seat.

Tubs glanced at me as I sat and scooted the chair closer to the table.

"Have a good time with your girlfriend?" she asked.

My stomach flopped again. Stiffly, I said, "She's not my girlfriend."

A delighted smile lit Tubs' face. "Relax. It's just a turn of phrase. That's how we referred to friends of the same gender back in the last century." Differentiating between Tubs' teasing side and her serious side sometimes took more work than I was prepared for.

I bared my teeth in a faux grin and prayed for the night to end.

CHAPTER 2

"Hey, Flynn!" A familiar but unexpected voice startled the crap out of me. The pizza dough I'd been whirling hit the edge of the counter and then dropped to the floor with a heavy thud.

"Bombs away!" Joey of Joey's Pizzeria hollered. "Dough is money, ya know." He scrunched up his sweaty, red-cheeked face to let me know he was mostly kidding. Joey was a family friend, a beefy guy of maybe fifty, jovial, and always shiny from the heat of the huge oven that dominated the tiny boxcar-shaped store. The pizzeria might have been small, but we produced some mighty tasty pies when the dough didn't land on the floor.

Kate Goldsmith stood by the cash register at the end of the red-laminate counter that divided the minute kitchen from the equally minute waiting area.

I'd died when she'd said my name, and now, as she looked around at the aged interior of my part-time job, I died again. She wore a black choker, a rhinestone tank top, and designer jeans with artful frays that probably cost more than I made in a whole month.

I had on Levi's 501 jeans that were ripped, but that was because I'd worn them out and didn't feel the need to buy replacements until school was back in session. A flour-dusted, sauce-speckled apron covered my T-shirt and thighs, and I knew there had to be white smudges of flour on my face. Just the way I wanted someone like Kate to see me.

"Joey," I said, "can I take five?"

"Yeah, sure, kid."

I peeled the dough off the floor, tossed it into a garbage can, and approached the girl I hadn't been able to get out of my mind for the last week. On the way, I grabbed a damp rag, wiped my hands off, and then rubbed them dry on the inside of my apron.

"What are you doing here?" I asked.

"Well," she drew the word out, "I meant to ask you for your number last Saturday, but things happened too fast. So, here I am."

I leaned against the counter and crossed my arms. Might as well be direct. What's the worst that could happen? "I was thinking the same thing."

A smile spread across her face.

"How'd you find me?" I wondered if I was being chick-stalked and didn't even know it. Where was the fun in that?

"My mom talks to your—Tubs, and Tubs talks about you all the time."

"Awesome." Just what I wanted to hear. "So—"

"So," she echoed and, for the first time, looked somewhat uneasy, "I was um...wondering...if you might be interested in a date—no!" She slapped a hand over her mouth, and I raised my brows. Her words came out in a rush. "Not exactly a date, I mean...er...wanna hang out sometime?"

This time, I couldn't stop grinning. "Yeah. I'd like that."

"When do you get off?"

"Off?" My voice actually squeaked. "Off, as in today?"

"Yeah. Why not? I have nothing but time to waste."

Holy shit. A not-exactly-a-date sounded great after I'd had some time to panic and sweat and worry about what

I was going to wear, and in a perfect world, it wouldn't be my pizzeria duds. But then how often is the world perfect?

I glanced over my shoulder at Joey, who was working a new batch of dough to replace what I'd fumbled. "Hey, Joe."

"Yeah?"

"I'm done in an hour; you care if I bail early?"

"Nah. Go ahead."

"Thanks, man." I untied my apron and glanced at Kate, still stunned she was standing in front of me. "Give me five, and I'll meet you out front."

I snagged two slices of pepperoni pizza as we left the shop, and we munched on them as we meandered up Henry Street toward the Brooklyn Bridge. The pizza allowed me to keep my mouth busy so I didn't have to speak. I had no idea what to say.

It was unbelievable that Kate had sought me out. Me. The kid who tried to remain aloof, who hung on the fringe, who stayed as far away from the drama and bullshit that came from running with the "in" crowd as I could. I'd never been a follower. I was content to do my own thing. Moving to an uptight, one-upping environment hadn't altered that worldview.

Kate finished before I did, probably because she wasn't trying to delay the inevitable. She said, "I hope you don't mind me showing up like this."

I stuffed the last of the crust in my mouth and shook my head. Once I swallowed, I said, "No. Not at all. Bit of a shock, but a good one."

Her dimples dimpled again. "Whew. I debated for three days on whether or not this was a good idea."

"Good idea. Definitely a good idea."

We stopped at the corner of Henry and Cranberry. Ruffino's, one of my favorite corner stores, had its door propped open to let in the fresh air. It'd been a nice day—all blue skies and puffy white clouds, mid-seventies, and not so humid. At half past seven, the sidewalk cafes, bars, and eateries were in full swing. The pace of the neighborhood ebbed and flowed—unlike Key West, where things started slow, wound up through the day, and stayed crazy long into the night.

"Hey," I said, "want something to drink?"

Five minutes later, we exited Ruffino's with a bottle of Surge for me and a Diet Coke with Lemon for Kate and wandered down Cranberry toward the waterfront. She twisted the lid off her soda and took a swallow.

"How's that furniture polish?" I asked.

She gave me a nudge with her shoulder. "Smart-ass. I like my furniture polish just fine, thank you."

I tried to downplay the thrill that shot through me at her touch but couldn't think of anything more to say.

Thankfully, Kate did a better job of small talk. "So, I hear you're from Key West."

Wow. I shot her a sideways glance and downed some of the green stuff. "You've been busy, haven't you?"

"You're...intriguing. All tall, dark, and moody."

That did summarize me pretty well. I laughed. "Okay, then."

Kate's presence made my thoughts scatter, and I struggled to pull my head together. "Let's see. I actually lived here, in Brooklyn, with Tubs from when I was little until just after I turned six. My dad was in the military, and his position kept him moving around a lot. Once it was time for me to start school, Tubs convinced him he needed to settle down and be a real dad. He accepted a permanent post at the Naval Air Station in Key West and brought me down to live with him."

"He hauled you from here all the way to Florida? That must've been hard."

I shrugged. "I didn't think about the transition as being either easy or hard. Just the way it was. But when I look back at how things played out, it certainly wasn't always fun in the Florida sun. But I adapted. Sure missed Tubs a lot, though. My dad was pretty good about bringing me to visit." I went silent for a minute, thinking about that last trip I'd made with my father. It was just after school let out for the year, only a couple of weeks before that shit-ass day when my life blew up. When all our lives blew up.

Kate's gaze was glued to me, and I wondered just what she'd found out playing private eye. My best guess was, at some point, Tubs had told her mom and dad why she was suddenly taking care of her granddaughter again. What had gone down wasn't a secret, but also wasn't something I talked much about.

"Can I ask you another question?"

I gave her the slit eye. "Maybe." *Please don't let it be about my dad.*

"Where's your mom?"

Whew. That was an easy one. "Early in my father's first deployment, he'd been stationed for a while in western Italy. As the story goes, a pretty Italian girl from the town of Terracina worked in a café near the base. He fell for her long black hair and kind eyes. She fell for his charm. Nine months later I came along. Apparently, things were great for a while until she drowned while swimming in the ocean when I was about one and a half."

Kate's eyes went so wide it was almost comical. "Flynn. Oh, my God. I'm so sorry. I never would've asked—"

I held up a hand. "It's okay. I don't remember her, and it's a little like she was never there in the first place." Deep breath. "All right. Enough about me." I let that hang for a second. "There's an ice cream place off Water Street, near the piers. Then, it's your turn for the inquisition."

Those gray eyes searched mine. Once she realized I was good, she lit up like a sparkler. God, she was adorable.

She said, "Lead the way, my shiny knight in chocolate syrup. I'll tell you anything for a hot fudge sundae."

Fifteen minutes later, we were seated at a table on the patio of Dumbo Creamery with a bowl filled with enough ice cream, fudge, whipped topping, and cherries to choke an elephant—that's what my dad used to say every time he brought me here. When I was a lot younger, I thought Dumbo the Disney elephant made all the ice cream in the world. Much later, I learned that Brooklyn's DUMBO meant Down Under the Manhattan Bridge Overpass and regular old humans churned the cream. This had been our special place, and frankly, I was a little amazed I was sharing it with Kate.

Across the East River, the lights of Manhattan were beginning to twinkle, and the sight always sent a thrill down my back. "Your turn, Miss Goldsmith."

Kate licked ice cream off her lip. "What do you want to know?"

I tilted my head and regarded her. "It's Friday night. Why on earth are you slumming with me when you could be out with your friends? I'm sure they'd provide a hell of a lot more excitement."

Her eyes softened. "I've been watching you. In school, I mean. Not in a weird way."

"You have?" News to me. Interesting news. I'd had an eye on her too, somehow drawn to her energy. She was bubbly and cheerful and could change the tone of a classroom just by walking through the door.

"You're not like the kids from here." She spooned up some chocolate. "You're intense. You're really nice, even when others aren't."

"Tubs and Dad drilled that into me." I corralled one of the two cherries and popped it into my mouth.

"I saw you just before the end of the year helping that homeless person after a couple stupid football dickheads knocked her down in front of the school."

I remembered that incident vividly. We'd had a freak spring blizzard. Fat, heavy flakes deluged the city, and it was icy cold. Those two jerk jocks rampaged down the entire block before lumbering through the front doors of Stuyvesant.

A tiny elderly lady had been shuffling down the sidewalk, pulling a shopping cart through the snow. One of those idiots shoved her out of his way as they'd steamrolled past. She toppled in slow motion, like a bowling pin barely nicked by the ball. Her cart tipped over with her, scattering her belongings across the sidewalk. I helped round up her stuff and gave her the money Tubs had given me for lunch. She'd needed it way worse than I had.

Then, over the course of the next couple days, I'd hunted those two idiots down and made sure they'd paid for their thoughtlessness. One showed up to school with a black eye and the other a split lip. Neither talked about the fights they'd obviously been involved in. There were some benefits to being the daughter of a Special Forces soldier. Before my dad died, he'd taught me a lot about defending myself. "Just in case," he'd always said. "Better to know and never use the knowledge than find out you need the skill when it's too late."

I lifted a shoulder self-consciously. "It's what anyone would do."

Kate leaned toward me, her eyes intense. "No. It's not what anyone would do. I didn't see anyone stopping to help but you." She looked away. "I walked right by and did nothing."

How did this conversation become so serious? "Hey." I reached over and put a hand on her tightly clenched fist. Her skin was warm, and my stomach did its anticipatory flip-flop thing that I was beginning to associate with Kate. "Next time, I bet you'll be the one giving the assist."

"My friends laughed. Laughed at her and laughed at you for helping her. I told them to fuck off."

Holy shit. Kate Goldsmith told someone to fuck off? That made me feel...good? I scooped up a blob of whipped cream and swiped it on the end of her nose.

She laughed and grabbed a napkin to wipe off the white goo.

Time for a redirect. "What about you?" I asked and took another bite. The coolness of the ice cream soothed the not entirely unpleasant sensations that ping-ponged around inside me. "Hopes? Dreams? Big plans for the future?"

The smile that had tugged up the corners of her mouth vanished, and the playful twinkle in her eyes faded. Maybe I shouldn't have asked after all.

I opened my mouth to retract my words, but she said, "I have hopes and dreams, all right. But not so much big plans." She fixated on the napkin in her hands, twisted it, and huffed a sigh. "There's the great divide between what's assumed I'll do and what I want to."

"What do you mean?" This was the first time I'd ever seen such a serious look on Kate's face. Not that I'd studied her facial expressions up close before now.

She flipped her twisted napkin aside. "My father expects both my brother and me to follow him into the family business. The Goldsmith Foundation." She deepened her voice. "The Goldsmiths always do what's expected of them."

I raised a brow. "Your dad speaking?"

"Yeah," she said morosely and scooped up another bite.

"So, if you could do what you wanted, what would it be?"

In a heartbeat, her expression shifted from almost sullen to vital, animated. She leaned toward me. "I'd join up with International Volunteer HQ."

Okay. "Is that like the Peace Corps or something?"

"Kind of, but better. Check this out. It's based in New Zealand, but they do stuff in something like thirty countries. You can get involved in some crazy cool things. What I really, really want to do is go to Sri Lanka and help with a project involving wild elephant conservation. Or, if I can't get into that, they have another group working on Buddhist temple renovation and restoration." She practically bounced in her seat. The table shook as her foot vibrated like a jackhammer. "Animals and architecture. My two favorite things. Once I volunteer for a year or two, I want to go to architecture school so I can create spaces that mean something to people. I want to meld concrete and rebar and wood and glass into something that speaks to the heart. Maybe incorporate animals into it somehow. Or not."

Holy crap. I felt like I was watching a flower open in the summer sun. "Wow, that sounds cool."

"A friend of my mom's volunteered last year and had the most amazing experience. She went to Costa Rica and helped with a turtle conservation project. She said it was life changing."

"So why don't you do it?"

It was as if the power source she'd been plugged into was suddenly cut. She literally shrank into herself, and her voice dropped. "My dad would never okay something like that. He practically forced Will into a business degree. That's the same route he expects me to take."

I took another scoop of rapidly puddling ice cream and pushed the bowl toward her. "Finish it."

She slowly scraped her spoon against the bottom of the bowl. "I think that might be why Will parties as hard as he does. To block out reality."

That would suck. To know exactly what you wanted to do with your life and not be able to do it had to seriously bite. "Can't you explain how you feel to your dad?"

Kate licked her spoon off, tossed it into the bowl, and sat back with her arms crossed, gazing at a ferry on the river for a few beats. "I've tried. Mom's on my side, but he doesn't want to listen to her either."

I'd grown up under both Tubs and my father's expectation that I give my all to whatever I chose to do, but it was always clear that the actual choices were mine to make. Maybe that's why I felt so adrift now—lack of expectation?

Actually, knowing me, if anyone tried to force me onto a path I didn't want to travel, I'd fight tooth and nail anyway, so expectation probably wouldn't matter. I'd never be able to follow a predetermined path. I was way too stubborn, too independent. The thought of being told how to run my life made me feel antsy. And from watching Kate's personality shift now, it was easy to see the prospect of filling her dad's shoes drained the life right out of her.

"Can't you just say no?" I asked. "Tell him you're not going to do it? What's the worst that would happen?"

She ran a hand through those golden locks and pulled her hair away from her face for a second before letting it drop. "I don't think he'd pay for architecture school. And I obviously can't fund it myself."

"What about loans?"

"I don't even want to ask. I can't stand the thought of another lecture about the importance of our Jewish heritage and keeping the Foundation going."

"Couldn't someone else take over?"

"Not in my dad's eyes. It's Will and me." She thumped a fist against the table, and the empty bowl jumped. "Enough about my boring life. What about you? What's your future look like?"

My own prospects paled in comparison to either Kate's probable reality with the Foundation or her wishful future in architecture and animals. Yeah, Flynn. You're the one with choices. What are you going to do with *your* life?

It was my turn to stare blankly across the water.

"That you, Mikala?"

I rolled my eyes, closed the front door, and bolted it before tossing my backpack onto the recliner a couple of steps away. "Who else would it be?"

The top of Tubs' head was barely visible across the countertop separating the galley kitchen from the combined dining/living room. "You hush," she said.

The two-bedroom apartment wasn't large. In the living room, an old twenty-seven-inch TV that probably weighed a hundred pounds sat on a stand against one wall. A well-used green recliner and a couch—with pillows perfect for propping up one's head while reading—faced the TV.

An ancient quilt was folded over the back of the couch. It'd been there as long as I could recall. My great-grandmother had made the quilt from cloth scraps she'd collected in the ghetto, and baby Tubs had been swaddled in it when she was sneaked out of Lodz. In fact, a number of items harkening back to those dark days were scattered throughout the apartment.

In a tall hutch on the dining room wall was a collection of World War II memorabilia that went right along with Tubs' view of education. In her house, a broad range of knowledge and a solid understanding of history were, as she often repeated, "The keys to civilized society and insurance that history's mistakes aren't repeated. It's imperative we never forget the mistakes of the past."

When I was little and in the "why, why, why" phase, we'd take excursions to whatever location she thought might help illuminate her explanations. She knew staff at most of the museums throughout the city, and boy, did that open doors to places the general public rarely got to see. When I took the time to think about all the crazy things she'd done to indulge me, I realized I'd been a damn lucky kid.

In contrast to the heavy history behind some of Tubs' keepsakes, she'd decorated the walls with colorful Georgia O'Keefe prints, making the place a lot less museum-esque. While I missed my life in the Keys, this tiny apartment was home now.

A chest-high bookcase filled with the strangest mixture of books I'd ever seen, sat across the room from the hutch. The shelves contained tomes on looted art, the history of Hitler and the rise of the Third Reich, some Stephen King, Patricia Cornwell, Clive Cussler, and Sue Grafton mysteries, a few Harlequin romances, and my favorite, three collections of Snoopy cartoons.

I made a beeline for a bowl of peanut M&Ms that was ever-present on the round dining room table and scooped up a handful.

"Are you hungry?" Tubs asked from the kitchen as she set a hot casserole pan on the stovetop. "I made Sarmi."

"I am now." Ice cream or not, I'd eat her Sarmi—a Romani recipe for stuffed cabbage rolls—any time.

As a baby, when Tubs'd been smuggled out of the ghetto by her father's uncle, his family had taken her in, and they'd fled to Ireland, where she'd been raised in the Roma tradition. That's where she'd met my grandfather, Harlan Flynn, and left the wanderer life when she was seventeen. Luckily, she'd filed away in her head some of the ethnic recipes she'd learned as a child, and when she felt the need for comfort food, that's what she fell back on. After living with Tubs, those recipes had become my go-to comfort foods too.

Ten minutes later, we were both settled at the table, snarfing down the cabbage rolls and sopping up sauce with thick slices of homemade bread.

"So," Tubs said after she swallowed a bite, "you're home late tonight."

She was right. I was supposed to have been off at eight, and it was now a quarter past nine. "A friend showed up at the pizzeria, and Joey let me leave a little early. We went to Dumbo's."

Tubs surveyed my now almost empty plate. "You're full of ice cream, and you still managed to fit three cabbage rolls in that belly?"

I grinned.

"You." She gave my cheek a love tap. Her fingers were gentle, and I leaned into them. "Was this friend the same one you ran into at the Goldsmith ordeal last week?"

My ears flushed with heat. They were goddamn emotional beacons.

A delighted smile spread across Tubs' face. "It's about time you find someone your own age to hang around with."

"But I love you and your evil cronies."

Tubs had an inner circle of six close friends, and they called themselves the Art Squad. Each of them worked in different positions within the art world. They got together every other week or so for coffee and gossip. When that crew got going, holy cow, you never knew what stories you might hear.

Rich was an artwork conservationist who stuttered when he got nervous; Beni Higuchi was a police sketch artist—what a totally cool job, plus she told great stories; Anton, the walrus-mustachioed gallery director, was super nice and super boring; Elizabet, a special effects makeup artist at the Jewish Theatre of New York, could transform anyone into anything. It was amazing. Then there was Char, a crackerjack art historian and one of the kindest people I'd ever met; and Sahl Hadad, an Arab estate appraiser who could've doubled as a comedian.

A couple of weeks earlier, Char, the art historian, had told me about a painting that had been missing for something like twenty years. Stolen from someone's collection during a burglary in Philadelphia, it eventually turned up in the living room of an art collector in the Bronx. He'd unknowingly purchased it, along with a number of other pieces, from a crooked dealer who'd falsified provenance documentation.

Not long after the purchase, the duped collector had thrown a big party to show off his recently acquired prizes. The Art Squad had been invited, and Char recognized the piece. Beni brought it to the attention of the FBI's Art Crime Team. Thanks to their intervention, it was eventually recovered and turned over to the original owners, who now lived in France. The family had given up ever seeing the artwork again. That was freaking awesome. The collector had lost the money he'd paid for the piece. Definitely not awesome.

Tubs took a sip of coffee. "I know you like the gang, but one of these days, you'll appreciate a more youthful outlook on life."

I stuck my tongue out, and she whapped my knuckles with a fork. We finished eating, and I cleared the table while Tubs happily filled the sink with hot dishwater.

"Thank you, my dear." She bopped me with her butt, nudging me out of the narrow kitchen. "Wipe the table and go relax. I'll finish up." She was so weird. She actually liked doing the dishes.

"Thanks, Tubs. I'll take care of cleanup tomorrow night."

"Deal. Oh, wait a second." She wrung out the dishrag and tossed it to me. I snagged it from midair, and she hefted the dishes into the soapy water and began humming.

I headed for the table but paused, as I often did, at the bookcase. On the very top, all by itself, rested a wooden puzzle box made in the shape of a house. It was maybe five inches tall and three inches wide. Two windows and a door were inlaid on one side, and two more windows were inlaid on the opposite. Various pieces of the box shifted, sliding back and forth. If you did it in the right combo, the house opened up.

The wood was worn smooth, darkened with age and oils from fingertips poking and prodding and attempting to uncover whatever lay within. Once, years ago, Tubs' aunt managed to break the code and open the box. Inside were three photos of Tubs' family, a locket, and a letter written by her father outlining the horrors they'd had to deal with after they'd been relegated to the Lodz ghetto.

When Tubs was spirited from the ghetto, this and one other puzzle box were smuggled out with her, all wrapped up tight in that quilt that lay over the back of the couch. Tubs' dad had been a woodworker, and he'd made puzzle boxes in the evenings after grueling ten and twelve-hour shifts in one of the many Nazi-run factories. We were never sure why he'd sent these two boxes with his daughter, but family legend held that they were supposed to stay with her, no matter what. Speculation about the contents of the second box had been rampant.

Tubs kept hers on the bookshelf and had given my father that second, unsolved box. He'd kept his on a dresser in his bedroom. Occasionally we'd take the box, which was about the size and shape of a hardcover book, out to the living room and work on opening it. When I shook the box, whatever was inside rattled just enough that I could hear it.

Three sides of my dad's box were concave, maybe two or three inches high. The top and bottom of the box hung over those sides by about a quarter inch. The fourth edge bowed out like the spine of a book. Inlaid on the top was a brown, upside-down triangle surrounded by four diamonds, and between the diamonds were four spades. On the outside perimeter of the diamonds and spades were six hearts. We'd surmised the hearts represented Tubs' family. And the rest? Who knew.

I could picture that box so clearly in my mind's eye, and its loss speared me in the gut. Whoever stole my father's life had also taken that puzzle box and, along with it, whatever secrets were hidden inside.

"Honey," Tubs said, "let it go. Wipe the table and get a good night's sleep. You work tomorrow at eleven?"

"Yeah, I do." Sometimes it freaked me the hell out how Tubs knew what I was doing even when she couldn't see me. I abandoned the box, carefully wiped down the table, then swung back into the kitchen, and tossed the rag into the suds.

Tubs rinsed a handful of silverware under running water. "I'm working tomorrow, so if you need me, you know where I'll be."

"Okay." I threw an arm over her shoulder and gave her a squeeze. "Love you."

"Love you too, sweetie."

Once I was settled in bed, memories of Kate and the time we'd shared washed over me, making me thrum with a feeling that was absolutely foreign yet eerily familiar. I was still in shock that she'd come all that way to see me. To see *me*.

My head sunk into the pillow. I was exhausted and wound up all at the same time. I closed my eyes and replayed the exact moment I'd heard Kate's voice in the pizzeria. The thrill of the memory zipped down my spine again. It was a feeling that would be all too easy to become accustomed to. And that was a problem. What would happen when school was back in session and all her snooty friends surrounded her? Did I think for one minute that her summer distraction with me would mean anything then?

Fat chance.

Fat chance or not, I drifted to sleep with the vision of Kate sitting across from me at the ice cream shop with that dollop of whipped cream on the end of her nose and a giddy grin as wide as the East River plastered across her face.

Chapter 3

Since Kate had been brave enough to cross the East River and visit me at work, I figured I could be brave enough to call her and see if she wanted to get together to watch Fourth of July fireworks.

We agreed to meet at the corner of Waters and Pearl at six and bum around South Street Seaport until the rocket's red glare burst off the barges in the river. I was stuck working at Joey's until five and then hauled ass over the Brooklyn Bridge into Manhattan.

The sidewalks were literally crammed with people. Native New Yorkers walked fast, heads down, trying to get from point A to point B as rapidly as they could. Tourists wandered along at half-speed, taking pictures, talking to each other, mouths agape at the wonders of Gotham.

I worked my way over to Fulton, then trekked the four or so blocks down to Pearl Street. The temperature was in the mid-eighties, and I was sweating by the time I reached the Titanic Memorial in front of the South Street Seaport Museum.

We'd agreed to meet at the base of the relocated sixty-foot lighthouse that had been built in honor of those who perished with the Titanic on that icy night in 1912. I didn't see Kate, but there were a number of our classmates milling around the area. Great. Maybe if I didn't look at them, they'd ignore me.

The lighthouse had been built on the tip of a triangular area roughly the size of a basketball court, maybe a little larger. A sea of pavement hemmed in three sets of trees, and a number of benches were scattered around. Most of the benches were occupied, some by kids I recognized and a lot by people probably doing the same thing we were, biding their time until the fireworks started.

For some weird reason, boulders of varying sizes, mostly knee-to-hip high, had been placed around the base of the lighthouse. One of them was unoccupied, so I claimed it and climbed aboard.

From my perch on top of the rock, I watched the ebb and flow of humanity scurrying past. Too many people. So different from Key West, especially during the off-season. Even through the winter, when snowbirds flocked like hungry pelicans to the southernmost point in the US, I could find places on the island to be alone, or mostly alone, anyway. Here, no matter where I turned, it always felt like someone was breathing down my neck. Usually it didn't bother me, but right now, surrounded by my uppity peers, it did.

I glanced at my watch: Six sixteen. I wondered if I'd gotten the time wrong or if Kate forgot. Or maybe she was standing me up. Yeah, that was probably what happened. Why would Kate want to spend the Fourth with me? She was probably on some fancy rooftop with her friends, maybe even staring down at me. Me—who was stupid enough to have believed someone like her would want anything to do with a kid like me.

"Hey!" a voice called, ripping me out of my malaise.

I turned around so fast I nearly fell off my three-foot-high boulder.

"Whoa," Kate said and grabbed my arm. At the touch of her hand, my breath caught until I regained my balance. I slid off the rock, and she let go. My stomach dropped at the loss of contact.

Flynn, you need to get yourself under control. Jeez.

"Thanks," I said, and it was then I realized Kate had someone I didn't recognize with her. The girl was shorter than me, with long black hair pulled back in a ponytail. She had sparkling brown eyes and a big smile that I couldn't help return.

"Flynn, Ursula Thiebaux. Urs, this is Mikala Flynn, but don't call her Mikala. She might bop you."

If it was possible, Ursula's smile grew even wider. "I think I'm gonna like this one." She was wearing shorts and a yellow and black T-shirt. The logo on the front of the shirt was a bird with widespread wings. Above it read *Central Park*, and below, *Hawks*.

I said, "You go to Stuy?"

"Yeah, I'm a year behind you and Miss Poke Along here."

"Hey," Kate said. "Easy. Not my fault I couldn't decide what to wear."

It was then I registered Kate's attire. She had on blue jean short-shorts and a purple one-shoulder stretch top that didn't entirely cover her chest. The skin that was exposed was tanned and toned. I swallowed hard and tried to think clearly. Then I remembered I should probably look at Kate's face instead of studying her cleavage. God, what an idiot.

"You look great, Kate," I muttered, losing myself for a second until Ursula noisily cleared her throat.

I blinked and cleared my own throat. "Okay. What's on the evening's agenda?"

Kate bit her bottom lip and scrunched her nose at me. Could she be any cuter? Gah. What was I thinking?

She said, "How about we walk around awhile and then grab a snack." She pulled a pager out of a miniscule pocket and pressed the button to light it up. "Six forty-five. Urs, who's on the Fulton stage next?"

Ursula pulled out a piece of paper and unfolded it. "Moldy Peaches at 7:00. The big boom's at 9:20." She stuffed the paper away and rubbed her hands together gleefully. "I love fireworks. Can't wait."

"Come on." Kate slid an arm through mine and one through Ursula's. "Let's wander."

For the next forty-five minutes, we explored the seaport. I learned Kate had met Ursula a couple of years earlier when Will, Kate's brother, had played hockey at Central Park's Lasker Arena. Urs, as Kate called her, was a hockey ace, a left-winger who was talented and smart enough that she was probably going to score a full ride to either Boston College, Wisconsin, or Minnesota.

"Wow," I said. "You sure have your future planned out."

Ursula lifted a shoulder. "Have to. I was born in Michigan, but I'm First Nations. My mom moved home to Nova Scotia when I was two, and that's where I grew up. My family sent me to Manhattan to live with my aunt when I began outplaying the boys in my age group back home. They have a lot of hopes pinned on my hockey success. I'll do anything I can to honor them."

I'd been walking along the edge of the sidewalk next to the street as we talked. A group of eight kids approached from the opposite direction, so I stepped closer to Kate to get out of their way. My arm bumped into hers, and for a second I felt her fingertips against my palm. Then the whisper of her fingers disappeared, and I wondered if I was hallucinating.

I said, "From the sound of it, Urs, you're going to do way more than honor your family. Good for you. One day maybe I'll get my own life in order."

Ursula leaned around Kate to look at me, pushing her into me again—not that I minded—and said, "Don't know what you want to do when you're done with school?"

I was silent a couple of beats. "No. I don't. I—" My words were cut off when someone slammed into me. I stumbled a couple of steps backward.

"Hey, look," an unfamiliar, gravely voice said, "Kate! Lookin' good, babe." I narrowed my eyes and tried to place him. He went to Stuyvesant, and oh, yeah. Now I locked on. He was a football player, a teammate of the two jerk-ass jocks I'd taken to task over that incident with the homeless lady. With him was a girl, a friend of Kate's—blonde, made up, and oozing arrogance. She was all over Mr. Muscles, with her claws practically embedded in his probably steroid-infused biceps.

Beside me, Kate stiffened, and the hairs on the back of my neck jumped to attention. She said, "Hey, Nate. Stella Ann."

Stella Ann? Who'd name a kid that? No wonder she was wound so tight.

Stella Ann looked at me, then sized up Ursula before turning her attention back to Kate. "I thought you told me you had other plans tonight." Huge hoop earrings dangled from her earlobes, and they jiggled when she spoke. She was dressed in a super-low-cut halter and jeans so tight she probably had to grease herself to get into them. Yup, one of the popular, stuck-up, rich girls.

I felt Kate inhale, and she held it a second. Then she said, "I did have other plans, Stella Ann. Right here with these two."

Stella Ann laughed, a high-pitched sound that I imagined might burst from a squealing hyena. Her cackle was ear piercing. Made me want to clap my hands over her mouth. It took her three squawking breaths to get herself under control. "You're with," she pointed at me and Ursula, "these dumbass losers?"

My blood began a slow boil. Bullies pissed me the hell off. I took a step forward, and Kate put her hand on my forearm.

"They're not losers, Stell. They're my friends."

Stella Ann whooped again. This time, I shook off Kate's hand. "Listen, Little Miss Hypocrite." I stepped closer. "Leave Kate alone. Leave us all alone and back the hell off." At this point I was nose to nose with the little snot.

Ursula took a long step and came even with me, effectively pushing Kate behind us, which was exactly where I wanted her, well out of harm's way.

"Wait a minute," Kate said. She attempted to wedge her way between Ursula and me. I had to admit we made a pretty good wall.

"Words are just words," Ursula said. Her voice was calm, and in contrast to my tense, nearly vibrating body, she appeared almost relaxed. "Words cannot hurt unless we let them. If Kate wants to hang with us for the evening, then that's exactly what she's going to do. Call us whatever names you want, but just remember, what you fling at others tends to come back and smack you where it counts. Now, why don't you two continue your little date and walk away."

Oh, crap.

Nate frowned, and it looked like either he was trying to figure out what Ursula had said or suddenly had a bad case of indigestion.

Stella Ann actually humphed. "Kate, we'll talk about this later. I'll call you." She pulled Nate away, and they disappeared into the crowd.

"You might call, but I'm not answering," Kate muttered under her breath.

I exhaled and looked at Ursula. "Holy shit, you've got wicked skills."

She smiled, her teeth glowing white against her dusky skin. "*Verbal Judo*. It's a great book." She prodded Kate's shoulder. "If all your friends are like that, you need to start hanging out with some new ones."

Kate shook her head once, as if she were trying to clear it. "You're absolutely right, Urs. I think I've reached my limit of entitled, pigheaded bitches. Come on. Let's go watch some fireworks."

Chapter 4

The summer of 2001 was possibly the best summer I'd ever had. After that fourth of July, Kate, Ursula, and I became the Three Musketeers of the Big Apple. On the days Ursula and I didn't work—she stocked shelves at a bodega in the Bronx not far from where she lived, and I kept Joey on his toes at the pizzeria—we'd all get together and roam the city like a pack of curious wolves. We became intimately familiar with Central Park, the New York Public Library, the Museum of Modern Art, and Battery Park and even found time to make two trips to the Statue of Liberty and Ellis Island.

For each of us, there was something magical about the 354 narrow metal steps up to the Liberty's crown. To me, the journey represented everything my father had stood for—strength of character and the belief that the impossible could be overcome with persistence and determination. Kate viewed Lady Liberty as a symbol of the freedom she wanted but didn't believe she could have. To Ursula, the Statue was an emblem of purpose and courage—a talisman, of sorts, that she drew on when the going got tough.

Each of us learned something about our personal histories. We spent hours running family names through genealogical computers trying to map our heritages. I found Tubs when she and hubby Harlan emigrated to the US.

Urs was First Nations, the Canadian equivalent of Native American. In our research efforts, she managed to find a few far-flung relatives who'd brought their families into the country. She was of the Mi'kmaq, or, as it was more commonly known, the Micmac band. One of the coolest things we learned was that in the mid-nineteenth century, the Micmac created the world's first hockey stick. Ursula had followed in her puck-chasing ancestors' footsteps with her stellar biscuit-in-the-basket ways. I had a sneaking suspicion Ursula already knew all that but didn't want to burst Kate's bubble when she enthusiastically filled us in. Ursula possessed a patient gentleness with her friends that I very much admired.

During both Liberty trips, Kate made detailed drawings and notations about the statue in a notebook she'd brought specifically for that purpose. I could totally see her designing buildings that went beyond four walls and a roof.

All too soon, summer came screeching to a halt, and we found ourselves back at school. Nothing had changed, and yet, everything had changed. I was a junior, still adrift, although maybe not as wounded as I had been. For the first time, I had two good friends my own age, and that was a huge change. Needless to say, Tubs approved.

The other realization I came to was the reason for the funny feeling in the pit of my stomach every time I was near Kate. Why it felt like sparks flew each time our hands brushed. Why I felt both thrilled and breathless whenever she rested her palm on my shoulder.

I wasn't allergic to the girl. I was attracted to her.

Her touch literally sent shivers down my spine. I liked Ursula, too, but in an entirely different way. No fires were kindled when she put a hand on me, no charged flashovers happened when she slung her arm around my neck. She was totally my sister from another mister, and I'd do anything for her. For either of them, for that matter. These two, with such vastly different backgrounds from my own, had somehow become my best friends.

I'd never had a real boyfriend—never wanted one—although, on a dare, I had kissed the son of my dad's Army buddy. That experience had left me wondering what the hell the big deal was. Now, based on my physical reaction to Kate's very presence, I'd bet anything that kissing her would blow that experience sky high. In fact, I had to admit that a favorite distraction while I pounded pizza dough at Joey's was daydreaming about what Kate's lips might feel like against my own.

Was I gay? Straight? Bi? Was it nothing more than an oddity that Kate brought these strange but amazing feelings out in me? I just didn't know. I did know Tubs wouldn't care either way. She was cool like that—had a few gay friends of her own, both male and female. She'd love me no matter what.

Then there was Kate herself. I didn't know where she ranked on the Kinsey scale. She was a flirt, and she flirted with everyone. Yet, in all the talking the three of us had done, that was a topic no one had ever brought up. The looks and lingering touches made me think she was feeling exactly what I was. But if I was wrong and she didn't feel the same way, it could destroy our friendship. I wasn't about to take that chance.

Kate still hadn't found the courage to talk to her dad about what she wanted to do with her life. Most of the time, she didn't bring it up with me, and when she did, she said she tried not to think about it. But this was her junior year, and she had to make some big decisions soon. I didn't want to add my complicated emotional mess to her burden. I became good at boxing my feelings up when we were together.

The three of us weren't going to get a chance to hang around together at school, and that totally sucked. Ursula, entering her sophomore year, was laser-focused on getting herself in shape for the upcoming hockey season, which was scheduled to start in mid-October.

The only class Kate and I had together was Environmental Science. The topic wasn't especially exciting, but the opportunity to hang with Kate during the last period of each day was. Even though we didn't have classes with Ursula, we all shared lunch, so at least we'd see each other then. Before summer had ended, we'd promised to stick together no matter what, but who knew how that would go. Kids always promised friendship forever, especially in yearbook autographs, but I knew better. Nothing lasts forever.

The first week of school whipped by like a hurricane. Kate didn't fall back in with her old clique, and I was relieved. She'd grown into a stronger, kinder person over the summer. She was so much better than her old friends in so many ways.

I straggled into Enviro-Sci, dumped my books on the lab table, and collapsed onto a stool next to Kate. Kids slowly filed in, and there was much chattering about who had what plans for the weekend.

Kate's textbook was open in front of her, and she glanced away to survey me. "You look like hell."

"Thanks." I was too tired to even flip her the bird. "Pre-calc is going to kick my ass, and I have no idea why I decided to take Early British Lit. I'm already behind, and it's only been three days. I'm drowning in words." I closed my eyes and frowned. "And numbers." I dropped my head into my hands.

"Poor thing."

I felt her hand on my hair. My senses snapped to attention. Then she slid down and began massaging my neck. Holy shit. I might've skipped dying and shot straight to heaven.

I mumbled, "I might bring you home and never let you go."

"I'd be fine with that. As long as Tubs cooks."

"Mmm," I groaned as her thumb found a knot. "That means I can keep you 'til Monday."

She laughed. "Why 'til Monday?"

"Tubs leaves for a four-day conference thing in DC. I'd have to cook for you then, and we both know how that would end up."

Her hand stilled on my neck, but she didn't remove it. "She's gone until Thursday?"

Her tone of voice made me sit up. She gave the side of my neck a final squeeze and traced my jaw with her thumb before pulling away. I tried to analyze if my imagination had gotten the better of me or if that extra caress had really happened. Then I realized her gray eyes were narrowed, and she had an intensely calculating expression on her face.

"Yeah." My stomach did its Patented Kate Flip. Could she possibly be thinking what I was? In a light voice, I said, "What's rolling around in that brain of yours?"

Her eyes sparkled like they did when she was planning something delightfully devious. "You should stay over while she's gone. I have a queen bed. There'd be plenty of room."

I wanted to leap into her lap. I restrained myself. Kate had visited my apartment numerous times, and we'd been to Ursula's once. But I'd never been to Kate's place. She lived in the Financial District, probably in some posh condo, complete with doorman and security to keep out the riff-raff. Her family had a boatload of dough, and I was intimidated as hell at the idea of going home with her. And then, the thought of spending the night in her bed...holy crap. How would I keep my hands off her?

Of course, even more awesome would be for her to stay at my place while Tubs was gone, but my grandmother made it very clear I was to have no one over in her absence.

I cleared my throat. "What would your parents think?"

"They wouldn't care. I've talked about you and Urs all summer. They want to meet you. Up close and personal, not like at the Foundation fundraiser where they caught a glimpse of you and that was about it."

I opened my mouth to answer, but the teacher shut the door with a bang. The room quieted quickly. He said, "Don't forget about our field trip to Battery Park Tuesday. I need those permission slips back by Monday, people."

Kate elbowed me and whispered, "See? We can leave from my place together, and you won't have to get up so early."

She had a good point. I was so not a morning person. "Okay," I said under my breath, wondering if I'd lost my mind. Nothing like leaping directly into the gaping maw of my unfulfilled desires. "Check with your parents, and I'll talk to Tubs."

Monday after school found us hoofing it toward Kate's.

"Are you sure they don't mind?" I asked for the tenth time as we neared 90 Williams, a silver-sided, multi-windowed, fifteen-story building.

"No! Let me say it again. No, no, no, they don't mind. Now, shut up and come on."

The feeling low in my belly wasn't excitement or the Patented Kate Flip. It was terror. I was about to enter a world far removed from my own. I shaded my eyes and looked up. The sun and puffy white clouds reflected off the shiny exterior. The main floor was taken up by businesses: a dry cleaner, coffee joint, nail salon, and a barbershop. I followed Kate to a corner entrance, and a doorman opened the door for us. Just as I'd anticipated.

"Thanks, Hans," Kate said, and we slipped into the foyer, all dazzling white marble from floor to ceiling. I almost needed sunglasses. To one side was a security desk, and straight ahead were three banks of elevators.

Kate led me to the elevators and pushed the up button.

The elevator dinged, and then the doors slid silently open. Of course they were silent. I imagined any problem was dealt with lickety split, not in a matter of weeks or months as sometimes happened at home.

We climbed aboard and floated toward the fifteenth floor.

"You okay?" Kate asked.

No. I was not okay, but I said, "Yeah," and tried not to think about my queasy stomach. I was about to meet the high-society, rich-as-hell Goldsmiths of the prestigious Goldsmith Foundation. The parents of a girl I might have been falling in love with. I did not belong here.

A wry smile tugged up a corner of her mouth. "No, you're not okay." She grabbed my hand and squeezed it. I was so nervous I didn't feel the usual blast of heat from her touch.

"But you're going to be. Trust me. They'll love you. They already know you through Tubs, anyway."

It took me a moment to realize the elevator had stopped and the doors had opened. Kate pulled me out and down a hall that zigged one way and zagged another, past one apartment labeled 15A. We finally came to a stop at 15B.

Kate unlocked the door and swung it open to reveal an octagon-shaped, tiled entry. "We're home, Mom," she called.

"Hi, honey. I'm just about to leave for a meeting." Mrs. Goldsmith was decked out in a teal pantsuit, black heels, and a matching teal purse. She strolled down the hall toward us, all elegant and self-assured. "Mikala, hello, sweetheart."

"Hey, Mrs. Goldsmith." I'd occasionally spoken to her on the phone when she called Tubs but hadn't actually seen her until the Goldsmith fundraiser at the Museum of Jewish Heritage last June. Where this whole...thing...began.

"Make yourself at home. Dinner's in the fridge. Pop the casserole in the oven at three-fifty for forty-five minutes."

This family knew what a casserole was? Wow.

With that, she slid past us and crossed the threshold into the outer hallway. "I'll be back about nine, and your father won't be home 'til late. See you two later." With that, she wiggled her manicured fingers and disappeared around the corner.

Kate shut the door and locked it. "She's on too many boards. Come on, I'll give you the grand tour."

I followed her into a room immediately off the foyer.

"This is Dad's office." She abruptly stopped next to the desk. I put a hand against her back to steady myself. Her skin was warm beneath the cotton of her Moldy Peaches T-shirt. I let my hand linger as I looked around.

It could've been an office anywhere. The requisite desk was a behemoth, all glossy dark wood. Files were piled askew on one side, with a computer monitor centered in the middle. In front of the monitor were sheaves of papers, Post-it notes, and other bits of scribbling on scratch paper. A phone and a small lamp took up the rest of the space on the desktop.

Who knew? Apparently the rich and famous could be messy too.

A black leather love seat sat at a forty-five degree angle on one side of the room, and behind it was an entire wall of shelves full of war-related relics. Which only made sense, considering the foundation the Goldsmiths owned had risen like a phoenix from the rubble of *Kristallnacht*—the Night of Broken Glass—when Mr. Goldsmith's father's jewelry store had been looted and burned by the Nazis.

I stepped closer. There were so many objects—an old black shoe, a cracked pocket watch, various pieces of jewelry in clear boxes.

Kate said, "Each of those was recovered by my grandfather after his store was destroyed. Dad always says we can look, but if we touch, he'll find out and chop our fingers off."

"Man. Unbelievable." I felt like I was in someone's personal museum, which I supposed I was. "What horror people can inflict on each other..." I trailed off. Something on a lower shelf caught my eye, and I took a step closer. What? Was that—Oh, my God. I skirted the couch, put my hands behind my back, and leaned forward, trying to get a better look.

Plain as day, a carved puzzle box sat between an old cigar box and a tarnished silver beer stein engraved with German writing. The puzzle box looked exactly like the one that had been taken from my father's house in Key West.

Could it be... No way.

Absolutely no way was it the same one. I itched to reach out and pick it up and take a good look at it. My dad's box had a crack on one corner, not big enough to make it unusable, but enough to make it memorable. The corners on the front of this box looked intact, but I couldn't see the back of it. It nearly killed me not to reach out and grab it, turn it around, and check it out.

Really, what were the chances that my family's puzzle box could've made its way to Kate's father's collection? "All this stuff," I said slowly as I stood, "did it come directly from the store after it'd been ransacked?"

"Some, but not all. My dad's hunted for items that could be traced back to my grandfather's shop. I think in the last couple years, he's found two or three pieces. It's so weird. He has to buy them—buy them back, I guess."

Was it possible Kate's dad bought my family's ghetto heirloom? Could he have had something to do with the attack on my father? No. That was ridiculous. I needed to stop this train before it derailed me completely. No way could this be our puzzle box.

Abruptly, I spun around and nearly knocked Kate into the couch. I grabbed her, yanked her into me, and wrapped my arms around her. My frontal lobe told me it was to keep her from tipping over, while my lizard brain started cheering. God, she felt good. Too good.

Kate laughed, and I immediately stepped away. "I'm sorry." I said. My ears burned red hot. "For almost leveling you, I mean."

"Feel free to do that again. Any time. Come on." With that she flounced out of the room. It took me a second to realize I needed to follow her. Did she mean feel free to bodycheck her into the couch again or feel free to wrap my arms around her?

Jesus. I was completely discombobulated, and we'd been alone in her house for less than five minutes. Thankfully, Kate seemed blissfully unaware of my inner turmoil. She pointed out the bathroom next to the office and moved on. We followed the L-shaped hall past Kate's room on the left, kitty-corner from the kitchen on the right. Next came Kate's brother's bedroom. Since he'd left for college and lived in an apartment close to campus, Kate told me Mrs. Goldsmith had threatened to turn it into a sewing room. But for now, it still displayed the usual posters and paraphernalia of an adolescent boy.

At the end of the hall was Mr. and Mrs. Goldsmith's room.

We backtracked to the kitchen, which was as big as Tubs' living room and dining room combined.

"Want some soda?" Kate asked.

"Sure."

She opened the fridge. "Root beer or Pepsi?"

"Root beer's good."

While she did her thing, I checked out the rest of the kitchen. Black countertops with white speckles. Shiny pots and pans hung from a grid suspended above a butcher block-topped center island. Sure didn't look like something as simple as a casserole might come out of here. "Nice kitchen," I said.

Kate's voice echoed from within the silver behemoth. "Mom loves to cook. In themes. This week it's comfort-food-casserole week. Last week was Chinese. Kinda weird, I know."

Yeah, a little, but I was smart enough to keep that thought to myself.

In the middle of the island was a bowl of fruit exactly like you might see in a watercolor painting. Was the fruit real or fake? It all looked way too perfect to be edible. Curiosity overcame propriety, and I reached a finger toward a brilliant red apple. Kate closed the fridge door, and I jerked my hand back fast. By the time she turned around, it was safely stuffed in my pocket.

I cracked open the top of the A&W she handed me, took a slurp, and then followed her through the dining room, past a gigantic oak table that seated eight, and into the living room.

The living room was dominated by a window the size of a movie screen that looked west across the city. I could almost see the Jersey shore past the Twin Towers. They must've paid a pretty penny for that view.

A black leather, U-shaped sectional sofa surrounded a humungous projection TV. I sure wouldn't have minded settling in with a bowl of popcorn and doing some heavy-duty TV time in front of that monstrosity.

The framed works of art hanging on the walls weren't prints. They were the real things. At least this room was much brighter and lighter than Kate's dad's office with its dark wood, dark furniture, and dark memories. That thought brought me back to that damn puzzle box.

Kate said, "Let's bring your stuff into my bedroom and do a little homework."

"Okay. Lead the way."

Twenty minutes later, we lay side by side on Kate's bed, textbooks forgotten as she showed me brochures for the volunteer program she so desperately wanted to get into. Her arm pressed against mine, and my skin felt strangely sensitive to her every move. I ached for more. I wanted to caress her cheek and kiss those pouty lips.

"...and then if I can't—Flynn! Where are you?"

I ripped my gaze from those incredible lips. "What?"

She threw the brochure over her shoulder, rolled toward me, and shifted onto her side.

"Kate, what are you doing—"

The lips that I'd coveted for so long were suddenly on mine. My words died in my throat. Kate was kissing me. Holy shit, Kate Goldsmith was kissing me!

Once I recovered enough to realize this wasn't another daydream, I parried enthusiastically and pulled her body tight against mine. God, she felt good. As my lips memorized hers, I ran my hands slowly down her back and palmed her gorgeous butt. The movement made her groan, and that may have been the sexiest sound I've ever heard.

We eventually broke apart, breathless and wide-eyed. Kate propped herself on an elbow above me, a half-amazed, half-amused look on her face. Our legs were entwined, and one of my hands had found its way beneath her shirt. The skin on her back was amazing, so incredibly smooth, so incredibly hot. I felt like I was burning alive.

She dipped her head and kissed me again, gently biting my bottom lip, then soothing with her tongue before pulling away.

My brain was mush. "I...what? Wow."

"I've wanted to do that since last June."

"Buh—"

Jesus, Flynn. Pull yourself together. If I were a boy, I probably would've already shot off like a bottle rocket. I slid a hand up into her glorious hair and pulled her to me again. I took the lead, slowly investigating every inch of her mouth, her tongue, her lips. I'd always been better at showing than I was at telling anyway. When we broke the kiss, we weren't a frenzied, gasping mess. She'd calmed down; I'd calmed down. Holy shit, in that moment, I understood what people meant when they talked about fireworks between two people. And neither of us had done anything that went beyond PG-13.

"All I can ask," I said as I trailed my knuckles over her cheek, "is what took you so long?"

After a lengthy make-out session interspersed with a lot of talk about why didn't we do this sooner, we heated up the enchilada casserole Kate's mom had left us and chowed down like we hadn't eaten in days.

We laughed about the surprise of that first kiss and the longing gazes we both thought we'd hidden from each other. Kate told me she caught me checking out her ass more than once, and I admitted that, somewhere along the line, my feelings for her had shifted from simple friendship into something much deeper, but I'd been too afraid of losing her to tell her.

"You're a chicken, Flynn." She gave me a smirk. "But a pretty tasty chicken. I wonder if other parts of you taste like chicken too."

Holy shit. There was that deadly flirty Kate again. A bolt shot straight to my chicken parts, and I shuddered. "You're going to kill me." I paused, wondering if I even dared to ask the question that loomed in my head. At this point, why not? "Have you ever, uh..."

Kate waited a couple of beats and, when I didn't continue, said, "Done the dirty deed?"

I nodded. "You dated that lacrosse player last year." I hoped I didn't sound accusatory, but I probably did. Just the thought of that apelike boy-man touching her... I shoved that thought out of my head fast.

"Jack the Jock?" She rolled her eyes. "He would've loved it if I'd said yes. But no, things never went that far... Far enough to know he did absolutely nothing for me."

Her brow crinkled. "If fact, none of the boys I've ever dated came close to making me feel a fraction of what you do. And no, I've never gone all the way with anyone."

She drilled me with that killer gaze. Her eyes were filled with lust and longing and maybe something else. My breath caught in my chest. This was crazy. What were we doing? Was I a lesbian? Was she? Was this some experiment destined to blow up in our faces? Did I care? No, I decided. I cared about this person who was looking at me like she wanted to consume me whole.

Kate polished off the last of her enchilada and took a sip of water. "What about you?"

I burst into flustered laughter. This was crazy. Discussing our sex lives, or lack thereof, over enchiladas was insane.

"What?" Kate looked like she might throw her water on me to startle me out of my hysterics.

I explained my train of thought and, when I was done, waited warily for Kate to say something.

All humor drained from her face. "Flynn, I don't know that I've considered being with a girl before you came along, but this," she put a hand on top of mine, "feels right to me. Way more right than I've felt with any of the boyfriends I've had. I'm willing to play this out, see where it'll go. I like you, Flynn. I like you a whole lot."

I smiled, delighted, and I thought my heart might burst. I said, "Me either."

"Me either what?"

"I haven't, ah, slept with anyone either."

"Then we're two-of-a-kind, aren't we?" She leaned toward me, and I met her halfway to cup her cheek as I caught her lips with mine. She tasted of cheese and red sauce, and I couldn't get enough.

"Girls, I'm home!" Mrs. Goldsmith's voice floated into the dining room from the foyer along with the sound of the front door slamming shut. We jerked apart, scrambling to rearrange the expressions on our faces from guilty to innocent.

Kate grabbed our dishes as her mom rounded the corner into the kitchen.

"There you two are." Mrs. Goldsmith set her purse on the counter. "You're just eating now?" She apparently wasn't waiting for a response, because she followed that up with, "Anything left?"

"More than enough," I said and helped clear the table. "I think Kate left the casserole in the oven to keep it warm. The enchiladas were great. Thank you."

"Yeah, Mom, thanks." Kate scooped up the cups I'd set on the breakfast bar and stuck them in the dishwasher.

"You're both welcome. Glad you liked it." She pulled a clean plate from the cupboard and loaded it up.

I asked, "How was your meeting, Mrs. Goldsmith?"

Mrs. G gave me the kind of look an adult gives a kid when they've done something right. "Thank you for asking, Mikala. I've spent the last three months working with four different organizations to change city code. We want to encourage a shift toward sustainable development. I have one last meeting tomorrow, and I think everything's going to be a go."

I asked, "What's sustainable development?"

"It's a great idea," Kate said as she came out of the kitchen and sat back down. "It's one of the reasons I want to get into architecture."

I followed Mrs. G and her enchilada-laden plate to the table and settled into a chair beside Kate. I made a conscious effort not to touch her, and boy, was that hard. It was like once we let that genie out of the bottle, it was next to impossible to shove it back in.

While Mrs. G ate, we talked about green buildings and how they were good for the city. I'd never heard about environmentally responsible construction or how these kinds of green buildings helped use less fossil fuels. By the time Mrs. G finished eating, I thought the entire concept was a great idea.

"It can be quite complicated." Mrs. G pushed her plate away. "Coordinating everything between the client and the design teams, the engineers, architects, landscapers, electricians...all the pieces of the puzzle that go into it."

Puzzle. Puzzle box. Damn, was every little thing going to remind me of that box sitting no more than twenty-five feet away? Valiantly, I tried to shove it out of my mind while we talked. I totally gained a new appreciation for Kate's mom by the time we said our goodnights just after ten. What a really cool lady.

Once Kate shut her bedroom door, I asked, "Does your mom knock before she comes in?"

"What?" She looked at me, raised an eyebrow, and said, "Oh. Oh, yeah. Definitely."

I hoped she was right as I backed her up to the bed. Kate wound her arms around my neck, and I whispered hotly against her lips, "This sleepover business was the best idea you've ever had."

CHAPTER 5

My lids felt glued to my eyeballs. Where the hell was I? Why couldn't I move? Then memory slammed home, and suddenly I was wide awake. Holy shit. I was flat on my back in Kate's bed. She was half-sprawled on top of me, an arm across my middle and one leg over mine. Her head rested inches away, and I could feel her exhale against my cheek. In and out, the sound so even, so sure.

The room was pitch black. Trying not to wake her, I slowly rolled my head toward her nightstand—2:34 a.m.

We'd made out for a long time before falling asleep, tangled comfortably together. We were still fully clothed under a fuzzy blue blanket Kate'd tossed over us.

I needed to pee but was reluctant to lose the blissful connection we had. I tried to fall back to sleep, but the urge only grew stronger. If I didn't want to leave a puddle in Kate's bed, I'd probably better do something about it. Carefully, I wiggled out from under her.

She mumbled, rolled onto her back, and then quieted. Once her breathing evened out again, I slid off the bed and stumbled out the door and into the bathroom. I did my thing, and as I reemerged into the hall, the thought of that damn box—right next door—flared again. My fingers itched to touch it, to see if it felt as familiar as it looked.

I stood in the bathroom doorway and contemplated my options. I could go back to bed. I could walk into that office and take a peek. I could get busted taking a peek and get kicked out of the Goldsmiths' house with orders to never return, which might happen anyway if Kate's mom and dad found out what we'd been doing in her room.

Staying still, I listened hard for thirty seconds. Didn't hear anything. Nothing at all. Man, this place had to have some amazing soundproofing to drown out the noises of the city, even this late at night. The pull to solve this mystery was as irresistible as Kate herself. If there was even the slightest chance that box could be my family's lost heirloom, I needed to know. And then I'd need to find out how Mr. Goldsmith had ended up with it.

Finally, I turned right and felt my way down the dark hall and into the office. Did I dare turn on the desk lamp so I could actually see?

Ambient light seeped through the uncovered window, and I was able to find the lamp and switch it on without running into anything. The bulb was dim, illuminating a much smaller area than I'd expected. That meant I was going to have to pick up the box and bring it into the light.

No time like the present. I'd come this far. With a deep breath, I crept over to the wall of shelves and carefully picked it up. The box felt familiar in my hands; the weight seemed about right.

My heart began to thump harder as I held the box under the light. Holy freaking shit. The puzzle box was identical. It had the same wood inlay, worn smooth with age and handling. I slid my fingertips to the sections that I knew moved and felt the pieces slide.

My hands began to shake. Slowly, I turned it around, looking for the cracked corner. Then I did it again, carefully checking all the edges. Disappointment and confusion warred inside me. This wasn't my father's puzzle box. But it was identical in every other way.

A skritching sound at the front door—the office was directly off the foyer—scared the shit out of me. I nearly dropped the box. Then a key rattled in the lock.

Holy shit. Someone was at the door.

Heart lodged firmly in my throat, I hastily reached for the light. In my panic, I nearly knocked the damn thing over, but got it switched off.

The click and snick of the deadbolt retracting was incredibly loud. No way was I going to be able to replace the box and get out without being seen.

I was trapped.

Desperately, I searched for somewhere to hide. The couch and the desk were my only two options. I immediately axed the couch. Too open. A beam of light from the outer hall widened across the foyer floor as the door swung open. In a split second, I'd be completely visible to whoever was coming in.

I scrambled around the desk, shoved the chair out of the way, and slid under it. Thank God the desk was gargantuan or I never would've fit. I hugged the puzzle box tight against my chest and held my breath. What a cliché. Hiding under a stinking desk.

The door closed with a thump, cutting off the light. Another second, and the deadbolt was reengaged.

I remembered then that Mr. Goldsmith was coming home late. Goddamn, why hadn't I remembered that?

With any luck, he'd bypass the office and head straight for bed.

A heavy sigh and a thump on the desk above my head nearly made me scream. He was right fricking there. Then came the familiar click of the lamp and light illuminated the carpet outside the desk.

Shit, shit, shit.

I pressed the back of my head against the side of the desk. I was dead meat. So stupid. Why hadn't I gone directly back to Kate's room, snuggled up to her, and drifted off to sleep? Because I was too goddamn nosy, that's why.

Seconds dragged by like hours. I tried to guess what he was doing, where he was. Inches from the top of my head, a couple latches popped. His briefcase?

Paper rustled, as if he were sorting through the pages of a report. Then he yawned and mumbled, "Enough for tonight."

The light went out, and his footsteps faded away.

CHAPTER 6

The next morning, I stood in front of Kate's enormous living room window, looking out at a perfect September day while shoveling Froot Loops into my mouth. I'd already showered and dressed and was waiting for Kate to finish up.

Kate's parents had already left for work before we got up. I still couldn't believe I hadn't been caught last night. Though I'd found out the puzzle box wasn't my father's, I now had more questions than answers. Why did Mr. Goldsmith have a box identical to ours? Did his father somehow know my great-grandfather? I didn't dare ask because then it would come out that I'd been in the no-go zone touching the forbidden relics. Nothing like alienating the parents of my brand-new girlfriend right out of the gate.

Holy shit. Was Kate my girlfriend? We hadn't gotten that far in discussing our relationship last night. We were too busy getting busy. I couldn't bite back the grin or the rush of warmth. Sometimes I cracked myself up.

I spooned a heaping mound of cereal into my mouth. People on the ground looked like ants. I refocused on the Twin Towers. They were enormous. It felt like I could reach out and touch them even though they were probably five blocks away.

"Hey you," Kate said. She wrapped her arms around me from behind and nestled her chin in my neck. Sparks shot through my body and settled low in my belly. I still couldn't believe we were here. Literally and figuratively.

I swallowed my cereal and pressed my cheek against hers. "What time is it?"

She checked her watch. "Eight forty-five. We have plenty of time."

Sweet. The more time I had alone with Kate, the better. For once, the world looked bright and shiny, full of hope and possibility. I hadn't felt like that in a really long time. I scooped up more cereal and twisted around to offer it to Kate. As I aimed the spoon toward her mouth, she gasped. "Holy shit!"

"What?" I dumped the spoon back in the bowl and looked out the window. A huge, bright-red ball of fire spewed from one of the Twin Towers. Debris sailed from the building, and pieces of the façade peeled away to fall in huge chunks to the ground. "Oh my God!" I yelped. "What the hell?"

Kate shifted from behind me to beside me. I grabbed her hand. She threaded her fingers through mine and held tight. Her other hand was clamped over her mouth, and her eyes were wide. Between her fingers, she croaked, "I don't know. I thought I saw...no way." She shook her head.

I looked back at the incredibly horrifying, completely unreal sight. "Saw what?"

"A plane."

"An airplane?"

"Yeah. No. Oh my God. I don't know. What about all those people..."

The worst thought ever blossomed in my mind like a mini-explosion. "Kate," I said, my voice shaking, "where are your mom and dad?"

She turned her terrified stare on me and whispered, "I don't know. Dad. Oh God." She put a hand to her forehead and squeezed her eyes shut. "Today's Tuesday. He has a Foundation meeting every Tuesday at the museum..." She trailed off.

"At the museum. He's at the Museum of Jewish Heritage?"

"Yes."

"That's about ten blocks from the Trade Center. That's good. What about your mom? Where was she going for that meeting?"

I glanced away from the sickening sight to Kate, who pulled away from me and began pacing in front of the window, repeatedly glancing out at the devastation.

"Shit, shit, shit." She squeezed her forehead again and stopped abruptly, pivoted, and charged through the dining room into the kitchen. I followed on her heels. She raced to the refrigerator and ripped off a paper affixed to the metal surface with four apple-shaped magnets.

"Every week Mom leaves a list of appointments and phone numbers where she'll be, just in case." She slapped the sheet on the counter and ran her finger down it. "Here. She's here. At the National Development and Research Institute."

"Where is that?"

"Oh, God. I don't know." She yanked a drawer open and rummaged through it. "Her address book is in here. Maybe the...here." She yanked out a pale green address book with a gold band around it. She ripped the band off and frantically flipped through the pages. "Here. 2 World Trade Center. Thirty-ninth floor." She looked up at me, and I can now testify that when they say the blood drains from someone's face, it's true. "Jesus fucking Christ. Which Tower was hit?"

We dashed back to the window. Flames licked out between the columns, but now thick black smoke billowed from the impact site, or the bombsite, or whatever the hell had happened. The plumes of smoke were so dense it was hard to see the top of the structure. I had no idea which tower was which.

Kate dragged her fingers through her hair and studied the ceiling. "Okay. Okay. Okay. Dad always says the tower on the left is number two and the tower on the right is number one. All right. That means she's in the other one. She's okay—"

The ringing of the phone made us both jump. Kate made a dive for the cordless sitting on an end table next to the couch.

"Hello!" Kate's voice was up about sixteen octaves. "Oh. Tubs. Yeah, we're fine. Hang on; she's right here."

She thrust the phone at me. "Tubs?"

"Mikala. You're okay?" She sounded winded and worried.

"Yes. We haven't left for the field trip yet."

"Listen to me, honey. Both of you need to get out of there. Now. You're not safe. Head for our home. No subway, no cab. Walk as fast as you can. Okay?"

"But—"

"No buts. Leave the second we're off the phone. I'll be in touch as soon as I can. There's a cell phone in the bottom drawer of my dresser under my granny panties. Grab it and turn it on. Keep it on you, and keep it charged at all times, okay?"

My brain was whirling. "No subways and find the cell phone."

"Yes. I love you, Mikala. You're going to be fine."

Before I could get another word in, the line went dead. I hung up. "Kate, we need to leave. Now. Grab your backpack and get your shoes on."

The lobby was empty when we emerged from the elevator and tore out of the building. The tense silence we'd been suspended in was shattered as soon as we hit the sidewalk. Multitudes of sirens screamed, echoing through the streets. So many people stood facing the same direction, watching the black plumes of smoke pour out of the wounded skyscraper. Chills raced down my spine. We hustled at a fast clip toward the entrance to the Brooklyn Bridge. Before us was a picture-perfect day—the sky cloudless and bright blue. Behind us, the billowing charcoal clouds of death and destruction obliterated everything.

We made it about a quarter of the way across the bridge, run-walking around a horde of other terrified individuals intent on getting their own asses out of Manhattan, when a tremendous explosion made the bridge tremble. As one, every single person on the walkway turned around. A fireball shot out of the middle of the second tower.

"NO!" Kate screamed. "My mom!"

A tall Asian guy with muscles and tattoos next to us said, "Shit, man. It was a plane. I saw it. Maybe a 747. We're under attack."

I grabbed Kate's shirt in my hand and took off, dragging her behind me. I weaved through the stunned mob as fast as I could. Any moment, they were going to bolt, and I didn't want to be trampled.

Thirty hard-won minutes later, I was never so happy to see the familiar red and cream-colored entrance to our apartment.

Sirens still screamed, both from afar and nearby. The shrieking helped propel us the last few hundred feet to what I prayed was safety. We bounded up the four steps to the entrance of the complex and charged directly to the bank of two elevators. I repeatedly pressed the call button while Kate chanted, "Come, on, come on, come on," under her breath.

Finally, the doors squeaked open, and then we were on a slow, grinding ride to the ninth floor. With a shaking hand, I keyed the door to the apartment open, and we tumbled inside.

"Wait here just a second," I told Kate. I ran into my grandmother's room. Sure enough, hidden under her bloomers was a Motorola flip phone and a charging cord. What the hell was Tubs doing with a cell phone in her unmentionables drawer?

I keyed it on and found it fully charged. I grabbed the charging cord and stuffed it in a pocket along with the phone. Next stop, my bedroom. On my desk was shoebox-sized boom box. I unplugged it, hoping the batteries weren't dead, and hoofed it back to Kate, who'd wandered into the kitchen.

She handed me a glass of water, and I downed it. "Thanks," I gasped and dragged my forearm over my mouth. My mouth was dry and tasted like burned cardboard, and that water was sorely needed. "All right. Let's head up to the roof and see what's going on."

Kate stoically nodded and searched my eyes. "Thank you."

"Haven't done anything to be thanked for." I pulled her into my arms. She held on to me for dear life. I buried my face in her hair, breathing in whatever shampoo she'd used in the shower, and hung on to this one small moment of normalcy.

She pulled back and gave me a quick, solemn peck on the forehead. "You're my guardian angel."

I gave her a grim smile. "Come on."

The roof had fewer people milling about than I expected, and surprisingly, I didn't recognize anyone. We watched the hellish spectacle, all of us lined up on the west side of the building, mesmerized by the thick blue-black smoke pouring from each of the Twin Towers. Smoke from the two damaged buildings merged as it drifted at an angle toward us, caught on a current of wind.

We found an open spot along the waist-high concrete wall and hunkered down. I balanced the radio on the edge of the wall against a rusted metal safety bar of questionable integrity and tuned into New York's news station, 1010 WINS. In a tone of hushed horror, the announcer described what we were seeing. He speculated that two airplanes had been hijacked and used as massive bombs. The Pentagon had also been hit.

I felt like I was in the middle of the worst imaginable nightmare. My entire body trembled.

"Hey," Kate said. She wrapped her arms around my midsection. It almost felt like we were back at her place, looking out the picture window before the world blew up right before our very eyes. I wasn't sure I'd ever be able to look out that window again.

I whispered, "Aren't you worried about people seeing?"

She pressed her lips to my neck. "Seeing what?"

"Us. This." I pressed my back into her.

"Fuck 'em. If someone's going to bitch about this public demonstration of affection in light of that," she nodded toward the burning buildings, "I don't give a shit. You're all that's holding me together right now."

If she didn't care, I wasn't going to either.

For long minutes, no one took their eyes off the impossible. All of a sudden, it was as if the south tower was made of sugar and someone poured water on it. The building dissolved in on itself. With an incredible whoosh, it disappeared from view. In its place, an immense, roiling, dark-gray cloud of dust and debris rose, a mass of darkness filled with the detritus of death.

"Oh God!" Kate howled in my ear.

"Shit! Oh shit. Look at that," another person shouted.

I whipped around to face Kate and pivoted her away from the gruesome sight. She pressed her face against my neck. Her tears burned my skin. I held her tight and watched. Were we far enough away? Was that horrifying, roiling mass from hell going to reach us?

So many thoughts raced through my mind amid the chaos and destruction and terror. Was Kate's mom dead or alive? Was her dad far enough away? How was New York going to recover?

Numerous times, I tried to call Ursula on Tubs' cell phone and got nothing but a "the circuits are busy" response. In the end, I simply held onto Kate as we witnessed tragic history in the making. I was hyperaware of her fragility, her strength, her desperate fear, and her love.

With each second that ticked by, the feeling of fury inside me grew, solidifying, filling me with purpose. The aimlessness that'd overwhelmed me ever since my dad's murder evaporated.

In those moments, it was as if a blindfold had been ripped off. My mind became impossibly clear. One plane could have been an accident. Two planes was a planned assault intended to kill as many innocent people as possible.

I now knew without a doubt what I was going to do with my life. My grandfather gave his own life building what had just been taken down by absolute evil. I wasn't going to let the reason for his death be forgotten. I had two years of high school left, and I was going make the most of them. My father's footsteps led to West Point, and that was exactly where I headed once I graduated.

After that, I'd do whatever I had to do to hunt down the lunatics who did this. Then, I was going after the bastard who killed my father. Finally, goddamn it, no matter what it took, I was going to find and retrieve that cherished, stolen puzzle box and unlock whatever family secrets it held.

From the moment that first plane hit, all of our lives were changed. The path ahead wouldn't be easy, but like Tubs had always told me, I was stubborn and willful. My dad had often said that once I made my mind up to do something, no force of nature could stop me.

It was time to prove them both right.

It was time to prove to myself that I was capable of more than simply existing, that I could make decisions and follow through. That I could make a difference.

The time to begin that path was now.

About Jessie Chandler

Award-winning author Jessie Chandler lives in Minneapolis, Minnesota with her wife and two mutts, Fozzy Bear and Ollie. In the fall and winter, Jessie writes, and spends her summers selling T-shirts and other assorted trinkets to unsuspecting conference and festival goers.

CONNECT WITH JESSIE:

Website: www.jessiechandler.com

OTHER BOOKS FROM
YLVA PUBLISHING

www.ylva-publishing.com

Requiem for Immortals

Lee Winter

ISBN: 978-3-95533-710-0
Length: 284 pages (86,000 words)

Requiem is a brilliant cellist with a secret. The dispassionate assassin has made an art form out of killing Australia's underworld figures without a thought. One day she's hired to kill a sweet and unassuming innocent. Requiem can't work out why anyone would want her dead—and why she should even care.

Book one of *The Law Game* is a dark lesbian thriller with a twist in its tale.

If Looks Could Kill

Andi Marquette

ISBN: 978-3-95533-721-6
Length: 207 pages (52,000 words)

Eleanor O'Donnell, an investigator with NYC PD, must determine the link between fashion mogul Marya Hampstead and a Russian crime family. Ellie goes undercover as an aspiring designer and intern at Hampstead's fashion empire. In addition to runway gossip, Ellie uncovers secrets that will kill far more than a bad outfit.

"If Looks Could Kill" is the fifth and final installment of *The Law Game.*

FOUR STEPS

Wendy Hudson

ISBN: 978-3-95533-690-5
Length: approx. 92,000 words

Alex Ryan lives a simple life. She has her farm in the Scottish countryside, and the self-imposed seclusion suits her until a crime that has haunted her for years tears through the calm and shatters the fragile peace she'd finally managed to find.

Lori Hunter's greatest love is the mountains. They're her escape from the constant hustle and bustle of everyday life. Growing up was neither traditional nor easy for Lori, but now she's beginning to realise she's settled for both. A dead-end relationship and little to look forward to. Her solution when the suffocation sets in? Run for the hills.

A chance encounter in the mountains of the Scottish Highlands leads Alex and Lori into a whirlwind of heartache and a fight for survival as they build a formidable bond that will be tested to its ultimate limits.

COMING FROM YLVA PUBLISHING

www.ylva-publishing.com

THE LAVENDER LIST

Meg Harrington

Aspiring actress Amelia Maldonado finds herself embroiled in the affairs of mobsters and spies in post-war New York, and the only ally she has is the mystifying girl she's got a crush on.

UNDER PARR

(Norfolk Coast Investigation Story - Book #2)

Andrea Bramhall

December 5th, 2013 left its mark on the North Norfolk Coast in more ways than one. A tidal surge and storm swept millennia-old cliff faces into the sea and flooded homes and businesses up and down the coast. It also buried a secret in the WWII bunker hiding under the golf course at Brancaster. A secret kept for years, until it falls squarely into the lap of Detective Sergeant Kate Brannon and her fellow officers.

A skeleton, deep inside the bunker.

How did it get there? Who was he...or she? How did the stranger die—in a tragic accident or something more sinister? Well, that's Kate's job to find out.

The Law Game

Archer Securities © 2016 Jove Belle
Daughter of Baal © 2016 Gill McKnight
Evolution of an Art Thief © 2016 Jessie Chandler

ISBN 978-3-95533-736-0

Published by Ylva Publishing, legal entity of Ylva Verlag, e.Kfr.

Ylva Verlag, e.Kfr.
Owner: Astrid Ohletz
Am Kirschgarten 2
65830 Kriftel
Germany

www.ylva-publishing.com

First edition: 2016

Credits
Edited by Jove Belle & R.G. Emanuelle
Cover Design by Dirt Road Design
Cover Photos:
Archer Securities: © bluebay2014 | Dollar Photo Club; © Paul Hill | Dollar Photo Club; © kirill4mula | Dollar Photo Club
Daughter of Baal: © 3dmitry | Dollar Photo Club; © Katalinks | Bigstock Photo
Evolution of an Art Thief: © chesterF | Dollar Photo Club; © kuco | Dollar Photo Club